STRONG WINE

Sword Dance Book 3

A.J. DEMAS

Strong Wine

A.J. Demas

© 2021 by A.J. Demas
Published October 2021 by Sexton's Cottage Books.
All rights reserved.

Cover art by Vic Grey
Cover design by Alice Degan

CHAPTER 1

It started to rain when Damiskos was halfway home, just a light mist beading in his hair, which was still damp from the baths. He quickened his pace, swinging his cane, and arrived at the pink door in Saffron Alley only a little wetter than he had been when he set out.

The house was quiet, and he paused a moment in the hall as usual, wanting to call out but not sure what to say. "I'm home"?

It had been a month since he first walked through the door of Varazda's house. Every so often in moments like these when he was alone, he had the odd idea that the house was cradling him like a pair of cupped hands, an extension of its master's love. Maybe it was because it was so obviously Varazda's house, the comfortable, eccentric elegance of it so precisely adapted to him.

Varazda had never said, "I love you," but he had said Damiskos was loved. He felt loved all the time, out in the city by himself or working in the garden or lying in bed next to Varazda.

Or—as last night—underneath Varazda. Damiskos grinned in the dim hallway at the memory.

"Damiskos?" Yazata's voice was hushed as he looked out from the kitchen. "Oh, it is you. You've got wet! Let me fetch you a towel. Remi is asleep in the sitting room."

Damiskos came through into the kitchen, and Yazata brought a towel and made him sit on a bench while he dried his hair for him as if Damiskos were a little boy.

"There, that's better." Yazata ran his fingers through Damiskos's hair, then abruptly snatched his hand away. "Are you cold? I'll make you some tea."

"I'm fine—I was swimming. It warms you up."

Yazata gave him a disapproving, grandmotherly look until Damiskos said, "Tea, yes. Absolutely."

Damiskos rested his cheek on his hand as he watched Yazata bustle to the workbench and scoop tea leaves. Yazata was very physically affectionate; so was Varazda, for that matter. The whole family hugged and kissed and snuggled with each other. Lately Damiskos had noticed Yazata starting to treat him the same way, then catching himself and stopping, still wary around Damiskos. But they were making progress.

"Varazda's not back from his thing?" He couldn't remember what it was called: a celebration in honour of the birth of a friend's child.

"Not yet. Ariston went out, too. To the fishmonger's."

"You're letting him buy fish now?"

"Goodness, no. He needs to sketch some for his new piece."

"Ah."

Yazata finished making the tea and checked on the rain, then, finding it had not increased to a downpour yet, went out to visit Maia across the street. Damiskos took his cup into the sitting room, where Remi was curled up on the cushions of one of the divans, sleeping with her bottom in the air. He settled into his usual seat in the corner and looked out the half-open door at the light rain sparkling with unexpected sunlight in the garden.

He had planted a couple of shrubs in pots against the far wall and built a trellis to train vines on in the spring. He and Ariston had dug a hole for a fountain and lined it with bricks as a substrate for the veneer of marble chips that Ariston had planned. Ariston's workbench in the corner had expanded and become much more cluttered since he had left Themistokles's studio and begun building a clientele of his own. Pieces of his first commission, a series of aquatic-themed reliefs to decorate a new public toilet, were propped against the wall in various stages of completion.

Damiskos himself had been officially jobless for two weeks now. He had managed to leave his post at the Quartermaster's Office without returning to Pheme, because his deputy had done well enough in his absence to warrant a promotion. It had all been accomplished by letter, a strange way for his military career finally to end, but in a way it also seemed fitting. Every so often in the past two weeks he had thought about it, and a kind of unmoored feeling would come over him, as if part of his identity had been cut loose, and he wasn't yet sure how he felt about it.

Then the other day Varazda had introduced him to someone, quite naturally, as a retired soldier. And Damiskos had thought, with a sense of shock, *That's what I am*. Finally, after five years of pretending that he hadn't left the legions, he really had.

He would have to return to Pheme at some point to see about his pension.

He would have to return to Pheme at some point because he was still paying to rent an apartment on the Vallina Hill, and to board Xanthe at a stable nearby, because he had come to Boukos a month ago with only a small bag, thinking he was staying a week, and because he hadn't seen his parents in a month or adequately explained to them what he was doing in Boukos.

But if he were to go back to Pheme, that would, surely, be the moment when he'd have to ask Varazda what came next. He had no idea how he was going to do that.

What was the question, even? Were they still at the stage where it would be appropriate to ask, "Can I stay a while longer?" Or was it time to say, "Can I stay forever?" But there was always the risk, with the latter question, that Varazda might say—well, not "No," but at least "Maybe." And then what? "Can I stay for the time being, at least?"

Yesterday had been Damiskos's thirty-third birthday. Zashians liked to celebrate birthdays in style, and so as soon as he'd let slip the date, Damiskos had been expecting something. Yazata had cooked a sumptuous meal and invited Marzana and Chereia and their sons. Ariston had given Damiskos a clay statuette of Terza and the Bull that he had made himself. Varazda had given him a pair of warm pyjamas—and later, when they were alone in their bedroom, a blue glass bottle of expensive scented oil. They had put that to use immediately.

Damiskos sipped the last of his tea and leaned his head back against the cushions of the divan. Outside the rain was coming down harder.

It was pouring by the time Varazda got home. He ran all the way from the end of Fountain Street with his hands in fists inside his coat sleeves, and stood in the front hall catching his breath and dripping on the tiles. Yazata appeared with a towel and held a finger to his lips, nodding toward the sitting room.

"Can you help me with my hair?" Varazda whispered, displaying his freshly hennaed hands.

Yazata *tsk*ed genially. He helped Varazda strip off his wet coat and unbraid his hair, and rubbed it dry with the towel. Varazda gave him a kiss on the nose.

"Is Dami back yet?"

"In there. Take a look."

Varazda followed Yazata's gesture and went to look in through the sitting-room door. Remi was sleeping in a chubby-limbed heap, face down on the divan, and Dami was stretched out on the corner seat, one arm flung out on the cushions, head tipped back, equally deeply asleep. Selene was hunkered on the floor nearby.

Varazda smiled, looking in at them. He felt a ridiculous sense of pride. Remi was his daughter, whom he'd raised since she was a few weeks old, so it was all very well to feel proud of her. But Dami didn't belong to him, wasn't his responsibility. Yet Varazda found himself sometimes wanting to nudge their friends and acquaintances, point, and say, "You see how happy he is now? You see how the strain is gone from his eyes, how much more easily and genuinely he smiles? *I* did that."

Dami even looked fitter—something Varazda wouldn't have thought possible—after a month of exercising in the pool at the Baths of Soukos, pushing himself hard without overtaxing his knee. He walked more easily, carried his cane more but needed it less. He was relaxed and at ease around Varazda's family now. Neither he nor Varazda had spoken about how much longer he was going to stay.

Varazda thought about the night before, after Dami's birthday dinner. They had retired as soon as their guests left, the rest of their household considerately melting away, and in the lamplight in their bedroom, Varazda had danced for Dami, with Dami, moving around him, shedding clothes as he went, until they ended up on Dami's bed, with Dami on his stomach …

"How is Babak's baby?" Yazata asked, coming up behind Varazda.

"Hm?" For a moment he couldn't think what Yaza was talking about. "Oh, healthy and adorable."

"And the mother?"

"Overwhelmed, clearly. Having a son seems to have made Babak return to his roots, and I don't think she was ready for it."

Yazata winced sympathetically. "She will need to brace herself for the wedding."

They heard the door on the other side of the house open, and Yazata rushed off to proffer towels and shush Ariston and Kallisto, whose voices could be heard in the front room.

Varazda stood a moment longer looking at Dami lying on the divan and remembering the night before. He shivered.

The name for it in *The Three Gardens* had something to do with a pomegranate, but Varazda knew how Dami would have described it: Varazda had fucked him. Dami would have said that to flatter Varazda, of course, even though Varazda had only used his fingers, with Dami lying on his stomach, which was probably not the best position—and finally he'd had to shift to get his hand down to touch himself. Varazda had deliberately not done it for him.

Dami was usually happy to cuddle and talk after making love, but last night he had just lain there with a smile on his face, looking ... fucked. It had given Varazda that same feeling of pride. *I did that.* It had been a good birthday present.

He went through into the room that he still thought of as Dami's to change his clothes. In the recent reorganization of the household, Varazda had lost his bedroom, and indeed more or less the upper floor of his house. Remi had decided that she wanted a room of her own, so Varazda had moved downstairs to the new room he'd added for Dami, and they'd gotten the builder in again to put a door through to connect the upper floors of the two houses so that Remi wasn't upstairs on her own. It had worked well.

Dami and Remi were still napping when Varazda came back out into the sitting room. He could hear whispering coming from Ariston and Yazata's front room, and when he went into the kitchen to get himself a drink, Ariston appeared in the doorway. He wore a green mantle that Kallisto had given him the other day, wrapped in a style that made him look elegantly tall and lean rather than gangly. He beckoned to Varazda mysteriously.

"We want to talk to you," he said unnecessarily, when Varazda had come in and closed the door behind him. "Have a seat." He indicated Yazata's large wicker chair, then dove in to plump the cushion before stepping back.

Varazda gave him a puzzled look and sat. Ari sat on the edge of his desk, and Yazata perched on the stool in front of it. Kallisto lingered near the window, looking like she wasn't sure she wanted to be there.

Ari cleared his throat and flicked back his hair, which he was growing out in accordance with the latest fashion. "It's about Damiskos."

"Oh?" Varazda tried hard for a neutral tone, and thought he just about managed it.

"We don't want him to leave!" Yazata blurted out.

Varazda blinked. He wasn't sure what he'd expected, but it was not this. "That's ... good. I don't want him to leave either. But it's really up to him."

"We want him to stay," Ari reiterated, presumably thinking Varazda might not have understood the first time. "We've talked about it and we all agree."

"Yes," said Varazda patiently. "I also agree. I'm not thinking of turning him out, if that's what you're worried about."

Kallisto turned away from the window. "They're worried

you're not doing enough to make sure he stays," she said, looking embarrassed.

She was a courtesan who specialized in flogging and choking her clients for their pleasure, and *this* embarrassed her.

"Yeah," said Ariston, shooting her a grateful smile. "Are you, you know, meeting his needs? In bed, I mean. He's a man—you've got to—"

"That is *not* what *I* meant!" Yazata yelped, jumping to his feet and knocking over the stool in his haste. "Holy God, Ariston, what do you mean talking about such things? Such things are private!"

Ari spread his hands hopelessly, glancing between Yazata and Kallisto. "What? That's what I thought we were talking about."

Kallisto shook her head in a clear *keep me out of this*.

"What *I* meant," Yazata spoke before Ari could go on, "was—can we afford to keep him?"

"To, uh, *what*?"

"No, no, that was not what I meant to say—forgive me. Can we afford for him to remain with us … indefinitely? We —Ariston and Kallisto and I—have discussed it, and we all agree that we very much want him to stay, and so if there are any economies to be made, I am quite willing—"

"Yazata, immortal gods," Ari groaned. "He's got a pension. He can *work*. He was First Whatever of the Whatever! Have you not noticed that he's good at basically *everything*?"

"Of course I know that," said Yazata, almost hotly. "He is the best of men—I think I scarcely knew men like him existed until he came into our lives. Of course if he wants to work, if Varazda wants him to work—but if not," he ended, his voice dropping shyly, "I—I like having him around the house."

"Yaza," said Varazda, holding up a hand. He got up from

the chair. "Ari." He glanced at Kallisto, whom he suspected of being more involved in this than she wanted to admit. "I'm glad to know that you want Damiskos to stay. I'm sure he will be glad to know it too."

"I don't—" Kallisto began, then put her hand to her lips. "Er. I don't necessarily think you should tell him about this conversation."

Varazda gave her a look. "I wasn't thinking of it. But thank you."

They all jumped at the sound of a knock on Varazda's door.

"I'll get it," Kallisto offered eagerly, already starting across the room.

Varazda glanced between his two friends after she had left. They were still giving him earnest looks.

"You really have to make sure you're—" Ari started.

"If there's anything we can do," Yazata said at the same time, then heard what Ari had been saying. "Not in *that* regard. Holy angels."

Varazda rubbed his fingertips between his eyebrows and said nothing.

"It's a letter," said Kallisto, reappearing. "For Damiskos. From Pheme."

CHAPTER 2

"It's from my parents," Dami said, holding the tablet loosely in his hands and looking down at it as if something about it bothered him.

Remi looked up from the floor where she was feeding Selene crumbs of stale biscuit. "You have parents?" She sounded surprised.

Dami smiled down at her, a little sadly. "I do. They live in Pheme. They want me to come see them." He looked up at Varazda. Apologetically? Varazda couldn't tell.

"Anything wrong?" Varazda asked.

Dami frowned down at the letter again. "Hard to say. They claim it's urgent, but I'm afraid with them that likely means they don't want to tell me what it is because they know I won't like it." He looked up at Varazda again, and this time his expression was definitely apologetic. "I'm sorry," he said, in case that hadn't been obvious. "I think I'll have to go."

Yazata had been hovering in the kitchen pretending—or, knowing him, really trying—not to listen, but now he looked in the doorway.

"Is anything the matter?" Yazata ventured. "At home? Er—in Pheme?"

"My parents want to see me about something," said Dami, putting on one of his tired, don't-worry-about-me smiles. "I daresay it's nothing serious, but I do owe them a visit. And it's a good time to go, before the stormy season."

"You're going away?" Remi cried, looking desolate.

"Just for a little while." Dami didn't meet Varazda's eye. "It doesn't take long to get to Pheme."

"You're coming back?" Remi pursued.

"Yes," said Varazda. "Of course."

"You're leaving?" Ariston appeared in the sitting-room doorway. "What—already?"

"Oh, for the love of God," Varazda grumbled. "He's going to see his parents, who have asked him to come."

"It's not anything—" Ari started.

"Probably not, but they don't say," Varazda cut him off. "Anything else?"

Ari wrinkled his nose discontentedly. "Well, remember what I said before, that's all."

"Thank you," said Varazda crisply.

Dami closed the letter and set it on the table, then got to his feet. He looked out through the door to the yard.

"The rain's stopped," he observed. He looked at Varazda. "Come outside with me a moment."

Varazda followed him out into the yard, a space almost entirely transformed in the time Dami had been living with them. Ari's half-finished carved fish and the newly-laid paving stones glistened with rainwater.

"I'm sorry about this," Dami said, looking out at the yard rather than at Varazda.

"Don't be. You were always going to have to go back to Pheme. And if your parents need you … "

Dami looked Varazda in the eye. "Should I give up the lease of my apartment in Pheme?"

And there it was.

"Yes," said Varazda. He could feel his heart beating faster.

Dami nodded. "All right," he said, his tone still grave, still the old Damiskos. "I will."

They stood a moment longer in the wet yard, looking at one another, and it was a strange, weighted moment. Varazda thought he understood. The letter from Dami's parents had forced his hand, but it had also brought his old life in Pheme back into view, and it must not have felt to him like the time, soiled and sullied as the moment was, for passionate declarations. In a way, Varazda agreed with him.

Varazda smiled. "Good."

Dami smiled too, although it was still that old, sad smile. He drew a breath. "Last night was really something."

Varazda laughed a little unsteadily. "It was, wasn't it?"

"You're all right?"

"I? I'm not the one who—who—"

"Oh, honey, you didn't *hurt* me. You did a beautiful job."

"I'm glad. I … borrowed a copy of *The Three Gardens* from Babak and studied the, um … But there were some hard words, so I couldn't get much out of the text." He had been learning to read Zashian a little in the past month, but the Cinnamon Grove was still largely beyond him.

Finally Dami laughed, in the easy way that made Varazda feel pleased with himself. "You were perfect," he said. "I just wanted to make sure you felt all right about it, after. I know I passed out pretty quickly. Which I try not to do, if I think you might need me."

If he thought Varazda might need him to hold and gentle him, to bring him back to a place and time of safety. That was what he meant. And to tell the truth, Varazda didn't always need that, by any means, but last night it wouldn't have been unwelcome.

"It was your birthday," said Varazda with a smile. "You are entitled to put yourself first for once."

Dami laid his hand on Varazda's hip and drew him into a warm, gentle embrace. Varazda reached up to touch Dami's cheek.

"Oh, you've got henna again," Dami observed delightedly, drawing Varazda's hand away from his face to look at it. "I didn't notice."

"They often do it at birth celebrations. There were a lot of Pseuchaian girls there who were very excited about it. So *exotic*, you know. So *Sasian*." He gave the Pseuchaian pronunciation an exaggerated hiss.

Dami gave a disapproving grunt. "Your designs are beautiful. Can I touch?"

"Sure."

He ran a thumb lightly over Varazda's palm. "I'll be back before it wears off. I promise."

There was a thunderstorm the night before Damiskos left, but the next day dawned clear and cold, and the ship was set to sail. The whole household came down to the harbour to see him off, everyone wrapped in thick cloaks, Remi dozing with her head on Yazata's shoulder. It was Kallisto who rounded the others up and herded them away so that Damiskos and Varazda could have a moment together on the dock.

"I'll write as soon as I can and let you know what's going on," Damiskos said, unable to think of anything else.

"If there's anything we can do to help … " said Varazda.

One braid of his hair trailed out from under the hood of his cloak. Damiskos reached out and tucked it back in. Varazda smiled.

"You could … we could kiss," he offered. "If you want."

"Yeah?" They didn't ordinarily kiss in public, and this place was very public, with sailors and dock hands and passengers passing and Varazda's family standing nearby, very obviously watching.

Varazda nodded serenely.

Damiskos slid his hand in under Varazda's hood, cupping the back of his neck, and leaned in and kissed him, firmly and deeply. Varazda staggered a little when he let go of Damiskos's shoulders. It may have been for effect—or it may not. It had been a good kiss.

It was pretty much the only thing about their parting that Damiskos could reflect on with satisfaction as the ship moved away from the dock and he watched the waving figures of Varazda and his family grow smaller. The last two nights they had tried and failed to make love; the first time they had been interrupted, and the second time Varazda hadn't been able to get hard, and when Damiskos had pointed out that this was obviously because he was forcing himself when he didn't feel like it, they had almost quarrelled.

And before that and colouring all of that, his stupid, *stupid* question in the yard after he got his parents' letter. But even thinking back on it now and hating himself for the way it had come out, he couldn't think of any better way he might have said it. Should he give up his apartment in Pheme or not? That was the practical matter.

The truth was, in the moment he had expected Varazda to say, *No. No, if it's not too much trouble. No, I don't think it would be a good idea just yet—do you?* He hadn't expected their future to be settled in that curt and unromantic question. He owed Varazda better than that.

The journey from Boukos to the city of Pheme took a little less than two days in late autumn. It was broken at Anthousa on the north coast, where the passengers got off and had a bad night's sleep in an overpriced hostel, and everyone arrived bleary-eyed on the docks in Pheme around the seventh hour the following afternoon.

Damiskos had always had mixed feelings about arriving in Pheme. He didn't dislike the city the way some people did, but he didn't love it either. He'd liked almost all of the other places he'd lived better, so coming home always had an air of vague disappointment for him.

As they drew within sight of the city, all the grandeur of its marble buildings was still muffled up in a grubby-looking fog. By the time they reached the harbour the fog had burned off, but the sunlight was cold, the air damp. Damiskos made his way up through the warehouses and factories of Lower Goulina to the Vallina Hill, and headed straight for Kleon's stable.

"Kleon!" he called, recognizing the hostler in the stableyard from behind by his broad shoulders and bald head.

Kleon turned and gaped, his expression looking quite genuine. "Damiskos Philionides? I—I didn't think I'd been seeing you again." He looked, honestly, a little as if he was seeing a ghost.

"You didn't? What, have rumours been circulating?" It was possible, given the unusual way he had left the Quartermaster's Office, that some people had been saying he was in exile or disgrace—but he didn't think it would have been a major piece of gossip.

"Well, you dropped off the face of the earth for, what? Two months?" Kleon was beginning to sound defensive. His eyes darted around the yard.

"One month. I've been in Boukos, visiting a friend."

"One month, still—that's four weeks' payment missed. I'd like to do a favour for you because you're a friend, but I'm running a business, and—"

"Wait a minute. Four weeks—you mean to tell me you haven't been paid for Xanthe's board in *four weeks*?"

Kleon shrugged hopelessly. "What was I to think? I thought you'd dropped off the face of the earth."

"What did you do?" Damiskos felt sick. He knew the answer before Kleon said it.

"I sold her." Kleon looked as if he felt sick himself. "The day—the day before yesterday. I held on as long as I could, but—" He spread his hands hopelessly. "I have to pay rent myself. I'm sorry."

"No," Damiskos managed. "I'm sorry. I sent money to—someone—to pay Xanthe's board while I was away, but obviously … "

"Shit. They cheated you. Damiskos, I'm so sorry. It wasn't that bastard Dromo, was it?"

"No, no. I don't suppose, if you only sold her two days ago—do you know where I might find her?" Not that he could afford to buy her back. He didn't know what he was going to do.

"Ah, well, actually—there's some hope there. I sold her to a friend of mine, who has a place out in Thumia. Keeps retired racers, sort of a hobby. I let him have her for the price of four weeks' board, not an obios more—it didn't feel right profiting from the situation, whatever'd happened to you." He shrugged. "He *might* be willing to let you have her back cheap. Though he knows what she's worth, so I can't make any promises."

"Thanks, Kleon. You've been more than decent."

"Nah, I feel like an asshole." The hostler shook his head. "If only I'd held out a couple more days."

Thumia was all the way out beyond the city limits on the other side of the Skalina. Damiskos had only a light bag with him, so he didn't bother to return to his apartment. He ate a greasy meat pie and an apple in the Vallina Market, then set off across the river. He had a little money on him—most of what he'd taken with him to Boukos, in fact, since Varazda had not let him spend much of it—and he would have access to more when he could get to the Bursar's office. For the time being, he hoped he would be able to arrange something on credit. At least to prevent the man from selling Xanthe on to someone else. She wasn't worth as much as all that, he told himself by way of comfort. She had been a spectacular horse in her day, Zashian-bred, as brave as she was elegant, but she was old now. Well, she was thirteen. She wasn't *old*.

It had been years since Damiskos had been through the Skalina neighbourhood, and it hadn't improved from his memories. If anything, it was worse. It was a rambling slum of cheaply-built apartment blocks, many leaning and sagging against one another as if about to collapse, which they routinely did; the sky opened up in ominous patches here and there above piles of rubble. Many doors were boarded up, but many others had had the boards torn off. The streets stank of piss and rotting things.

Passing the door of a grimy wineshop on the main through-street, Damiskos was startled by a voice, vaguely familiar, hailing him from the shadows under the awning.

"First Spear! Oh, I'm sorry—I recall you don't like being called that."

Damiskos turned and shot a stern look at the man getting up from the bench in front of the wineshop. He took an involuntary step back when he saw who it was.

It was Helenos Kontiades, former student of the philosopher Eurydemos, failed plotter of the restoration of Phemian purity through pointless war with Zash.

He had an empty wine cup in his hand as he strolled out into the street. He had clearly spotted Damiskos's step back, and an unpleasant smile spread on his lean face.

"Damiskos Temnon. How unexpected, and yet how

fitting. First Giontes, then ... and now you! Surprised to see me?"

He had been drinking in the middle of the afternoon, and in fact the way he stood there smiling slyly at Damiskos, wine cup dangling from his fingers, suggested that he was already rather drunk. He looked thinner than he had two months ago at Laothalia, and he'd grown a thick, dark beard. His tunic and mantle were both stained, and his hair looked greasy.

"I thought you were in exile," said Damiskos, not moving from where he stood in the middle of the street.

Helenos tried to take a swallow from his empty wine cup, gave it an aggrieved expression, and laughed. "No, not really. Not officially. I can't even claim that dignity. I'm simply in hiding."

"I remember now," said Damiskos flatly. "You escaped prosecution in Boukos and used your connections to weasel out of being sent home to Pheme to answer for your crimes here."

Helenos gave him a bored look. "If you want to put it like that." He ambled toward Damiskos. "It's been wretched. I can't tell you. I've been living on Pyria most of the time—do you have any idea what a shit-hole that place is? Full of savages. The water gives you diseases." He waved his cup. "I've had no choice but to drink wine instead. Speaking of which, I don't suppose you'd like to buy me another bottle?"

Damiskos gave him a long look. "You don't suppose. Do you remember a couple of months ago when you seized my friend's villa by force and killed several members of her household?"

"I?" Helenos widened his eyes exaggeratedly. "I have never personally killed anyone."

"I bet."

Helenos gave him another sly smile. "Oh, yes, you're a man of action, Damiskos Temnon—don't I know it? I see you've brought your sword." He snickered. "Looking to use it?"

"Not particularly."

"Mm. We could do something else. After you buy me that bottle, of course."

Damiskos looked at him, wide-eyed. He was now frankly alarmed. This was not how Helenos had behaved at Laothalia.

Rather against his better judgement, because he knew that any prolongation of this conversation inevitably played into Helenos's hands somehow, Damiskos said, "What are you doing in Pheme?"

"Oh, you know. Irons in the fire and so on." Helenos had advanced close enough now for Damiskos to smell the boozy scent emanating from him. He waved a hand. "Don't worry, don't worry. My fangs have been very effectively drawn. I'm in hiding, as I said. My little band of fanatics has been dispersed—poor Gelon was executed, did you know? And my lovely Phaia was sent to Choros Rock, which is a fine old Pseuchaian institution, to be sure—who better than an ancient order of priestesses on a windswept rock in the sea to be the guardians of gentle womanhood gone astray—still, you can't deny that she was a useful firebrand. And I do mean that in *every* sense." He licked his lips.

He was revolting, but Damiskos almost felt sorry for him. This Helenos was pitiable compared to the slick, charismatic fellow he had been in the summer. But it was hard to feel truly sorry for a man who'd had you dumped headfirst into a fish-sauce vat and left to die.

"Don't come any closer," Damiskos said, because Helenos appeared about to.

"What's the matter?" Helenos leaned in. "I thought you liked men."

"I don't like assholes."

Helenos leaned closer still, the alcohol on his breath

pungent in Damiskos's face. "Neither," he snarled, "do I. You ruined me, Damiskos from the Quartermaster's Office, you and that fucking Sasian cunt of a—"

"Don't"—Damiskos's hand was fisted in the front of Helenos's tunic so tightly he almost lifted the other man off his feet—"speak of him."

"Whuh?" Helenos looked completely, genuinely surprised. "Oh, immortal gods, I remember now! You were fucking him! Are you always so loyal to your whores?"

Damiskos threw him across the street.

He hit the bench in front of the wine shop with a crash, thudded against the shop counter, and slid to land in a heap on the ground. For a moment, Damiskos wondered if he was dead. Then Helenos pushed himself shakily up, groaning. He wiped blood from his mouth, where he must have bitten his lip, and did not rise from the ground. His wine cup lay shattered on the pavement.

There were people watching—an old woman and a little boy sitting on a doorstep, a couple of other patrons in the dim interior of the wine shop—and Damiskos did not like to think of himself as the type of man who would beat a drunk in the street and leave him there, even if he very much wanted to. He stalked over to where Helenos sat slumped, and hauled him up with a hand under his armpit.

"Where are you staying?"

"You want to come home with me after all?" Helenos blinked at him. At close quarters like this, he stank. "I'm not sure I can withstand your attentions, but—"

"I want," said Damiskos crisply, "to kick your head in, but I'll settle for dropping you on your doorstep and never seeing you again. Where are you staying?"

Helenos squirmed, wincing. "You really hurt me, you know."

"Good. Where?"

"Across the street." Helenos jerked his chin. "The door with the peeling paint—the one that's *not* hanging off its hinges. I'm on the top floor. You can manage?" He batted his eyelashes again.

"Fuck you."

Damiskos half-marched, half-dragged him across the street, through the door with the peeling paint—not a very helpful description, all the doors around here had peeling paint—and up three narrow, badly listing flights of stairs. A thin, white-haired man, carrying what looked like a bundle of dirty grey fur, squeezed past them on the last flight with a nod and an odd, cringing smile, and darted in one of the doors off of the small landing at the top.

One of the remaining doors stood open, but Helenos waved grandly at the third and said, "My abode. If you would be so good." He dug in his mantle and produced a purse, from which, after some fumbling, he extracted a key, which he promptly dropped.

"Terza's cock," Damiskos muttered, propping Helenos against the wall before bending to retrieve the key.

Of course the key didn't fit the lock; it was evidently a key for something else entirely, and the door was not locked. Helenos went off into fits of laughter and clutched his ribs dramatically. One of his neighbours put a grizzled head out her door, swore incoherently at them, then froze in terror when she saw Damiskos's sword and retreated inside, closing her door as quietly as possible, as if she thought this might prevent them from noticing her.

"Charming neighbourhood, isn't it?" Helenos drawled.

"Go sleep it off," Damiskos recommended sternly.

"You know," said Helenos, suddenly sounding more sober, "I really did have hopes for you. Such a principled man. I would have expected you to be easily won to our cause."

Damiskos had already turned toward the stairs, but he

stopped and looked back. Helenos still leaned indolently against the wall, but his gaze was keen.

"I thought you didn't believe in any of your own bullshit," Damiskos said.

Helenos's eyebrows rose and he smiled unpleasantly. "Really? You thought I couldn't look out for my own interests and at the same time desire the restoration of Phemian glory? How simplistic. How—one might even say—naïve."

"I should have left you in the street," Damiskos muttered, and went back down the stairs.

The hostler's friend in Thumia didn't want to sell Xanthe back to Damiskos, but not for the reason he had expected.

"She was miserable, stabled in the city—she needs space and freedom to roam," the man said, and looking at Xanthe trotting across the pasture toward him, of course Damiskos could see that it was true. He'd paid—thought he'd paid—Kleon to take Xanthe out regularly, to make sure she was ridden and had a chance to roam and graze freely, but once the money stopped coming, she had probably been neglected.

"I'll sell her back to you," the farmer said, "if you've got somewhere better to keep her, but not otherwise."

Damiskos did have somewhere in mind: the meadow at the end of Saffron Alley, and its adjoining farm and stable, which were owned by a friend of Varazda's. Damiskos had been to visit and talked horses with the man, and knew he'd be excited about Xanthe. But he hadn't mentioned this to Varazda, and he hadn't thought of bringing Xanthe over this trip. He hadn't thought of making this trip at all at this point, though in respect of his horse it was lucky he had.

"I understand," he said, "and I'm glad you have got the care of her. I'll pay you for her now—half today, and half when I've been to the Bursar for my pension—and you keep her for me until I have a place for her."

They agreed on a price, and Damiskos walked back over Skalina Hill and across the river, feeling ashamed for having neglected Xanthe. Just because he had been wrapped up in his own feelings for Varazda didn't mean he should have forgotten about her. Varazda managed to care for his whole family and his network of friends across Boukos, all while pursuing the only love affair he'd ever had in his life. Damiskos apparently couldn't even manage to look after a horse.

CHAPTER 3

Damiskos woke in his apartment on the Vallina Hill for the first time in a month, and stared at the ceiling, remembering where he was.

It wasn't a depressing place like the hole Helenos was hiding in; it was a pleasant room in a decent part of town, with an alcove for his bed and a privy down the hall and a respectable landlady who kept the place clean. But it wasn't Varazda's house in Saffron Alley. It might as well have been a hovel.

He got up and began packing his things in the bags and trunk he had bought yesterday. Outside, the view from his third-floor window was foggy again down toward the river, and the room was cold, but he didn't bother to light the brazier. Packing didn't take him long. The clothes that he hadn't taken with him were folded in a trunk already, including the thick winter cloak that he had begun to miss the last week or so in Boukos. He nestled his lute in on top. He had a few books, the box of his grandmother's jewellery, an ugly bronze lamp that his brother had given him once as a joke, and a collection of things from Zash—a couple of inlaid daggers, a small bottle in the shape of a pomegranate, an enamelled statuette of a horse—all gifts from people long gone from his life, some gone from the world of the living altogether.

When he had packed everything, collected it all into the centre of the room, and secured his favourite stool to the larger of the two trunks with cords, he went down to knock on his landlady's door. His rent was paid until the end of Eighth Month, and the remainder of his furniture—his bed, a table, and a couple of chairs—he offered to the landlady. He should probably have tried to sell them, given the current state of his finances, but the landlady had been good to him, and he'd have given her some other kind of present if he could. He arranged to have his packed belongings transported to his parents' apartment, and finally, since he couldn't in good conscience avoid it any longer, he set off there himself.

His parents lived in Upper Goulina, an old neighbourhood in the heart of Pheme, full of big houses in ill repair, many of them former city estates now divided up into apartments. His parents' place was in a smaller house, in better shape than some. It had three stories, and they rented the whole of the middle one. Their downstairs neighbours ran a barbershop in the front of the house, and were engaged in a constant feud with the Temnons over the use of the garden.

The downstairs door, next to the barbershop, was normally unlocked, so Damiskos walked in and up the stairs to the first landing, where he knocked on his parents' door. It was opened, after some hurrying footsteps and the thump of something being set down, by Gaia, his parents' sole remaining slave.

"Oh! Damiskos! Mistress, it's Damiskos!" she yelled back inside the house. "Come in," she said, holding the door wide and beaming at him. Her hair was coming down untidily around her face, and the thing she had set down was a large, unopened jar with the seal of an inferior olive merchant. She had a blunt-looking knife in one hand.

"We haven't seen you in so long," she went on, closing the door behind him and picking up her jar again. She began hacking at the seal with the knife. "They're in the d—in the winter dining room."

"Would you like a hand with that?" Damiskos asked.

"Oh, would you?" She passed off the jar and the blunt knife. "Oh, but you've got a bag. Let me take it for you." She tried to take the bag off his shoulder while he was still holding the knife in that hand. He switched hands hastily in order to pass the bag to her.

He pried the seal out of the jar and waited until she had found a place to put his bag before handing her back jar and knife.

"It's so nice to have you back," she said, beaming at him again.

"Blessed Orante, girl, why are you standing there babbling?" Damiskos's father, Philion, strode out of the dining room—the only dining room in the apartment, which they insisted on calling "the winter dining room"—and clapped Damiskos on the shoulder.

"My boy! Here you are at last. We're just finishing breakfast. Come see who else is here."

"I am glad to see you well, sir." For a moment Damiskos did not move from where he stood.

He wanted to say, "What did you do with the money I sent you for Xanthe's board?" But he knew he wouldn't get a straight answer if he did. It would be his mother's fault, he'd be told, or they'd made a mistake and thought all the money was for them, in spite of the clear instructions he had sent every week. And he would be justly rebuked for greeting his parent with complaints instead of filial affection.

His father was bustling toward the dining room now, so

Damiskos followed him. Gaia took the olives back to the kitchen.

The dining room was surprisingly full when Damiskos entered; he'd expected perhaps one guest, but there were three, along with his mother, lounging on their couches with fruit-peels and bowls of yogurt littering the tables between them. Myrto, Damiskos's mother, started up with an expression of mock-surprise, gold bangles chiming, as he entered. She was dressed in a deep purple gown, her hair arranged in the crisp waves that she favoured.

"Mother," he said awkwardly, hurrying to clasp her hands and kiss her on the cheek. "I'm sorry it has been so long." He looked across at the occupants of the other couches. "Sir, Madam. Ino. This is a surprise."

Korinna and Simonides were older than his parents, or at least they looked it now. It had been nearly fifteen years since Damiskos had seen them. Korinna's hair showed a stripe of silver along the roots, where it needed to be dyed, and Simonides's face looked even more like a candle left in a hot room, slowly sagging as it melted. He was looking at the floor, but Korinna looked at Damiskos, with an expression of undisguised pity.

"Poor Damiskos," she said. For a moment he had no idea what she meant by it.

Their daughter, Ino, was alone on the third couch. She had the same slim figure as she had at sixteen, the last time Damiskos had seen her, and the clinging folds of her lavender-coloured gown showed off her long legs. She wore her golden-brown hair in a sleek style now, looped back from her face, with a veil of a lighter shade of lavender in the back, trailing from an elaborate gold comb thing.

She glanced up at him and then away, with a little nod of greeting. He remembered that little nod, the way she avoided meeting your eyes if she could. She was Damiskos's age, and he supposed she looked it, but really she had not changed much at all. He was glad to see that; perhaps it meant that life had not been too hard on her.

Belatedly he realized that Korinna had called him "poor Damiskos" because of how much he had changed himself. He had forgotten about that.

"Sit next to Ino, Damiskos," his father instructed him, hauling himself back onto the couch with his wife and rearranging his mantle with a grunt. "Come now—you haven't eaten, I suppose?"

He had eaten, hours ago. He sat at the end of Ino's couch —she tucked up her feet, further than she needed to—and took off his own sandals before someone could bawl for Gaia to come and do it for him. His mother reached over to offer him a dish of cheese drenched in honey.

"We got that Kossian cheese that I remember you always used to love," she said.

"Oh," said Korinna, with an artificial brightness. "I remember that too. We used to serve it whenever you visited." She laughed. "Such expensive tastes!"

There was a moment's awkward silence, probably filled by everyone remembering why Damiskos used to visit Korinna and Simonides's house, and why he had stopped. That was certainly what Damiskos was doing. He ate some cheese. It was as good as he remembered, though rather drowning in the honey. He wondered if you could get it in Boukos; he thought Varazda would like it.

"How was Boukos?" Philion asked, mouth full of bread.

"It's—" Damiskos didn't know how to answer. "Much as it always is. It's a lovely city."

"It's so close, really," said Korinna quickly. "It's a shame we don't visit more often."

"We've never been," said Simonides. His voice sounded rusty, as if he hadn't used it in a while.

Out of the corner of his eye, Damiskos saw Ino glance at her father, a tiny smile on her face.

Philion snorted. "All very well to visit, but I wouldn't want to live there. Their damned public watch crawling all over you, brothels on every street-corner, and the way they run their government! Dreadful place."

Korinna laughed, flashing Philion a toothy smile. "You're so like Simonides, with all your opinions!"

This was so far from true that Damiskos realized his eyebrows had risen before he could stop them. Ino's father had opinions, certainly; you hardly ever heard about them, and in Damiskos's experience, when you did sometimes you wished you hadn't, but at least they were consistent and deeply held. Philion Temnon just repeated things he'd heard other people say. He'd reveal massive logical contradictions in the course of a single conversation and wave them away grandly. He just didn't care.

"Simonides," Korinna went on, "says that the Sasians will be the downfall of Boukos." She shrugged. "I've no idea, but that's what he says."

"Foreigners," Simonides creaked. "Full of bad ideas."

Ino was no longer smiling at her father. She looked down at the cup in her hands, and Damiskos heard her give a little sigh.

"Oh, I *like* the Sasians," said Damiskos's mother with a bright, unselfconscious laugh. "They're so interesting, with their beards and things. I'd love to go shopping in Boukos some time."

"The trade agreement has been good for the local economy," said Damiskos, feeling like a character in a badly written play.

"That reminds me," said Myrto, "did you bring me back a present, darling?"

"Yes," said Damiskos. "Only I … er."

He hadn't wanted to produce his mother's present in front of Ino and her parents, because of course he had nothing for them. He got up, feeling that it didn't matter what he did, and went to get the bottle of perfume he had bought for his mother, while his father yelled for Gaia to come do it for him, and Korinna *tsk*ed archly about "that girl of yours."

Myrto exclaimed delightedly over the perfume. Korinna sniffed at it and said it was heavenly. Ino flinched and made a face when her mother shoved the bottle under her nose.

"It smells like sick," she said in a tight voice.

"Stupid girl," Korinna hissed, with a look of such violence that Damiskos thought if the bottle of perfume had not been Myrto's, she would have thrown it at her daughter.

"Sorry," he said, giving Ino an apologetic smile. "You don't like strong smells. I remember that."

It was very clear that something was up, and Damiskos both desperately wanted and feared to find out what it was. His parents and Ino's had been friends once—their fathers had briefly been in business together—but all that had ended spectacularly sixteen years ago, and as far as Damiskos knew none of them had spoken to one another since. He'd heard that Ino had married, and his parents had made disparaging comments about her husband, but he had not listened.

"Have you gone to see any friends since you got back?" said Damiskos's mother, ploughing gamely ahead with the next stilted line in their script.

"No. I had some business to transact yesterday." After a moment he added, neutrally, "It was about Xanthe."

His parents exchanged puzzled glances.

"Who's Xanthe, dear?" his mother asked finally, a little fearfully.

"My horse."

"Oh! Oh, goodness, I thought for a moment you were talking about a daughter!"

Philion Temnon roared with laughter. "I was about to say that sounds more like a name for a horse."

"I asked you to pay for her board at Kleon's stable in the

Vallina with some of the money I had sent from the Bursar's office while I was in Boukos," Damiskos went on. He shouldn't say this in front of Korinna and Simonides, but he could not help himself. "Yesterday Kleon told me he hadn't received anything. What did you do with the money?"

"Darling," said Myrto, "I think we probably spent it. You know how it is."

Korinna made a little noise that sounded like satisfaction, and Damiskos regretted his lapse. There was no question that Korinna and her husband knew what his parents were like, but it was still unfilial of him to put it so plainly on display.

"We were determined to be here when you got home," Korinna was saying, and Damiskos realized she was talking to him. "Weren't we, Simonides?"

Simonides muttered something, which Korinna ignored.

"They don't keep a house in town any more," said Philion. He wiped his mouth with a napkin, tossed it at the table, and missed. "So they're staying with us for the moment."

Damiskos did his best to keep the look of incredulity off his face this time. Incredulity and alarm, in fact. The Temnons' apartment did not have enough rooms to accommodate a whole extra household. Were Simonides and his family in such straits that this was really their best option?

"Did you hear that poor Photios died?" said Korinna.

"Did he?" said Damiskos helplessly. He had no idea who poor Photios was.

"My husband," Ino supplied in an undertone.

"Oh! I'm so sorry. I didn't know."

"It was six years ago," she said. He'd always found it hard to tell if she was being deliberately deadpan or just not expressing emotion because it didn't come naturally to her. He thought it might have been the former here.

Well, that explained why she wasn't dressed in mourning. Had she been living in her parents' house for the last six years? He was surprised they hadn't made another attempt to marry her to someone—surprised she hadn't jumped at the opportunity to get away from them, as she had before …

Then he realized what they must be doing here.

His most vivid memory of the whole awful business sixteen years ago was sitting with his mother, eating stale leftovers from what was supposed to have been his own wedding feast, because it had all been bought and paid for before Ino's parents decided to call off the wedding and withdraw their consent. His father, out in the atrium of their old house, had been loudly supervising the removal of another load of furniture and art that was going to pay off the most urgent of the debts.

"I feel sorry for that girl," Myrto had said, looking critically at a shrimp pastry she had just bitten into. "You would have made her a good husband." She nibbled a little more of the pastry. "Not many would."

That was more or less all she'd ever said on the subject, but at least she had said it. Damiskos's father had not stopped talking about the insult to himself and his family for months, but it never seemed to have occurred to him that there might be any reason to pity anyone else involved.

And now Simonides and Korinna were sitting in the Temnons' dining room as if they had all been the best of friends for the last decade and a half.

"It was never a happy marriage," said Korinna, with a soulful look at Damiskos rather than at her daughter. "We would often talk about how it might have been different."

"Oh."

"Wouldn't we, Simonides?"

Myrto gave a tiny snort of laughter, presumably at the idea of Korinna and Simonides talking "often" about anything.

Philion shot her a look. "Here's what it is. Ino stands to inherit a fortune."

"Oh, well ... " said Korinna, simpering.

"A fortune," Philion repeated. "A business, to be precise, that stands to do very well, very well indeed. Her great-uncle in the colonies left it to her, and she needs a husband to manage it for her. Of course you couldn't expect a woman to run a business. So, here we are."

You *could* expect a woman to run a business, Damiskos thought, and in fact he could imagine Ino being pretty good at it, though she might want someone to help her with the parts that involved a lot of talking to people. But that wasn't the main point here.

Damiskos was still holding the napkin which he'd been using to wipe honey off his fingers. They were still somewhat sticky.

"I'm sorry, sir," he said. "I'm sorry, Ino. I'm not in a position to marry. If—if that's what you're suggesting."

"Oh, pssh," said his father. "I knew you'd have some kind of scruples about it—didn't I say so, Myrto? Didn't I say he would have some kind of scruples?" He sounded indulgently proud of it, in fact.

"You did, dear."

"But you see, it's perfect. We all know you and Ino should have married years ago when you were young. We all see that now."

Korinna murmured agreement.

"And," Philion went on, "there really is a lot of money to be had. You needn't worry on that score."

"Sir, I am not concerned about money. I am not in a position to marry because I am not free to do so." It sounded better than, "Because I don't *want* to."

"Myrto!" Korinna cried, in a way that was probably meant to sound arch but just sounded angry. "You *assured* me that he wasn't married or engaged!"

"All a waste of time," Simonides muttered.

"He isn't," Philion declared. "Xereus's head. He'd have told us if he was."

"Of course he would," said Damiskos's mother. "Oh, but perhaps he was about to. Darling, did you meet a girl while you were in Boukos? How exciting!"

"I'm not engaged," he said, because he wasn't about to begin spinning a web of lies. "But I am not free to marry."

Once or twice Damiskos had thought about how he might tell his family about Varazda. It would be in the context of explaining why he was moving to Boukos, and it would be nicely vague. Varazda's whole family could be invoked, in fact, as a household of Zashians with whom he was going to live. Later, perhaps, they could meet Varazda and be free to wonder just what was going on there—but it wouldn't matter, because they would be resigned by then to their once-brilliant son living out his days as a pottering bachelor in a backwater republic. Except that evidently they weren't. And he had never imagined he would have to explain Varazda as his reason for not being free to be anyone's husband.

"The business is flourishing," Damiskos's father was saying. "Expanding—lots of profit in it, and it's a sure thing, not like real estate. It's in Kargania, so you'd have to go there, at least for a couple of years, to oversee it."

"But Ino will like that," said Korinna. "Won't you, dear."

Ino looked at her hands in her lap.

"She'll like to get out of the public eye, I expect," said Myrto. "With the charges being laid and everything."

Korinna shot Myrto a poisonous look. "They're nothing to do with us. I assure you." Turning to Damiskos with an attempt at a smile, she said, "Ino was briefly engaged to Sosikles Phostikos."

"The politician." Damiskos was glad he didn't have any food in his mouth to choke on. "I didn't know he was—um —engaged. To Ino."

"Of course not," Philion scoffed. "And it won't come out. He wasn't about to advertise the fact that his bride-to-be was a commoner. Not that—you know. Nothing to be ashamed of."

Damiskos sighed. If it had been possible to sell aristocratic status the way you could sell decrepit country villas and ancestral lands, they would have been a family of commoners themselves long ago. In practice they might as well have been.

"And, as Korinna said," his father went on, "nothing he did has any connection to Ino or her family."

"All the same," Myrto persisted, "it might be nice for her to get away from Pheme while the trials are going on."

"Quite," said Philion, "quite."

"Phostikos is a two-faced shit," said Simonides in a violent mutter.

"Language, darling," Korinna hissed.

"Never should have trusted him." He lapsed into silence again.

For a while they were all awkwardly silent. The things that Damiskos might have said to his parents couldn't politely be said in front of Ino and her family. The things he might have said to her weren't really appropriate for their parents' ears. He didn't have anything at all to say to Korinna or Simonides.

"It's so nice to have you back, Damiskos," Myrto said finally. Her smile was just a little sad. "What were you doing in Boukos? Work?"

"No. I'm thinking of moving there."

"Oh!" His mother looked surprised in a mild way. "I've heard it's a nice place to live."

Korinna gave a little gasp. Ino was trying to hide the fact that she was moving her fingers up and down in her lap, over and over again. She was rocking back and forth a little, too, but her mother hadn't noticed yet.

"Don't be ridiculous," said Philion. "What about your career?"

"I've already left my post at the Quartermaster's Office. It wasn't going anywhere."

"Poor Damiskos." Korinna slid back into the conversation, loudly. "You had such a bright future, when Ino and you were young. But, you know, that's perfect in a way. You can travel to Kargania with her and run the fertilizer business, and—"

"Fertilizer?" Damiskos repeated, feeling hysterical laughter bubbling up his throat. This thing got worse and worse. "Fertilizer—you mean ... "

"There's serious profit in it," his father repeated sternly. "Don't be silly."

"It is a little funny," Myrto murmured. "But it's ... you know ... it's very important to the farmers. And you liked living in the colonies."

"I liked living in Zash. Kargania is a whole different situation."

"It's a perfect place to make a fresh start." Korinna took over again. "And a perfect start to your political career."

"My political career," Damiskos echoed.

"If you wanted to have a political career," said Korinna, in a tone which Damiskos had heard her use before with her husband. The words *which you do* were strongly implied.

The silence stretched out again. Damiskos realized, with a feeling like a dark mouth slowly swallowing him, that he was not going to go on saying, "No." How could he? His parents were asking for his help; Ino, from the look of things, actually needed his help. He should have realized that his life with Varazda couldn't last.

The front door rattled in the silence, and hobnailed boots clattered in the hallway. Damiskos looked up.

"Timiskos is home?"

"Mm," said his father, sounding uninterested. "Didn't we tell you?"

Damiskos tossed the sticky napkin onto the table, swung his legs down from the couch, and was out of the dining room in a couple of strides.

His younger half-brother was in the hall, getting his boots off with one hand while holding a couple of writing tablets in the other. He looked up.

"Damiskos, you're back! What brings you—just coming to see the parents, I guess."

"And you! Well, except I didn't know you were in Pheme."

"Yeah. I got back a couple of weeks ago."

Timiskos looked older, although it had been less than a year since Damiskos had seen him. He was dressed in civilian clothes, aside from the boots. He wasn't wearing a sword, and he was clean-shaven. He'd left his legion, Damiskos guessed, and he probably didn't want to talk about it.

"You're staying here?"

Timiskos shrugged wanly. "I've got nowhere else. Father and Myrto borrowed money in my name while I was away, so I've got debts now that I didn't know about. And I didn't manage to save much from my pay. Can't afford to go anywhere else."

"Wait," said Damiskos. "They did what?"

"You know. They did what they do. You're all right? I heard you went off to Boukos without telling them what you were up to."

"I told them what I was doing, they just didn't pay attention. I was visiting a friend. A lover, actually."

"Oh. Sounds fun! I was never able to get into all that."

"All what?"

"You know. In the army. Brothers in arms and that sort of thing. I mean, with women it's fine, I guess, but with another man?" He shrugged again. He was doing too much shrugging, Damiskos thought, and not enough meeting his brother's eyes. "Just couldn't see it. It's great for you, though, I bet. To have someone like that."

"It's not someone from the army, actually. How much debt did they run up in your name?"

"I don't even know, Damiskos. At this point … "

Damiskos folded his arms to keep from grabbing Timiskos's shoulders to stop the shrugging.

"Gods. Don't look at me like that—you look like my commanding officer."

"That's just how I look. Let's go in before they come out here looking for us."

CHAPTER 4

When breakfast was finally over, most of the household melted away. Myrto and Korinna went out to the market, Philion went down to the barbershop, apparently to pick an argument with their neighbours, and Simonides and Timiskos retired to their rooms. It left Damiskos and Ino alone in the dining room, obviously by design. He moved to the couch opposite her, and they sat a little while in silence. She looked calmer, but still uncomfortable. As well she might, he thought. He felt uncomfortable.

"It's good to see you again," he said finally.

She gave him a look which suggested she thought that was a lie.

"It is," he insisted gravely. "I always wished you well, and I wondered how you were doing. I guess ... you've been back in your parents' house for a while now?"

She nodded, guardedly.

"Do you still paint?" he asked after another silence.

At that, her face lit with a tentative smile. "Yes. But not as much as I used to. I found something else I love even more."

"Really? What is that?"

For a moment she seemed to be weighing whether she should tell him. It was probably—certainly—something she had been told she shouldn't love. Even her painting had never met with approval from her family; she'd been too interested in the technical details of mixing pigments and making her own brushes, and she had wanted to repaint all the frescoes in the house. He wondered if she'd ever gotten to do that.

She said, "My late husband was a silversmith. He taught me his trade."

"No! You know how to make things out of silver?" It was both entirely unexpected and somehow obviously perfect. "I've always thought that was sort of like working magic. What kinds of things do you make?"

"Cups and bowls. I like the round shape because you can incorporate a whole scene with people and a background, just as you would in a painting, only in relief rather than in colours. I sometimes do smaller things—I made this bracelet." She held out her wrist. "But I don't enjoy the small work as much."

Damiskos leaned across the table to look at the wide silver bangle, decorated with an impossibly intricate tangle of leaves. On one of the leaves there was a little snail. All he could think of was how much Varazda would like a bracelet like that.

"It's gorgeous," he said finally. Ino never minded if you took a while to figure out what to say.

"Do you want to hear about how you make things out of silver?" she asked shyly.

"I would love to."

She glowed and swayed to and fro as she described in incredible detail, with historical anecdotes and an exhaustive list of all the books that had ever been written on metallurgy, the craft that she had learned from her husband. He listened, smiling and nodding and trying to ask interested questions, because he remembered that this was a way of being nice to her—and it was easy enough.

When she had finished describing the process of chasing a silver bowl and stopped for breath, he said, "Is it true that your marriage was unhappy?"

She looked surprised, then shook her head. "Oh, no. Mother says that. Because we didn't have children, I think? And she never wanted me to marry Photios. I had to pretend to be carrying his child to get her to let me."

"I'm sorry," said Damiskos. From the way she'd described her husband teaching her his craft, it had sounded as if they had been something like soulmates. "You must miss him."

She nodded. "We were happy. He was a very good husband to me. But he was old, and his health was always weak. We had ten years together—we were lucky."

"That's a good way of looking at it." After a moment he said, "What do your parents think about the silversmithing?"

"They don't know about it." She spoke with an almost alarmingly fierce satisfaction. "I pretend to visit a friend, and instead I go down to Photios's son's workshop—Photios had a son, before he married me, who's an adult now, and carries on his trade—and I help him with commissions. He always says that he'll give me my share of the proceeds, but I tell him to spend it on more materials—the business is not doing as well as it used to, and Photios would want me to take care of his son. Besides, I don't know what I would do with the money." She was silent for a moment. Then she said, "Do you want to hear about the commission I got from the Temple of Kerialos?"

"Of course," he said. "Tell me."

"So you're out for good, are you?" said Damiskos, as he sat with his brother in a Lower Goulina wine shop that afternoon.

"What?"

"You've left the legions."

"How did you know? Father told you, I suppose."

"No, I just guessed. What happened?"

Timiskos, of course, shrugged. "I don't know. Nothing. Nothing happened—I just couldn't ... I just didn't want to do it any more. Don't worry, I am ashamed."

"You think I want you to be ashamed?"

"Well, you should. I was doing it for you. I was trying to have the career that you couldn't have any more, I guess, but it was impossible. Not just because I don't have your talents, but I ... hated all the regulations, the discipline, the way you never had any time alone. And I hated Sasia. Immortal gods, Damiskos, I tried to like it there because I knew you did, but the people are so strange, the food is strange, the politics are strange—I could never pick up more than a few phrases of the language—there was just no way I could stick it out there. And I know there are plenty of other places to go, but I just wanted out."

"I'm glad you got out. Sincerely. You should've—it's not your fault, but you should've given up sooner if it was making you miserable. I should have paid more attention and realized something was wrong."

Timiskos shook his head. "No, I was determined not to let you know."

"I don't care, you know. You don't owe it to me. Divine Terza, I—you don't, Timiskos. I encouraged you to join because it was good for me, it was a respectable career that Mother and Father were happy for me to take up, but it got me *out*—out of their house, out of the city, off the island—and that was what I wanted. And I stuck with it because it turned out to suit me, but I didn't necessarily think you'd want to do that. I just hoped it would help you get some distance."

"I guess it did," said Timiskos, frowning. "Yeah. For a while."

They sat in silence drinking their wine for a few minutes. Damiskos looked out the window at the street, where sailors passed on their way up from the harbour, their shadows beginning to lengthen over the pavement. He wondered where Varazda was, what he was doing now.

Dancing, maybe, swords in his hands, black hair swinging loose, in some nobleman's house. Or at home in his own house, playing with Remi while Yazata cooked dinner. Damiskos would have given anything to be there.

"About the debts," he said. "I know you don't know exactly, but roughly how much are we talking about?"

"Oh. You mean my debts?" Timiskos shrugged. "Two thousand or so."

"Divine Terza. Who to?"

"A couple of shops and a jeweler—but most of it to one of Gorgion Pandares's gaming houses."

"Terza's fucking—" Damiskos pushed his hands into his hair. "He's gambling again. I thought that had stopped."

Timiskos shook his head. "He stopped betting at the races, but he started going to these places ... I'm not sure they're even licensed, and the fellow who owns them, Pandares—"

"Yes, I remember him."

"Bad news."

"To put it mildly. Look, I ... I'm not sure how much I can help right now. I was sending them money to pay for Xanthe's board—"

"Oh, gods, they spent it."

"They did, and the hostler sold Xanthe. I had to pay a deposit toward buying her back, so I'm cleaned out at the moment. I should be able to start drawing my pension again soon, but it's not an awful lot of money."

"I don't know. It's not your responsibility."

"They're my parents."

A young man with bright red hair was waving to Timiskos from the door of the wine shop. Damiskos nodded in his direction. "Someone you know?"

"Soukios!" Timiskos hailed him with a bad attempt at cheer. "Come, join us!"

Soukios slid onto the bench beside Timiskos, flagged a waiter for an empty cup, and helped himself to wine from their bottle.

"I knew I'd find you here," he said, elbowing Timiskos. He looked a little older than Timiskos and spoke with a slight Kossian accent. His red hair and his tunic were lightly powdered with marble dust. "This must be your brother."

"Do we look alike?" Timiskos asked. "We're only half-brothers, really."

"You look alike," said the friend. He reached across the table to shake Damiskos's hand. "Soukios Sousiades."

"Damiskos Temnon. Are you a sculptor?"

"Eh? No, I do mosaics."

"Ah, that explains it. I have a friend who's a sculptor," Damiskos explained. "He's always covered in marble dust too."

Suddenly he wished Timiskos's friend would ask about this sculptor, giving him the opportunity to talk about Ariston, whom he had begun to think of almost as a nephew or —well, a brother-in-law.

Soukios, who said he had just finished work for the day, polished off their bottle and called for another one. They refilled their cups, and Timiskos's friend began a salacious story about the family that had commissioned his master's latest work. Outside the light was beginning to fail, and Damiskos wondered if they should order some food.

"Soukios was a school-mate of mine," said Timiskos, interrupting the story. After a moment, Damiskos realized that he'd felt the need to explain why he was friends with a mere mosaicist.

"That's right," said Soukios humorously. "I've got an education—and here I am working with my hands. Oh, the *shame* of it! Nah, I'm joking. I make good money. My folks are proud of me."

"That's great," said Damiskos sincerely. He thought of Ino and her silversmithing, and wondered if he should ask some leading questions to express an interest. But Soukios didn't seem to want to talk endlessly about his craft; he seemed more interested in the wine.

Damiskos turned to his brother. "Do you ever think of taking up a trade like that, Timiskos?"

"What? No, I couldn't. No."

Soukios wiped his mouth and made an emphatic gesture. "I keep telling him he should, though. You know he helped his stepmother redecorate her apartment? And he did a great job. You can make money doing that, for wealthy clients. And it's pretty genteel—it's not grubbing around with mortar and marble dust. Not that I mind that, I'm just saying."

"I don't want to decorate people's houses for a living, Soukios. Just leave it, will you?"

"All right, all right."

"Sorry, did he just say Mother's redecorating?" said Damiskos. That was probably where the money for Xanthe had gone.

"So I didn't get to finish my story," Soukios went on. "There they were, bent over the couch, him with his—"

"Damiskos is just back from Boukos," Timiskos interrupted again. "So he probably has some stories of his own." He gave a rather forced laugh.

"Yeah?" said Soukios eagerly. "Did you visit any of the Pigeon Street girls?"

"I did not."

"Oh, right, I forgot," said Timiskos. "You were there to see your, uh. Your brother in arms or whatever."

Soukios frowned. "I'd've thought an old army buddy would have taken you to sample all the—"

"He's not an 'old army buddy.'" Damiskos suddenly felt very tired.

"What was it the parents wanted you to come back for, anyway?" Timiskos asked. "It has something to do with Simonides and his wife, or something?"

Damiskos sighed. He found himself pinching the bridge of his nose and realized it was a gesture he had picked up from Varazda. "They want me to marry Ino because she's inherited some shit business in Kargania."

Timiskos blinked at him. "What is it? The business."

"Shit. It's shit. It's literally shit, selling shit. In Kargania."

"What?" demanded Soukios. "They sell shit in Kargania? They *buy* shit?"

"For fertilizer. I think people buy and sell it here, but there's a lot more farming in Kargania, so there's probably more, you know, shit-selling."

"What kind of shit? Karganian shit from—what? Mountain goats? What do they have there?"

"I have no idea. Maybe."

"Mountain goat shit, seriously?"

"Shut up, Soukios," said Timiskos. "Yeah. I don't know. It doesn't sound great, but it's a business, though, isn't it? It would mean a steady income. And Kargania's not that bad these days—it's peaceful compared to fucking Sasia, and you *liked* it there. And Ino's nice-looking, right? Weren't you going to marry her, when I was little? Or was that someone else?"

"No, that was her."

"I mean, she's definitely weird—"

"No, she's not. You just have to be understanding with

her—I mean you just have to try to understand her. It's not even that hard. It's just that her shitty parents have never made an effort—even though her father's obviously the same way she is."

Terza's head, he hated both of them. He should never have left her with them sixteen years ago. But at the time there had seemed to be nothing he could do. And he remembered something else, something she had said to him at the time.

"So there you go," Timiskos was saying. "You like her. You'd be happy together."

With no warning, tears started to leak out of Damiskos's eyes. He covered his face with his hands. He felt his brother's hand on his shoulder.

"What is it?"

Soukios groaned. "He wants to marry someone else, you moron! Ah, Anaxe's tits, I'm going to get us another bottle of wine."

Damiskos scrubbed at his eyes. "I shouldn't—sorry—shouldn't drink any more. We should get home, Timi. They'll want us to be there."

"Home?" Timiskos repeated. "You're staying with Father and Myrto?"

Damiskos levered himself up from the table. "Like you, I've nowhere else to go."

"Uh-uh, you can't go yet," said Soukios, reappearing with a wine bottle. "I can't drink this all by myself."

Damiskos took another swipe at his eyes and sat back down.

"Tell us about her," Soukios said as he filled Damiskos's cup.

Damiskos looked into his wine cup. Varazda wouldn't have minded being described as a mistress; Damiskos could even imagine that there were situations in which he would like it a lot. It was Damiskos who didn't want to do it just then—didn't want to talk about Varazda at all.

So it was Timiskos who corrected his friend: "It's a 'he.'"

"Ohhhhh," said Soukios. Then, after a moment, "You know, I've heard a lot of wives don't care—or, I guess if they do, there's nothing they can do about it, because you're the husband."

"Kargania," Timiskos reminded him. "Shit business? It doesn't matter whether she cares or not. Anyway, leave him alone."

Soukios shrugged, and topped up Damiskos's cup after he had taken a swallow.

"So," Soukios began again, "there he was, with his dick … "

In the end, they did not stay much longer. Timiskos saw someone entering the wine shop to whom he—or rather, Damiskos's parents—owed money, and made a discreet exit. Damiskos paid for the wine and followed him. The brothers walked most of the way home together in awkward silence. It was not quite dark, the streets emptying as the shops' shutters closed.

Timiskos cleared his throat. "Look, I'm sorry I was callous, before. About Ino and the whole thing. I guess sometimes you just want someone to be happy, so you try to come up with reasons why their situation isn't so bad. You know?"

Damiskos nodded. "I know. I was doing that with you and the army. When I think back now, I should have been able to tell you weren't happy."

"I guess," said Timiskos after another moment, "you want to stay in Boukos with your, your guy?"

Damiskos ran his knuckles along his jaw, rasping over his beard. He wondered if Varazda had picked up *that* habit. He found himself hoping absurdly that he had, and that he laughed about it when he found himself doing it, because he didn't have a beard. ("Neither do you," he could hear Varazda saying. "You have *stubble*.")

"Nah," he said. "It's not that kind of thing. Couldn't last."

It could have lasted. He could so easily picture himself as an old man in Varazda's house, tottering around while Varazda—old too but still poised and elegant, all silver hair and gold jewellery—looked after him.

He didn't tell his brother that, for the same reason Timiskos hadn't told him why he went into the legions. Maybe it was stupid, but he couldn't bring himself to say, "Yes, I want to stay in Boukos, more than I've ever wanted anything—I feel like an animal in a trap, desperately looking for a way out, and I don't know if I'll ever stop feeling that way."

They arrived on their parents' street. The barbershop at the front of the house was shuttered, but there were a pair of men standing outside the door that led up to the Temnons' apartment. Damiskos stopped in the street as soon as he caught the glint of light on their helmets and naked swords, but he had seen it too late. The men started forward into the street.

"Which one of you is Damiskos Temnon?" one of them demanded.

CHAPTER 5

"Holy angels, it's cold in here!" Varazda announced to anyone who had perhaps not noticed. He had crept out of the bedroom with a blanket around his shoulders to light the brazier in the sitting room.

"Have you heard from Damiskos yet?" came the usual question from the kitchen.

"Yazata, I just got up! I don't get messages from him in my sleep." He snickered at the idea of a dream messenger from Dami. It would have been kitted out in a crisp uniform, and would probably have marched.

"I just thought something might have come last night, after I went to bed," said Yazata. "It's been nearly a week, hasn't it?"

"Five days," Varazda corrected him. "And *I'm* the one who's supposed to be counting them, not you."

Remi bounced into the room and tried to wrap herself up in the trailing end of his blanket. He scooped her up and walked through into the kitchen.

"Are you sure there wasn't a letter last night after you got in?" Yazata persisted.

"I got in at midnight. I'm sure."

50

"Have you written to him?"

Varazda deposited Remi at the table and slid in next to her, rewrapping the blanket around both of them. "Twice. Once in Zashian, to show him that I was practicing. It said, 'Hello how are you we are all well here Yazata misses you.'"

"What?"

"It didn't."

"Oh." Yazata brought over bowls of porridge, two large and one small. "Don't touch, Remiza, it's hot. I do, though. Miss him."

"Blow on it, blow on it!" Remi demanded. "Not you, Yaza—Papa."

Ariston and Kallisto came down as Varazda was cooling Remi's porridge for her.

"Brr! It's as cold as Anaxe's, uh, private parts," said Ariston.

Kallisto gave him a quelling look. "Still rude. You should not swear by any of Anaxe's body parts."

"Yes, my lady," said Ari meekly. "Varazda, has there been—"

"No! Five days. And yes."

"What?"

Kallisto pushed him toward a seat at the table. "No, he hasn't had a letter from Damiskos. It's been five days since Damiskos left. And yes, Varazda has written him. You and Yazata really need to stop pestering him. Damiskos is *his* lover."

She sat next to Ari, which put her directly opposite Varazda. He finished blowing on Remi's porridge and returned it to her.

"I think you should go to Pheme after him," said Kallisto.

Varazda looked up, surprised. She accepted her own bowl of porridge from Yazata, and blew on a spoonful.

"It's just my opinion, and you don't have to listen to it

any more than to these two. It isn't *any* of our business. But personally, I think, if you can make the time, you should go to Pheme. You know his address. You could show up and surprise him. Of course I don't know him as well as you do, but he strikes me as the sort of man who might not write because he doesn't know what to put in a letter, but would be overjoyed to see you."

"We all know he would be overjoyed to see you," said Yazata.

"Duh," said Ariston.

He left later that morning. He hadn't really needed to be convinced. The truth was, he was worried. He didn't think Kallisto was quite right about Dami not knowing what to put in a letter. Dami had written three times in the first month they'd been apart, and they had been rather ridiculous letters to send your lover, but Dami knew very well Varazda had appreciated them. Varazda had been expecting more of the same, maybe with some stilted military terms thrown in, to make it clear that it was a joke. To have heard nothing at all … well, it was probably because a letter had gone astray, that was all.

Yazata, Ariston, and Kallisto had all been eager to help Varazda clear his schedule by conveying messages and cancelling engagements for him after he was gone, and he preferred to get on the ship as quickly as possible so he wouldn't have too much time to dread it. He hated sailing and had never made the trip from Boukos all the way around the island of Pheme to the city. But he judged all sea travel against the journey across the open sea to Boukos from the south-west coast of Zash, and compared to that, this was not so bad. He passed most of the time during the day-and-half and the uncomfortable night of the journey trying not to worry about Dami.

Their parting had been so unsatisfactory. They should have been able to make love the night before Dami left, and it was entirely Varazda's fault that they hadn't. But he shouldn't have snapped at Dami for trying to insist he didn't mind. It wasn't as if Dami had been lying. With his generosity, he probably *didn't* mind. Why was it so hard to accept that you needed your lover to be generous in order for the whole thing to work?

And *was* the whole thing working? Varazda wondered, as he had several times in the intervening days, whether he should have turned that grave conversation in the garden into something more tender, more monumental, after all. He did want Dami to stay forever. He should have said so.

The fog shrouding the harbour of Pheme thinned as the ship approached, and Varazda had as good a view of the biggest city in the world as anyone ever got. It was the first time he had seen it. Against a background of dramatic green mountains, the city sprawled over a series of hills ringing the harbour, a huge jumble of rooflines and walls chequered with windows, streets winding up hillsides like dark fissures. An especially wide fissure held the river, winking in the sun as it scrolled down from the mountains. Here and there, columned temples or civic buildings peeked out from behind tiled roofs, as if the city had grown up willy-nilly around them, hiding their prominence. There was, of course, no hill-surmounting, gilt-roofed palace, as there would have been in a Zashian city. But Varazda could see now why Dami laughed about the size of Boukos. Pheme made it look like a village.

Disembarking in the harbour after taking in that view of the city from a distance, Varazda felt rather like a bird walking on the floor of a forest that it had just flown over.

He could still look up and see some of the city's hills—it had seven, didn't it, famously?—past the buildings bulking around the harbour, but he couldn't orient himself toward any of the things he had seen from the ship. Not that it would have helped him much if he had.

He had come in Pseuchaian dress: his plainest tunic and boots, with a dark green mantle of Dami's and his hair tied back simply, no jewellery at all. Trousers and a coat would have been warmer in this weather, and he was far from the only foreigner on the docks, so perhaps he needn't have bothered. His kept his hennaed hands tucked inside Dami's mantle, all the same.

He looked around the crowded quayside, and decided to follow the clearest current of traffic flowing up into the city. He knew where he was going, roughly. Dami lived in a place called Vallina Hill. Varazda had seen a map of Pheme at the Palace of Letters once, but he hadn't had time to consult it before leaving Boukos, so he was relying on his memory that it was near the river Phira to the south. He would find the river and follow it into the city until he thought he might be close and then ask for directions.

It was a longish walk just to get from the harbour to the mouth of the river, and he began to get the feeling that he was probably going out of his way. He was also hungry, but he passed up several insalubrious-looking wine shops full of sailors before he found one he wasn't afraid to enter. He was surprised by how unsafe the city made him feel.

"Am I near Vallina Hill?" he asked the man behind the wine-shop counter after he'd paid for a greasy sausage on a skewer.

"Not really," said the man, and rattled off a string of directions that made Varazda decide to stick to his original plan of following the river.

He walked through a neighbourhood of warehouses and shipyards, where the Phira was so wide that the other bank looked like an island in the distance, and boats ferried passengers across. The river narrowed, and the warehouses gave way to smart-looking shops and houses. Then it forked around a small, built-up island, and the two streams became narrow enough for bridges. Varazda, looking to his right, away from the river, caught his breath at a sight of gleaming marble buildings and statues in a wide open square, just visible down one of the crooked fissures of streets. He turned into it and emerged in the Phemian agora, the heart of the biggest city in the world.

Varazda had been to Suna—briefly, on his way from Gudul to Boukos—and seen the inside of the Great Palace of the King of Zash. This, he thought, should not have impressed him. It was just a big square—not square, in fact, but irregularly shaped—with buildings all around it. There were market stalls in the middle that ought to have looked tacky, and crowds of people, slaves and labourers and well-dressed women, coming and going. And all around them were soaring, columned porches, painted statues of winged deities, marble inscriptions commemorating the victories of the Republic. It was not harmonious, but it was alive. It ranked easily among the most impressive sights Varazda had ever seen.

He could tell that one building was a temple—to Amphiaraos, the patron god of Pheme? Another would be the Civil Assembly, the main seat of government. And was the Marble Porches, the philosophy school, located here too? He only realized how long he had been standing gaping around at the agora when someone bumped into him and swore, and someone else—probably working in tandem—tried to steal his bag.

He whirled and let the thief get a good look at the knife he had been carrying in his belt, then put it neatly back when the man scurried away.

He had overshot Dami's neighbourhood, it turned out,

but this time he got clearer directions, and it didn't take him long to retrace his steps and find himself on the right street, then in front of the right building, looking up at the windows of the place where Dami lived. He found he was oddly nervous.

He greeted the woman sweeping the steps of the building. "I'm looking for Damiskos Temnon—I believe he lives here?"

She looked him up and down curiously. "He did. He moved out, oh—a week ago?"

"Oh," said Varazda. "Do you have any idea where?"

"No, he didn't leave an address. I didn't hear where he had his things taken, either. Oh, but if you see him, tell him some letters came for him."

"I—do you mind if I see them?"

She looked uncertain for a moment, then disappeared inside the building and returned with two small, sealed rolls of paper. Varazda recognized them with a sinking feeling.

"I sent these," he said. "Do you mind if I take them?"

"I suppose you might as well," she said.

He spent some time sitting on a doorstep near Dami's apartment building, holding his unopened letters, fighting back panic. Finally he collected himself, reminding himself sternly that Dami had *said* he was going to give up his apartment, so of course he wasn't there. And as for Varazda, he was an adult, and this was just a Pseuchaian city—so long as he kept his wits about him and avoided bad neighbourhoods, there was nothing to be afraid of.

The only question was where he should go now. Where *could* he go now?

Dami's parents lived in Pheme, of course, but Varazda had no idea where. And while he was sure he could find a reasonable inn—probably—to spend the night, the sun was still high in the sky, and that wouldn't do him much good now. He needed to find someone he knew. Surely he did know someone in Pheme, besides Dami.

He was trying to remember the names of any of the Phemian diplomats he had met at the Basileon, when it occurred to him. He did know someone in Pheme; he even knew, roughly, how to find her house. She had written Dami a long letter, which he had read out to Varazda, in which she said she was staying at a house in the city, and described its location: near the Maidens' House, overlooking a park.

An hour later, after only a couple of false starts (apparently when you asked for directions to the Maidens' House in Pheme, people thought you were coyly asking to be directed to a brothel), Varazda arrived on a doorstep in a quiet street. The sun was beginning to go down, the shadows of buildings already making the streets dark. He hoped he was at the right door.

It was opened to his knock by a servant he did not recognize, a young woman with dark brown skin and black curls who struck him as looking like Remi might when she grew up.

"Is your mistress in?" he asked, trying not to smile too obviously at her.

The girl laughed. "Which one?"

"Oh, I am sorry. Perhaps I have the wrong house." A distinct possibility. The neighbourhood was confusing, and the house's door was tucked in between shop-fronts. "I'm looking for Nione Kukara."

"She's in the dining room," said the girl cheerfully. "Have you eaten?"

"I ... haven't," said Varazda, coming inside at her gesture. "But shouldn't your mistress—one of them—be the one to ask me to dinner?"

"Should she?" The girl closed the door behind him. "I

would have said so, normally, but she freed us all two weeks ago, and since then we don't know whether we're coming or going."

"Congratulations! May—may the gods smile on you." That wasn't the right expression, but it conveyed the general idea. "I remember that feeling. I was freed as part of a group, too. We all wandered around in a daze for a while, not knowing what to do with ourselves."

"That's exactly how it is here. Let me announce you. Oh, who are you, anyway?"

"Say 'Pharastes from Boukos.'"

The girl's mouth fell open. "No! Not *the* Pharastes? I've heard so many stories about you! I was in town when everything happened out at the villa, but the other girls told me about it. I thought you were just terribly Sasian, from the way they talked—but you look quite normal. Sorry, sorry—off I go!" She turned and pelted away into the house, where he heard her breathlessly announcing him from the door of the dining room.

"Pharastes is here! You know, Pharastes from the summer —*the* Pharastes?"

He followed her in. Nione was just sitting up on her couch, from where she been snuggled up against her companion, a big woman in a beautiful blue dress, with tiny gold butterflies sparkling in the dark cloud of her hair. Aradne, who had been Nione's steward in the summer.

This was what the girl had meant when she asked *which* of the mistresses of the house he wanted to see. Varazda had to restrain a ridiculous urge to bounce and clap his hands excitedly, the way his daughter might have done.

"Ph—Varazda," Nione corrected herself carefully. "What a pleasant surprise! Are you and Damiskos in Pheme together?"

"No," he admitted, the desire to bounce draining away.

"No," said Aradne, pushing herself up to sit too, serious and alert. "Something's happened to Damiskos."

"It has?" Nione glanced between Aradne and Varazda, momentarily confused. "What?"

"I don't know," said Varazda. "It might be nothing. But I've come here because I'd nowhere else to go."

"Sit down, for the gods' love," said Aradne. "Have you eaten dinner?"

He sat and rearranged some food on a dish while he explained why Dami had come to Pheme and what had happened when he went to Dami's apartment. Nione and Aradne sat listening intently, and did not resnuggle themselves on their couch. Varazda felt guilty for interrupting their cozy meal, and sad that the moment for bouncing and hand-clapping had been preempted by his own trouble.

"It is probably nothing," he said. "Dami didn't write because he didn't get my letters, and he didn't get my letters because he's given up his apartment. He—he said he was going to."

"Oh!" Nione clasped her hands delightedly. "Did he—is it because—"

"He's moving in with you," said Aradne.

"Yes."

"Hooray!" said Aradne, grinning. "That's the best news."

"Oh, I'm so glad," said Nione. "He seemed very happy in his letter."

"*You* both seem very happy," Varazda got in at last.

They exchanged glances and smiled. "We are," said Aradne.

"How long have you … " He gestured vaguely, Zashian-style.

"Oh, twenty years, give or take," said Aradne with a smile, reaching across to squeeze Nione's hand. "And about a month."

"Might Damiskos be at his parents' house?" said Nione.

"That seems most likely," said Aradne. "Do we have any idea where they live?"

"None," Varazda admitted. "I have generally avoided talking to him about his parents."

"They had a house on the North Bank, near the Tortina Bridge, when I first knew him," said Nione, "but I believe they sold it, or … " She winced.

"Lost it," Varazda finished for her. "He said something about that. I gather they rent a place now. Actually, I do recall that he said it was in a neighbourhood that is … somehow tacky?"

"Upper Goulina, maybe?" said Aradne.

"Is Upper Goulina tacky?" Nione asked.

"So tacky," said Aradne. "How do you not know that?"

"I don't know anyone who lives there. What about the Rina?"

Aradne shook her head. "That was *sketchy*, not tacky, and it's improving, anyway. It's almost fashionable now. I say start with the Goulina. We'll send one of the boys to ask around first thing tomorrow. What's Damiskos's father's name?"

Varazda winced. "Phil-something. He never uses his patronymic, so I'm not sure. His family name is Temnon."

"Oh, that's right," said Aradne, "he has a family name. So they're aristocrats who lost their city house and live in a tacky part of town—it'll be Upper Goulina for sure."

"His father is Philion Temnon," Nione supplied, a little apologetically. "Philionides is his patronymic."

"Ah yes," said Varazda, embarrassed.

He wondered if Dami remembered *son of Nahaz son of Aroz of the clan Kamun*, which Varazda never, ever used but had for some reason trotted out when Dami asked about his name the first time. He also never remembered that Dami was an aristocrat. It wasn't a status that seemed to have much meaning in Boukos, but that didn't, just then, strike Varazda as being a very good excuse.

"Do you have anywhere to—" Aradne started. "No, of course you don't." She swung herself off the couch and went to the dining-room door to call for the girl who looked like Remi.

"Have a room made up for Pharastes, will you? The one with the peacock on the wall, maybe."

"Yes, ma'am." The girl glanced over Aradne's shoulder to smile at Varazda.

"And get Niko for us too, will you? We'll have a job for him tomorrow." Aradne turned back to Varazda. "Now—eat something."

Niko, a boy whom Varazda remembered from Laothalia, arrived and at first didn't recognize Varazda in Pseuchaian clothes, then was almost as excited to see him as the door-keeper had been. Aradne explained his errand, and he had to be sternly forbidden from setting off on it then and there—"because it's not *quite* dark yet, is it, ma'am?"—instead of waiting for the following morning.

Varazda forced himself to eat some dinner, and then Aradne said, "Let me show you around my house."

Nione made a little noise of protest. "Maybe not just now, my dear. I won't say you look like you need to rest, Varazda, but I'm sure, in your position, *I* would need to rest, and perhaps you would like to."

He smiled gratefully. "That's quite a good idea."

"Oh, all right," said Aradne, getting up. "I'll take you to your room. You're my first guest, did you know?"

"Really? I'm honoured."

"First guest in my own house. It's quite special."

Nione remained in the dining room, and Varazda followed Aradne out into the atrium. When she closed the door behind her, he grinned at her.

"Can I give you a hug?" he asked.

61

"I was just about to ask if I could give you one."

She was built a little bit like Yazata, and she gave excellent hugs. When she let him go, he said, "Did she … "

"Buy me a house? Yes, she did. Come on—she's right, you do need to rest, and all flattery aside, you look it, too. I'll tell you all about it tomorrow."

CHAPTER 6

It took Niko a couple of hours to find out the Temnons' address the following morning, but as he set off at dawn, he was back by the time Varazda was eating breakfast. The house was in Upper Goulina, as Aradne had predicted.

"I can take you there myself," she said. "I'll make myself scarce after we get there, of course. And if you don't want company on the way—"

"Oh, I do, profoundly. Thank you."

He finished dressing after breakfast in the Zashian-style suit he had brought with him. If he had to show up unannounced on Dami's parents' doorstep, he thought he might as well let them know straight away what they were dealing with. Aradne, wrapped in a warm mantle, with the gold butterflies winking in her hair again, spent the first part of the journey to the Goulina Hill interrogating him about the construction, fashions, and customs surrounding trousers.

"How did you know where to find us?" she asked finally.

"Nione wrote to Dami a couple of weeks ago. I guess they had been corresponding, and she knew where he was staying. She said she was at a house in the city, and described where it was. She didn't mention she'd bought it for you."

Aradne smiled. "She didn't mean to, at first. We were renting it, to get away from Laothalia—that was my idea, actually, because I was afraid … After that business in the summer, she was spending all her time praying, and of course I'm in favour of a certain amount of praying, but I was afraid she was going to make some kind of rash decision. Well, to tell you the truth, I was afraid of her taking a new vow of celibacy." With a reticence that was unusual for her, she said, "I'd waited so long for her to be free of the first one. And then that gods-cursed Phaia got to her first and broke her heart."

Varazda winced sympathetically. "You didn't blame Nione for that?" he asked after a moment. He would have, in Aradne's position.

"Oh, I did. When you came to the villa in the summer, I wasn't too pleased with Nione, and she, bless her heart, had no idea why." She sighed. "And then all that happened, and Phaia turned out to be a snake in the grass—sometimes I still regret I never got my hands on her. They sent her to Choros Rock, didn't they? She deserved worse." She shook herself slightly. "Anyway, it was my idea to come here, and I picked the house and everything, just asked—well, told, really—Nione to give me money to rent it.

"So we came here, and it was a brilliant idea, if I say so myself. One thing led to another, and when Nione found out the house was for sale, she bought it for me. She was hung up on the difference in our status and wanted me to have a place of my own, so I didn't feel dependent on her. She was afraid I wouldn't accept the house as a gift, too!" Aradne laughed. "That kind of thing doesn't bother me. Would it bother you?"

Varazda considered that. It was a very hypothetical question. "I'm afraid it might, a little. But I'm, well, probably more male than you."

Aradne shouted with laughter and slapped him on the back. "Probably! It wouldn't take much."

"But look here—'one thing led to another'? You can't possibly expect me to be content with that."

"Oh." She looked surprised. "I don't know. Most people would be. It wasn't a romantic thing, with declarations and … well, I suppose there was a *little* bit of that, with the freeing of all the slaves and that."

"She did that for you?"

"Obviously. Well, in a way. It wasn't as if she didn't think it was the right thing to do." She was silent for a moment, then she seemed to have marshalled her thoughts, and she said, "I don't know if you can really understand what it was like for me. I've known her since I was a little girl—she was a girl then too, but I don't think I ever noticed. She was always … like a goddess to me. Sort of—sort of literally. I thought I was the steadfast, loyal one, but when she retired from the Maidens … I didn't know how to love her as an ordinary woman, and so Phaia got to her before me, and I couldn't even explain why that upset me so much.

"She didn't know that I wanted her, because I'd spent so many years worshipping her as if she wasn't really human. Why are you looking at me like that?"

"You said it wasn't romantic. You get to be with your goddess, and that's not romantic?"

Aradne scowled at him. "It's terrifying, is what it is. You don't believe in deities that can walk the earth—that's why you can't understand."

"Oh." That brought him up short.

"Mind you," she said after a moment, with a small, secretive smile, "it's also *wonderful*, and I'm—we're both—very, very happy. Anyway, here we are."

They stood in front of a barbershop on a street of big, decrepit-looking houses, and Aradne said, "We're here."

Varazda looked up at the building. It had a facade of

dirty pink stucco that was falling off in places, and an indecipherable mythological fresco in between the windows on the second storey. The barbershop, which had a clean new awning and customers waiting outside, was the only prosperous-looking part of the place. There was a door to the side of the barbershop with a lion's-head knocker and a guard in a military-style helmet lounging against the doorpost.

Aradne frowned. "That's odd. Let's go see if we've got the right place."

They approached the guard. "Excuse me," said Varazda, with a little Zashian flair to match his clothes, "can we go in?"

"That depends," said the guard, without moving from his slouch against the doorpost. "Are you a friend of Damiskos Philionides?"

"I am." He said it before stopping to think about whether it was the right answer or not.

The guard shook his head with obvious satisfaction. "Then no. You can't."

"Why?" Aradne demanded.

The guard looked at her as if deciding whether she deserved an answer. "Because I say so, and I'm allowed to say so, because I'm guarding the door."

"Why are you guarding the door, though?" Varazda asked, as politely as he could, before Aradne could snarl at the man. He felt cold. He didn't want to hear the answer, but the question had to be asked.

"Your friend's confined to the house awaiting trial. He killed a man."

"Bullshit!" Aradne spat. "Who's he supposed to have—"

"You wouldn't happen to know," Varazda cut in, his voice sounding surprisingly normal, "who was the victim?"

"Of course I know. My master brought the charges. Your friend killed his son. Helenos Kontiades Diophoros."

"That's—"

Varazda put a hand on Aradne's arm. "That's very surprising. We're quite shocked. And you're sure we can't speak to him?"

"Yeah. I'm sure." The guard smiled unpleasantly.

"We'd better go, then, hadn't we?" said Varazda, and dragged Aradne away.

They had got some distance up the street, and she was beginning to gasp for breath, when he finally slackened his pace and let go of her arm. Feeling guilty, he stopped altogether.

He was glad she was with him. Having someone more volatile than himself to control had helped him stay calm himself. He wondered how long he would be able to keep it up.

"Helenos—that's—" She paused to catch her breath. "That's the goat-fucker from the summer, isn't it? So he's dead! I wish I'd had the chance to kill him myself. Do you think Damiskos did it?"

Varazda shook his head. "No. Helenos isn't—wasn't—the fighting type, and Dami wouldn't kill anyone unless it was a fair fight. Or an accident—but you don't *accidentally* kill a shit like Helenos. What was he doing in Pheme?"

"No idea. Orante's tits, what if Phaia is here too?"

"'Don't sheathe your sword too soon,' is what they say where I'm from. But no, I don't see Helenos springing her from Choros Rock and coming back to live in hiding in Pheme. They didn't part very well."

"Pharastes, what are we going to do?"

He grabbed both her hands. "Thank God—or Orante, or whoever—that it's not worse. He's not—" He almost choked on the word. "—dead, or sick, or even sentenced yet. We'll figure this out."

She nodded resolutely. "You're right. Wish we were a bit more discreetly dressed, the two of us."

"Mm. We might be able to use that to our advantage,

actually." He scanned the street and pointed to a shop opposite the Temnons' building, selling cheap-looking lamps. "Are you dressed like a woman who might shop in a place like that, do you think?"

She considered it. "Yeah. It looks like stuff for freed slaves with more money than taste. I could pass for that." She flashed him a crooked grin.

"Well," he said sceptically, "if you're sure. You go see if they know anything there. I'll try to strike up a conversation with the assistant at the barbershop, the one who's just emptied his dustpan in the street over there."

He watched her go into the shop, and reminded himself sternly that he had a mission now. It was no time to fall apart. No time to worry about what Damiskos was—what he had—

He turned toward the barbershop. It always helped to have a mission.

When he rejoined Aradne in the street a few minutes later, she had a tacky lamp to show for her errand and an incoherent story about how one of the young men across the street was a murderer, and maybe he was the one who had killed that fellow in Bridge Street last week, you know the one who'd had his throat slit, but which of the young men was it now anyway? Varazda had learned something more to the purpose.

"Let's walk," he said, "before that fellow at the door notices we're still here. Around the back of the building, if you don't mind—I want to get a look at the walls. So the barber's man was full of information—some of it irrelevant. For instance, the building's owner is trying to sell, and it's felt this scandal will drive down the price. Some of it was more to the point. It turns out Helenos is the son of a fairly powerful family, and the guards his people have set on the Temnons' door are very chatty. One of them told the barber that Helenos was found dead in a seedy part of town, that he was poisoned—"

"Poisoned!" Aradne repeated in disbelief.

"Yes, and as far as Dami having killed him, 'There are witnesses.' Our man didn't know quite what that meant."

"I'd say it meant they were seen drinking together, except—Damiskos, drinking with that goat-fucker?"

"No," Varazda agreed. He looked up at the windows of the second and third stories of the Temnons' building. "They have good wide sills and quite solid-looking cornices. The trouble is, I don't know which floor his family's on."

Aradne looked at him sharply. "You're not thinking what I think you're thinking. Are you?"

He cocked an eyebrow at her. "Probably."

"They're at it again," Philion Temnon announced. "Moving the statuary around. Look." He stood in the open door of the balcony at the back of the apartment, beckoning to his wife.

"Close the door, dear, you're letting in a draught," said Myrto, not looking up from the game of robbers she was losing to Korinna. "We'll have the boys go down and put them back where they were later."

"I can't leave the house, remember?" Damiskos called from the doorway of the kitchen, where he was picking over lentils while Gaia went to bring back water.

"Surely you're allowed out into the garden, though. It's our garden."

"It's a shame it's such a small one," said Korinna, taking another of Myrto's tiles off the board.

"Myrto," said Timiskos wearily, from where he slouched on one of the couches, "it's not your garden. That's why your neighbours keep moving the statues—they're not *your* statues."

"Ridiculous." Philion was still standing in the open doorway watching the activity below. Dusk was falling outside, and the air coming through the door was bitterly cold. "That's a ridiculous place to put that Soukos and the Dolphin."

"It's a ridiculous statue," Timiskos muttered.

Korinna glanced up from her game and gave Damiskos a suspicious look through the kitchen door.

"He spends a lot of time with your slave girl," she remarked. "Do you think it's quite tasteful, Philion? Oh, that's not a legal move, my dear. I'm so sorry."

Philion laughed uncomfortably. "Oh, you know. Boys will be—I mean, haha, men, you know. Gaia's a pretty girl. I can tell him to tone it down if you'd like."

"Slave bastards are expensive," said Simonides out of nowhere. "Better to expose them."

"Yes, yes," said Philion. "Absolutely."

"He's *sorting lentils*," Myrto remarked dryly. "Gaia is not even there."

Philion looked in through the kitchen door, frowning. "Couldn't Ino be doing that?"

"Yes, sir, I'm sure she could, but she's out visiting a friend."

Korinna gave a loud sigh. "I *tried* to forbid her, but you know how she is. Everything has to be exactly the same, or … " She waved a hand dismissively. "There we go, that's the game. Poor Myrto! I expect you couldn't concentrate for worrying about your poor son. But I *know* this will all be resolved soon. They'll find him not guilty, and then we'll sue them for slander. Won't we, Philion? You come have a game with me now."

"Ah yes, good idea. Yes—it's a disgrace, but it will be sorted out soon." Philion had said this easily a dozen times in the last four days. "When my friend Olympios gets back from Anthousa, he'll sort it all out. He's a first-rate advocate, and we won't have to pay him much, because he's a friend."

"Oh, that must be a relief!"

"Most advocates are crooks," Simonides put in.

Damiskos picked out the last bit of debris and swept the lentils off the counter into a bowl. In the last four days, he had moved from feeling desperation to being almost amused by the grotesqueness of his situation. He felt as if his heart had taken too much and simply gone numb. It was a bad state in which to be making tactical decisions; he remembered that from his army days.

He'd expected Korinna and her family to melt away at the first sign of trouble, and perhaps if the trouble had not arrived so suddenly and spectacularly they would have. Instead they seemed to feel—Korinna, the decision-maker of the family, seemed to feel—that they were stuck here and that their best gambit was to "stand by" Damiskos for the duration of the trial and its aftermath. She wasn't happy about it, and was doing her best to make the Temnons feel that she was doing them a favour, not to say martyring herself for their benefit. No doubt when it came to dividing up the profits from the Karganian fertilizer, this would be taken into account.

The day after the guards from Helenos's family had arrived to deliver the charge, Ino had knocked on the door of Damiskos's room and said, "If there is anything I can do to help, I hope you will tell me. I don't believe you did it. You have always been a good friend to me."

He had wanted to give her a hug—in that comfortable way that everyone in Varazda's family was always hugging each other—but he knew she didn't really like that kind of thing, so he just nodded and said, very seriously, "Thank you."

Damiskos retired early and fell asleep while the rest of the household was still up, and he could hear their voices buzzing in the atrium. When he woke, it was full dark, and the house was still.

He had a bedroom to himself, the one which was normally Timiskos's. This was not by choice. The first night, he had set up a camp bed in a corner of Timiskos's room, as the house was already overfull of guests, with Ino sleeping in Gaia's room and Gaia evicted to the dining room. The second night, he had found the camp bed moved out to a storage closet, Timiskos ordered to sleep there, and Timiskos's room freed for Damiskos's sole use. He tried to protest but got so many significant looks that he stopped, afraid that Korinna was going to say, in front of Ino, how she expected her to make use of his newly private sleeping quarters.

He'd been woken by a noise, a small, stealthy noise. He felt muzzy, and his mouth tasted sour. He pushed himself up on his elbows and tried to locate the source of the noise.

There was a window near the foot of his bed—Timiskos's bed—and as Damiskos looked at it, one shutter swung noiselessly inward, and a figure appeared poised on the sill, ready to spring down into the room. Even in the dark, it was a figure Damiskos would have known anywhere.

Varazda hung there for a moment, half-in and half-out of the window, as if making sure Damiskos had seen him and that it was safe to come inside. He was dressed in black trousers and a plain black shirt, with his hair pulled back in a knot. Dressed, in fact, for breaking into second-storey windows.

He made a little gesture, visible in the moonlight, drawing an arc with one finger, down into the room, and raising his eyebrows questioningly. In answer Damiskos just sat up and opened his arms. In a moment Varazda had dropped down onto the bed and scooted up into Damiskos's lap, straddling his thighs and wrapping Damiskos in his arms. His hands were cold through the fabric of Damiskos's pyjama shirt.

"Are you all right?" Varazda whispered. "More or less?"

"More or less. Much more for seeing you."

Varazda tightened his grip. "Tell me what happened."

"I, uh." Damiskos loosened the embrace to lean back a little and look at Varazda. "How are you here?" he whispered. "What is this? Are you really here?"

"Yes, I am, my darling. This is what I do."

"Rescue me?"

Varazda shook with silent laughter. He was in Damiskos's bed, in the middle of the night, when Damiskos had thought he was far away and maybe lost forever, and he was laughing.

"Sneak about people's houses without being caught," he said. "Usually I don't have to scale walls, but I'm pretty good at that, too."

"You are." Damiskos remembered. "How did you know where to find me?"

"I didn't. I just found you. It was a lot of work." He grinned.

Damiskos drew Varazda's face down and kissed him, harder than he intended. Varazda kissed back just as fiercely, but then he drew back and laid his fingertips on Damiskos's lips.

"Tell me what happened. I know Helenos died by poison, I know his father brought charges against you, and you're confined to the house—I assume because you couldn't raise money for a bond?"

"Mm," said Damiskos from beneath Varazda's fingers. Varazda took them away. "They wanted 600 nummoi."

"That's a lot. Why do they think they have witnesses?"

"Well, they do. Not to me killing Helenos, because I didn't—"

"Obviously."

"—but I did meet him in the street the day he died.

Shortly before he died, I guess. I was seen by several people, we had an altercation—"

"As you would."

"—and he shouted out my name in the street. I knocked him down—"

"Good."

"Well, not good, because he fell harder than I expected—he was at least half-drunk—and *for some reason*, which I've kicked myself for ever since, I felt the need to see him safely home. People in the building where he was staying saw us there, too."

"Hm. Awkward. And then he turned up dead."

"Apparently. Poisoned with something called thorn-flower. I was able to find that out by talking horses with one of the more friendly guards. But that's about all I got. Most of the guards are not at all friendly."

"Thorn-flower," said Varazda thoughtfully. "I believe that's the same thing they call Nepharos's Bell in Boukos. You know they use that for executions?"

"Huh. I didn't know that." After a moment, he added, "In Pheme, er, people of my station are often exiled instead of … you know."

Varazda nodded, expressionless. He probably knew that didn't apply in cases of deliberate murder—certainly not the murder of a fellow aristocrat by poison.

"Well," he said, "since you didn't commit the crime, why don't we focus on proving that, and it will be immaterial."

"I think the defense will hinge on my character, and how strange it would be for me to poison someone when I was carrying a sword at the time."

"What? No, the *defense* will hinge on finding out who really killed Helenos, and bringing them to justice."

Damiskos shook he head. "Darling, this isn't Boukos. There's no public watch here."

"I know that. I'm here."

He said it so simply, his bravado so matter-of-fact that it almost didn't seem like boasting. Damiskos wanted to say, *Don't do this for me. I'm not worth it.* But that wasn't true; somehow, as wrong as it seemed, to Varazda he was worth it.

"So," said Varazda, "how long ago did this happen?"

"Uh. It was last Xereus's Day. So … a week? Six days."

Varazda nodded. "And you've been at your parents' house since?"

"Since Bread Day—the charge was laid that night."

"Is the trial scheduled?"

"Not yet."

"Right. Well, let me know as soon as it is."

"How? I mean, how can I—you shouldn't be—"

Varazda put his fingers on Damiskos's lips again. "I'm staying in Orchard Street, at Aradne's house."

"You mean Nione's house?"

"No, I mean Aradne's house—there's a whole story there, and it's a good one, but there's no time. What else do I need to know? Where did you run into Helenos?"

Damiskos told him, and answered several more questions about what had happened and who had been watching. Then Varazda withdrew a couple of tightly rolled scrolls from his sash and pressed them into Damiskos's hand.

"I wrote to you," he said with a little smile, almost shy. "Your landlady kept them for you."

"I'm sorry—I couldn't risk—even if I'd been able to get anyone to carry a letter—"

"Shh. I know."

"But also," Damiskos ploughed on, "I didn't know what to say because there's this whole other situation—"

They heard a small sound from the atrium, a door opening and shutting quietly. Varazda made a face.

"You'll have to tell me about that later," he breathed.

He leaned in and kissed Damiskos one last time, lightly, then sprang back to the window. There was a soft tap at

Damiskos's door. When he looked back at the window, the shutter was swinging closed.

He waited another moment, and tucked the two letters under his pillow, before he said sleepily, "Who is it?"

The door opened. Ino stood on the threshold in her nightgown.

CHAPTER 7

Varazda couldn't hear what the female voice said until its owner had come inside the room and shut the door behind her. But he could tell she had come inside the room and shut the door behind her.

Perhaps it was his mother.

"What's the matter?" Dami asked.

"Mother was watching from the hall to make sure I came in. Sorry." The woman's voice was glum and affectless.

Varazda clung tensely to the masonry outside Dami's window, frozen lest he give himself away with the inevitable slight scuffling of descent.

"Oh," said Dami, obviously dismayed. "That's—that's all right. But, Terza's head—watching from the hall, really?"

There was someone passing in the alley below, pushing a wheelbarrow that rattled over the stones. It would have offered good cover for any noise Varazda might make, but the person might see him if he moved. He remained stuck where he was.

"Mm-hm," the woman was saying. "She found out about Kleisios. Photios's son. I don't know how. She doesn't know about the smithy, yet—she thinks Kleisios and I are lovers. Lovers!" she repeated bitterly. "He's my *stepson*."

"Shit. Sorry. I mean, I'm so sorry. Did she forbid you from visiting him, or … "

"Leaving the house. She's forbidden my leaving the house. And made me come in here 'to see if you wanted company.' She said, 'If you can't win him back, we'll have to do it the old-fashioned way. Don't take no for an answer.'"

The stupid wheelbarrow had got stuck in a crack in the pavement, and the person pushing it was kicking the wheel and swearing at it. *The old-fashioned way*? What was that? And win Dami back from what?

Oh. Varazda felt a moment of unaccustomed vertigo. She meant win Dami back from *him*.

On the other side of the window, Dami said, "Right, well —*no* is the answer, I'm afraid. I'm in love with someone else."

"Are you? Oh, that's nice." Varazda could hear the smile in her voice. "I was hoping maybe you were. And after all, if you do want to go into politics, you can marry this other person, can't you?"

The wheelbarrow unstuck itself and its owner trundled off down the alley.

Go into *politics*?

"Do you want to take the bed," Dami was saying, "and I'll make myself comfortable on the floor?"

"Oh, no. I'll go back to my own room. I'll tell Mother you said you weren't interested in having sex with me."

"Uh. All right, thanks. That's—I'd appreciate that."

Varazda climbed down, finally, still rather mystified by what he had heard, but wishing he could have gone back in and wrapped Dami in his arms for the easy way he had said, "I'm in love with someone else."

Aradne was still up when Varazda got back, sitting in the kitchen with her cook, listening to another young woman read aloud from a novel. Varazda heard something about doomed lovers as he came in from the passage, and he hesitated. He wasn't sure he was in the mood for doomed lovers. But they stopped reading when they saw him.

"Pharastes! How did it go with the breaking and entering?"

"What?" said the cook, staring between the two of them as Varazda pulled up a stool and sat down at the kitchen table.

"He was breaking into his lover's family home to learn the details of a false murder charge against him—it's the stuff of romantic fiction, Dria. It's as good as *Alkaios and Eudoxia*."

"Well, I guess I shouldn't be surprised, after what happened last summer," said the cook.

"So what did you learn, Pharastes?"

"Helenos died from drinking a tincture of Nepharos's Bell—thorn-flower, you call it here. He was staying in Crow Street on the Skalina Hill, and Dami knocked him down in the street when they met. Also, there's some woman who's trying to get her daughter into bed with Dami—I mean actually delivering her to the door of his room in the middle of the night—and I don't quite know what that's about. They said something about 'winning him back.'"

"Yikes," said the cook. She'd brought down a cup for Varazda and poured out some of the wine that she and Aradne had been sharing. She pushed it across the table to him. "He told you about it, though—that's a good sign."

Varazda didn't know what she meant. "He didn't get a chance to tell me—she came to the door, the young woman, I mean, and I overheard them talking."

The cook grimaced and shot Aradne a look.

"Don't be silly," said Aradne sternly. "I'm sure Damiskos behaved like a gentleman."

"What?" said Varazda.

"Oh, bless his heart, he wasn't even worried!" cried the cook. "Here, have a bun. They're still quite fresh, only left from yesterday."

"So who was the girl?" Aradne asked. "Not an ex-wife—he's never been married, has he?"

"No!" Varazda unpinned his hair and shook it out. "He's had, you know … " He trailed off, realizing he didn't know. Dami had certainly talked about male lovers, a fiancée in Zash, and visiting courtesans and things, but Varazda didn't know if he had ever had what one might call a regular mistress. He thought not.

"You know … " Aradne prompted.

"Um. Well, he's not like me."

"Addicted to cock?"

"Ew. Aradne, please."

She snorted. "What? He likes pussy, is what you're trying to say."

Varazda put his hands over his ears. That was when Nione came in, sleepy-eyed and wrapped in a shawl, carrying a lamp. The cook jumped instinctively to her feet.

"Hello, Dria. Aradne, what have you been doing to poor Varazda? He's red as a beet."

Aradne relayed Varazda's story in her own style, and Nione stopped her before she could finish a sentence that began, "What I think it must be—"

"Ino," Nione said. "She's not an ex-*wife*, she's an ex-fiancée. I remember her, slightly. She was around when Damiskos was still serving in the Maidens' Honour Guard, though they weren't officially engaged then. They were friends—her father was a business connection of his father. They got engaged just before he went into the legions, and then her parents called it off."

"Well, they've called it on again, I guess," said Aradne. "Or at least the mother has."

"The parents were both very cruel, I remember," said Nione. "I think Damiskos wanted to marry her mostly to get her away from them. She was shy—or something more than that. She had difficulty talking to people. I don't think they were in love, exactly. I'm sorry, Varazda—that must have been a distressing thing to hear."

"He started to tell me about it, before I had to dive out the window. He said there was a 'situation.' I don't think I understand very well what the 'situation' is, even now."

Nione and Aradne exchanged a glance. The cook, Dria, made a stifled noise.

Aradne said, "The awful mother wants him to knock her up—"

"Make her pregnant," Nione supplied with a wince.

"—so she'll have to marry him."

"Oh," said Varazda after a moment, realizing that he had reared back in shock. "I see."

Aradne shook her head. "I don't know whether it's worrying or cute that you're so innocent sometimes."

"Worrying," he said, rubbing his hands over his face. "It should definitely be worrying. And I'm not innocent, just—things like that happen at the Zashian court all the time, but I expect better from Pseuchaians." He shook himself slightly.

Nione kindly changed the subject. "I can go to the Hall of Justice tomorrow morning and find out the exact details of the charge, if you think that would be helpful. I'm afraid they wouldn't give them out to you, as you're not a citizen—but as a retired Maiden, I'm a sort of honorary man." She shrugged apologetically. "It's ridiculous, really."

"Don't worry," said Aradne. "There's nothing manly about you. Take it from me."

Dria giggled.

"And I suppose," Nione went on, mostly ignoring this, "that you'll want to visit the place where Helenos was living.

The Skalina is a very bad neighbourhood—you really must be careful there."

Varazda nodded. "Do they keep records of how people died here? When they die suspiciously, I mean."

"No," said Aradne. "They do that in Boukos?"

"Yes, there's a registry kept at the watch house. But it's a new thing—a friend of mine was responsible for starting it."

"There's nothing like that here," said Nione. "But we know how he died, don't we? He was poisoned."

"Yes, but I'd like to know how they know that." In Boukos it would all have been helpfully recorded in Marzana's Registry of Suspicious Deaths. "Damiskos said he was poisoned with thorn-flower, and as far as I know that doesn't cause any particular signs on the body, so they must have had some other reason to think that's how he died. I want to know what it was."

"Right," said Aradne. "In case they were mistaken or something."

"Or something," said Varazda. "What happens when someone is found dead, in Pheme? At home, the public watch would be called, and they'd take the body to the Temple of Nepharos—who does that here?"

"You can pay people," said Aradne. "I mean people who do that for a living. Or if you have slaves you'd get them to do it. In a place like the Skalina … " Her eyebrows went up, and she looked at Nione. "Gods, you know, I've no idea. Do you think the neighbours would do it?"

"Probably they would have," said Nione, "but they didn't need to. We know his family is involved—it was his father who brought the charge. And if they know how he died, and they could only know how he died by having been at the scene—they or their servants—then they were probably responsible for removing the body."

"You're right!" said Aradne.

"Brilliant," said Varazda.

Nione yawned hugely. "Thank you. I'm surprised I'm even coherent at this hour."

"I've often wondered how Pheme manages without a public watch *or* a royal guard, as they have in Zashian cities."

"Well, we have fire patrols at night," said Nione, "and the big houses and public buildings have guards."

"You can usually find *someone* to enforce the laws," said Aradne.

"I'm afraid I must be off to bed." Nione got up from the bench where she had been sitting beside Aradne. "I'll, um … " She hesitated.

"I'll be there soon," said Aradne, grinning up at her.

When she was gone, Aradne looked at Varazda and seemed to realize that she was still grinning. She looked embarrassed. Dria rolled her eyes and got up to put away some dishes.

"It's hard to get used to," Varazda offered after a moment.

"What is?"

"Oh, I was just thinking that I've been in Nione's position, more or less. It takes time to get used to. Sharing a bed with someone. Not that I ever took a vow of celibacy, just a general policy of avoidance, for, oh, a decade or so."

Aradne raised her eyebrows. "Is that so? And you were finally convinced to give it up."

"Oh, there was really very little convincing involved."

"Hah! Well, I've never been the least bit interested in men, but I can tell that Damiskos is a good one."

Philion Temnon's friend the advocate arrived, fresh from Anthousa, the following morning. He was a man named Olympios, with a square, pugnacious face and glittering eyes that roved restlessly over everything. He seemed unable to sit still for long. Damiskos had known officers like that in the army, and they were often very effective.

"Can't you just picture him in a courtroom?" Korinna exclaimed to Myrto, as Philion was showing Olympios the recent redecoration of the apartment. "He'll be perfect."

"He seems very energetic," said Myrto.

"Well, well," said Olympios when he had finished looking around the atrium, shaking Damiskos vigorously by the hand, "the distinguished soldier, accused of murder in the slums of Skalina—what a case, to be sure! And Kontios Diophoros's son, too. Between you and me, could you have picked your victim from a lesser family? It does make my job harder." Abruptly he roared with laughter. "I'm teasing you! I relish a challenge. I live for it. The higher the status of your victim, the better it is for me."

"I didn't kill him," said Damiskos, "so he's not *my* victim."

Olympios laughed as if Damiskos had said something witty. "I'll tell you, I have seen it all. There was one time I defended a man who was accused of killing his wife. Well, he told me he'd done it. What could I do? I mounted the best defense I could, and got him off. Yes, I did. I'll never forget the look on his face when the jury's votes were counted. This would have been ten, twelve years ago, before the fire at the Hall of Justice, when they had those awful frescoes—did you ever see those? Friend of mine knew a good story about how they were painted … "

He talked on, while Damiskos followed him on his second circuit of the atrium. Eventually he did return to the point of his story, which was that the wife had not been dead at all but somewhere abroad, and the man had actually wanted to be found guilty and sentenced to exile in order to join her; it had been an attempt at some kind of fraud. Damiskos wasn't sure whether he was supposed to be amused or impressed by the story. He was neither, and he remained grimly silent.

Olympios spent the whole morning with them and stayed to lunch although he was rather pointedly not invited. He talked for perhaps a quarter of an hour about Damiskos's defense and spent the rest of the time rehearsing past cases—sometimes acting out different parts, putting on voices—telling irrelevant stories, and dispensing unwanted advice about decorating. He liked to give people nicknames, and explained this annoying habit as if it was something he was particularly proud of. By the time he left, even Damiskos's mother had taken against him.

"Are you sure he's the right choice?" she asked Philion, in the silence that had descended after the advocate left.

"All crooks," Simonides croaked. "Advocates."

"Eh? Oh, he'll be fine," said Philion. "He pulls himself together. I've seen it before."

"Well, that's good," said Myrto. "But it is going to take an awful lot of pulling, isn't it?"

Her husband did not respond. Damiskos put an arm around his mother's shoulders and gave her a small squeeze. He wanted to tell her about Varazda, but not in front of his father.

"Well, *I* liked him," said Korinna, smiling at Philion. "He's a very good speaker."

Back in his room later that afternoon, Damiskos reread Varazda's letters. The first one was quite long and full of detail about events in Saffron Alley. He was glad, in a way, that Varazda had arrived before his letters, because reading this thinking that he might never see Varazda or any of the others again would have been too much to bear. He cursed again the fact that he hadn't had time to explain to Varazda about Ino and the shit business last night.

The rest of the household was still trying in increasingly awkward ways to give Damiskos and Ino time alone together.

Damiskos didn't bother trying to prevent them. Either he and Ino would sit together in silence, or he would ask her about the set of cups she was working on when she went out to "visit her friend" and enjoy listening to her talk.

He remembered her telling him sixteen years ago, "I don't want to marry someone who just wants to rescue me." He thought she probably still didn't want that.

Varazda's second letter was short and written in Zashian. It was a passage from the Tales of Suna, carefully copied out: the song of the moon fairy pining for her absent lover.

The wine shop where Varazda and Aradne had arranged to meet Nione was small and quiet, with frescoes of fruit around the front counter and a delicious aroma in the air. It reminded Varazda of home.

"There wasn't much to be learned at the Hall of Justice," Nione said as they sat down. "The charge is a simple one of deliberate murder. It was brought by Kontios Diophoros and is to be heard by a jury on the first—a week from today."

"That doesn't give us a lot of time," said Aradne. Glancing at Varazda, she added, "Er. Sorry."

"That's longer than I thought we'd have, actually." In Boukos the trial would have been heard days earlier; but Boukos was a much smaller place.

"There may be a little more I can do," said Nione. "Let me look into it."

"I can't tell you how grateful I am," said Varazda. "We have a bit more to tell, though it was a lot of work to get it."

"You can say that again," said Aradne, rolling her eyes.

The waiter arrived to take their order, and since none of them had so much as glanced at the menu, this took some time.

"We went to the Diophoros town house," said Aradne

finally, when they had ordered their food. "It's quite a grand place. We got in the back door by pretending to be fortune tellers."

"You *what*?" Nione started in alarm.

"No, no, we didn't actually use the sacred bones! Just made up nonsense."

"Oh, of course—I know you wouldn't, my dear. I'm sorry."

"I told you she wouldn't like it," Aradne said, looking at Varazda with a wry grin. "It was my idea, but credit where credit is due, Pharastes was much better at it than I. He told them these cryptic things that could have meant anything, all in a thick Sasian accent."

"If it's any comfort," said Varazda, "I don't think they really believed any of it. But the premise did allow us to bring the conversation around to what we wanted to know."

"He said, 'I can feel there has been a death—violence—a son of this house!'" Aradne did a bad imitation of Varazda's ramped-up accent.

"They were very eager to talk about it," said Varazda. "We met one of the men who had gone to retrieve Helenos's body. Apparently the murder was discovered by the neighbours, who didn't know who Helenos was—he was more or less in hiding. But he had been in touch with his father, and by chance one of his father's slaves had been sent there with money for him the morning after he died. They knew it was Nepharos's Bell that killed him because there was a half-full cup of wine laced with the stuff next to him."

"It has a strong smell," said Aradne. "You'd have to be pretty drunk not to notice you were swigging from a cup of it."

"Probably why the cup was still half full," said Nione reasonably. "Did the servants know what Helenos was doing in Pheme? It must have been risky for him to come back here. He must have had some reason."

"They didn't know," said Varazda, "but it wasn't to make contact with his family. He had done that, but only, from the sound of it, incidentally. His father had been sending him money but had not invited him to stay at the house."

Nione nodded. "So next ... "

"Next I have to visit the place where Helenos was staying."

The waiter returned with their food, simple dishes appetizingly presented on black-and-white plates that again reminded Varazda of Boukos.

"You have to try the sausages," said Aradne. "They're the best in Pheme."

"And the cheese," said Nione. "Oh, but I can't remember—can you have goat's milk?"

"Hm?" Varazda laughed. "It's been years since I even thought about that, actually." He felt guilty admitting to a pious person like Nione that he didn't observe the taboos of his own religion. "There's just so much goat everything in Boukos. And even in Zash, it's sort of ... an old-fashioned thing. Some people call it a superstition."

Of course then Aradne wanted to hear all about it, and Varazda blundered his way through an explanation of the doctrine of the Thrice-Holy Vaksha surrounding the Horned Beast, all the while suspecting that Nione could have explained it better herself. This took them through most of the meal, which was as delicious as it had looked.

"Now," said Aradne finally, "tell us how we can help with the investigation."

"Thanks. I don't know, yet. I think at first I should go look around the Skalina by myself."

"In case you need to scale any more walls," Aradne agreed.

"Do please be careful," said Nione.

"What else can we do?" Aradne mused. "There's no body to look at—he's been cremated and his ashes buried by this time. They told us that at the house," she added to Nione. "We didn't ask."

"Good."

"Oh, and the family's engaged an advocate called Eulios," Varazda added.

Nione winced. "Just what one would expect, I'm afraid."

"He's good?" said Varazda.

"Well, he's famous. He defended Dimon Auriadoros—do you remember him?" she asked Aradne.

"The parricide?"

"The man who was acquitted of parricide, I think you mean."

"Yeah, but everybody knows—oh. Right." She grimaced.

"I'll speak to my own legal man," said Nione. "I'm sure Damiskos's family will have engaged someone good, but … actually, you know, if I'm honest, I'm *not* sure of that. I'll send a message to Chariton."

It was raining when they left the wine shop. They parted ways because Nione and Aradne had an engagement on the Vallina Hill. Varazda intended to walk back to the house, change his clothes to something less ostentatiously Zashian than what he had worn to impersonate a fortune teller that morning, and go in search of Helenos's last place of residence. But by the time he arrived at Aradne's house the rain had become a stinging downpour, and a trip across the river was out of the question. He changed into dry clothes and sat in Aradne's peristyle, watching the rain soak her garden.

He wondered what Dami was doing, how he was coping, trapped in that apartment with his parents and the family of his former betrothed. Did his life with Varazda in Boukos already seem like a dream, like another world he feared he would never be able to return to? Varazda pushed his fingers into his hair, trying to shake the feeling that there might be some truth in that.

Some of the household women had come out to sit in the

peristyle with their spinning and to listen to another passage from the novel they had been reading in the kitchen the previous night. A character named Doris was making a long, impassioned speech to the hero, Alkaios, about why she must "set him free" so that he could be with another.

"*Eudoxia is young and pure. With her you could hold your head up in the agora—you need be ashamed no more.*"

The hero protested; he loved Doris with a passion that defied convention, he would go with her into exile if need be, into the Land of Dead, and so on. Varazda remembered that the novel was called *Alkaios and Eudoxia*, not *Alkaios and Doris*, so obviously he was going to change his mind at some point. Or she was going to leave him "for his own good." Or, because it was a novel, get tragically killed, leaving him free to be with Eudoxia.

Varazda got up and went back into the house. He sought out writing implements and composed a letter to his family —to Ari, really, with passages for him to read aloud to Yazata and Remi. With his audience in mind, he downplayed the gravity of the situation, made it sound as if he had it well under control. He put in some observations about Pheme for Remi and reassured Ariston that he hadn't forgotten his promise to visit the Temple of Xereus and admire the friezes.

CHAPTER 8

The following morning, Varazda was prepared to set out early. He rose before his hosts, dressed in Zashian clothes, and put in his earrings. He planned to create an impression in the Skalina neighbourhood.

He was eating a solitary breakfast, sitting cross-legged on one of Aradne's couches, when Niko put his head around the dining-room door to say, "There's someone here to see you, Pharastes."

"Yes?" said Varazda warily. He couldn't think who knew he was here. "Did they ask for me by name?"

"Yup. 'Someone named Pharastes,' he said. He has a message for you."

"All right. Ask him to step in, will you?"

"Will do."

Niko disappeared, and a few moments later a stranger came through the dining-room door. A stranger whom Varazda had no trouble identifying.

"I, uh—" The man glanced around the room as if expecting someone else to be there, then looked back at Varazda, his expression increasingly astonished.

"You must be Timiskos," said Varazda helpfully.

Dami's younger brother looked a great deal like him: the same strong nose, the same colouring, the same curly hair, although Timiskos wore his longer and was scrupulously clean-shaven. He was something like a decade younger than Dami, and they had different mothers (a situation Varazda had never inquired into, since he knew Dami's father and mother were still married). Maybe it was from his mother than Timiskos had inherited his heavy-lidded, sad-looking eyes and his softer jawline. He was slimmer than Dami, his presence far less intimidating.

"Uh. Yes, I—how did you know?"

"Damiskos talks about you." Varazda smiled. "And you look alike. Will you join me? I'm just having breakfast."

Timiskos came around the couches and sat down stiffly. "I'm afraid I'm rather ... er."

Varazda gave him a tolerant smile. "Did Damiskos send you with a message?"

"Oh. Uh. Yes. He said that if you wanted to get any message to *him*, you can send a message through me. Or—rather, if you want, I can carry—you know—I can come, and ..."

"Act as a go-between," Varazda suggested.

"Yes, that's it, yes. Sorry, I'm a little surprised, I'm afraid. I'm being quite rude about it, aren't I?" He laughed nervously.

Varazda shook his head, smiling. "Not at all. Did Damiskos happen to tell you who I am?"

"Well, roughly. But he definitely left out a few things! Did he—I guess he brought you back from Sasia?"

"No, we met on Pheme and I live in Boukos."

"Right, but—he does ... does he ... Uh. You're his lover? He was going to move to Boukos to live with you."

"Yes ... " Varazda wasn't quite sure how to take that last sentence. *Was* going to move to Boukos? "That's me."

"Blessed Orante. Well. I don't know what to say. Sorry, I guess."

"Sorry ... for what?"

"That he's going to marry Ino and move to Kargania to farm shit, or whatever. Oh. Anaxe's tits. You didn't know about that."

"I didn't know about that."

"Oh, shit. Oh, shit." Timiskos popped up from the couch then sat back down, wiping his palms convulsively over the skirt of his tunic. "How can I—what can I—"

"We didn't have much time to talk," said Varazda, rather resenting that he had to be the one to offer comfort after Timiskos had just dropped that on him. "I snuck in his window last night, and we were interrupted before he had time to tell me everything."

"You, uh ... what?" Timiskos shook his head as if he thought he must have misheard. "Well, here's what it is. Father and Myrto—"

"Are you allowed to bring guests into the house?" Varazda cut him off.

"Er. It depends who's on the door—some of them are stricter than others."

"If I were to accompany you back to the house now, say, would whoever's guarding the door be likely to let me in?"

Timiskos thought about that for a moment. "Yes. I think so. But—"

"Good," said Varazda, uncrossing his legs. "Let's do that."

By the time they arrived at the Temnons' home, Timiskos seemed to have become almost excited about the prospect of springing Varazda on his father and stepmother (he always scrupulously referred to her as his stepmother). From what Varazda knew of them, this was understandable.

Timiskos was also, Varazda thought, doing his best to be nice to his brother's lover. He wasn't doing too bad a job of it, though Varazda wasn't in any mood to appreciate it. Timiskos hadn't asked any of the usual rude questions about Varazda's clothes or general appearance. He asked what part of Sasia Varazda was from, as if aware that Sasia did have different parts to it. He did say, "You speak Pseuchaian so well," but he had the grace to look embarrassed about it afterward.

Varazda had not changed his clothes before leaving Aradne's house, though he had thought about it. Did he want to face Dami's family looking so aggressively Zashian? Did it matter?

He kept thinking about that novel the women had been reading. *With Eudoxia you could hold your head up in the agora—you need be ashamed no more.* Dami wasn't ashamed of him; Varazda knew that. But just then, he wanted to give Dami the opportunity to prove it.

The guard on the door beside the barbershop today seemed to enjoy his job less than the one two days earlier. He waved Timiskos and Varazda in with only a token raised eyebrow. They ascended a steep flight of stairs to a cramped landing with one door. Timiskos reached for the handle and paused to give Varazda an uncertain look over his shoulder.

"I, uh—I hope this isn't going to be too awful for you. They're going to be weird. They're … always weird."

"Thanks for the warning," said Varazda.

Timiskos opened the door, and they walked in.

The atrium of the apartment was large and airy and more tasteful than Varazda had expected. He had formed an impression of Dami's family as tacky people, but their home actually looked quite gracious. The walls were painted in a delicate peach, with small floral motifs. At the far end of the atrium, a number of wicker chairs and a couch had been placed in a casual arrangement, perfect for conversation, with a couple of potted trees to screen the area from the rest of the atrium, and an ornamental brazier for warmth.

The family, gathered in this area, looked up at Timiskos's entrance and went on looking, with wider eyes, when they saw Varazda.

They had obviously just got up, and from the look of them, this was earlier than they usually rose. There was a dark-haired, striking woman in late middle age, beautifully dressed but with her hairdo only half finished, easily identifiable as Dami's mother. There was his father, also recognizable, though mostly by his nose. His greying hair was standing up on the sides, his chin was unshaven, and his eyes were puffy. His tunic had crumbs on it.

There was another middle-aged couple, a man and woman sitting together on the couch, who must have been the ex-fiancée's parents. They had a subtly crumpled look to them, and when their eyes had finished widening, they narrowed suspiciously.

Finally there was a younger, very pretty woman, more put-together than the rest of them in a blue gown, with sleek blonde hair and a long neck. She was looking at Varazda with open fascination.

"Where's Damiskos?" his brother asked, approaching the family group. "I've brought—uh—someone to see him."

"He's in the bath," supplied a young woman with tumbling-down hair who peeked out from behind one of the potted trees. She began blushing and turned away to resume putting up her mistress's hair.

"Oh," said Timiskos. "Well, this is Pharastes. He's—" He paused to clear his throat. "He's the reason Damiskos was planning to move to Boukos."

Of course that was when Dami walked in, barefoot, with wet hair and a towel in one hand.

He looked at Varazda, and for a moment there was no

expression on his face beyond blank shock. Then he lit up with one of his warm, beautiful smiles.

"Hey," he said. "I wasn't expecting you."

He crossed the atrium to Varazda and took his hand.

"I couldn't stay away," Varazda said.

"May I?" Dami whispered.

"Sure."

Dami leaned in and kissed him lightly on the lips.

"You're up early," Dami said.

"Yes, well. I have work to do."

Damiskos felt as if a fog had lifted from his mind. It was like the clarity of the battlefield in the still moments before the troops clashed. His mission was to protect Varazda from his parents and from Korinna and Simonides; nothing mattered more than that.

Varazda would not hear any insulting questions or ignorant remarks. He didn't deserve that. He was the most splendid thing in the world, standing there in the Temnons' newly decorated atrium in his Zashian clothes, with his hair loose and his hands patterned with henna.

He had climbed through the window two nights ago, and that had been wonderful, but this—walking through the door—was more than Damiskos had ever imagined anyone doing for him.

"I could get breakfast," Gaia suggested in a small voice, looking out from the shelter of the orange tree. "Is—is everyone ready for breakfast?"

"Thanks, Gaia," said Damiskos. "That sounds great."

She scurried off to the kitchen. Timiskos was standing awkwardly behind Damiskos and Varazda.

"He, uh, wanted to come—" Timiskos started.

"To meet your family," Varazda finished for him.

"And here they are. Mother, Father—this is Varazda. You can call him Pharastes, if you like." He finished the introductions, to dead silence. "My parents' friends, Simonides and Korinna, and their daughter Ino."

"I am very pleased to meet you," said Varazda gracefully, making one of the little Zashian-style bows that Damiskos had not seen him do since the early days of their acquaintance.

"Will you ... join us for breakfast?" Damiskos's mother asked finally.

"I have already eaten," said Varazda, "but I would be very happy to sit with you."

As Varazda stepped forward toward the table, Timiskos looked at his brother. "Damiskos, you might have prepared me! I mean—"

Damiskos slapped him on the back. "I guess I should have! I didn't realize you were so easily overcome by the sight of a pretty face."

"That's not—"

"Sure that's what you meant."

"Do come sit with us," said Myrto, beckoning to Varazda, "while we wait for Gaia to bring our food."

Damiskos accompanied Varazda to the sitting area and pulled up a chair for him.

"This is a beautiful room," said Varazda as he sat. No one replied.

"Myrto," said Korinna, leaning forward across the table, "is this the sort of guest you regularly invite into your home?"

"Sure," said Damiskos. "I've brought a few of my lovers home before, right, Mother? You remember Memnon and Phoros."

"Yes ... " said Myrto vaguely. "I liked Phoros—he was very good-looking."

"But Phemian," Korinna suggested. "Not ... Sasian."

"Dirty dogs," Simonides muttered.

"Do you like the room?" Timiskos said abruptly, turning to Varazda. "I worked on the design."

"Did you really?" Varazda turned toward him with a sparkling smile, masterfully flaunting his appreciation of Timiskos's change of subject. "It's lovely. Elegant but comfortable. I like how you grouped the chairs over here."

"Oh. Thank you. I thought it was rather original." He began talking, somewhat randomly, about tables and frescoes, and Varazda listened with the same bright attention.

Damiskos glanced around the table. Myrto still looked confused, and Philion looked like he had just unsuspectingly bitten into a wormy apple. Korinna looked like she was ready to tear out someone's throat with her teeth, but was having a hard time deciding whose.

"What," Damiskos's father finally burst out, "in the name of Nepharos's hairy—"

"Sir," said Damiskos loudly. "Varazda learned that I was in trouble and came to see me. That's what he is doing here."

"What? But—but what the—"

"I understand your surprise, sir. I believe I had only hinted that I had a new lover."

"But he's—" Philion gestured wildly. "He's—"

"He's who I was visiting in Boukos."

"I don't care about that. I want to know—Will you shut up?" Philion growled at his younger son. "Nobody cares about your wall-paintings and your gods-cursed potted trees, you—"

"I know a few words in Sasian," Ino said suddenly, in the overloud voice that she sometimes used accidentally—though this time Damiskos would have bet it wasn't an accident. "Kusko, santia, pasavina, shas."

Varazda's eyes widened slightly. "Those are all ... metal-working terms, I think. I'm afraid I don't know what they mean."

"Oh, that's all right," said Ino, as if the two of them were alone in the room, "because I do. Could I look at your earrings? Are they from Sasia? I mean Zash. I want to see what technique was used."

Varazda beamed at her and reached up to unhook one of his earrings. "Of course."

"Don't encourage her!" Korinna snapped, shooting out a hand to keep Varazda from passing Ino the earring. He started and dropped it.

Varazda didn't even glare, in any way worthy of the name —not like Damiskos knew he was capable of glaring—but his look was enough to make Korinna shrink back in her chair. It was deeply satisfying.

"Here you go!" said Gaia, darting forward and picking up the earring from the floor. She hesitated a moment, then passed it to Ino, with a wary glance at Korinna. For a moment there was excruciating silence as Ino studied the earring.

"It's silver-gilt," she announced finally. "Not gold all the way through. Did you know that?"

Korinna *tsk*ed as if she herself were not wearing brass and glass beads.

Varazda smiled. "I did. I have a few solid gold pieces, but I find gilt much more economical."

"Oh, it *is*. Do you know how it's made? It's an interesting technique. What you do is—"

"How—how do you know about that?" Damiskos interrupted, flat-footed but desperate to keep Ino from revealing too much of her technical knowledge in front of her mother, who would eventually put two and two together. "Oh, I guess your late husband must have talked about it sometimes."

"Yes," said Ino after a moment, slowly, "and I—wanted to be a good wife, so … I always listened."

"Oh, he talked about nothing else," Korinna scoffed. "He was the most tedious man."

Ino swallowed hard but said nothing. She held onto Varazda's earring, and he didn't ask for it back.

"Breakfast is, um … " said Gaia, gesturing vaguely.

"Splendid," said Myrto, standing up. "Varastes, I think it's lovely that Damiskos is attached to such a … such an interesting person. Do please come into the winter dining room with me and tell me about that *fascinating* paint on your hands. It isn't tattoos, is it, like they do in Kargania?"

Almost as soon as they had decamped to the dining room, Olympios, the reason they had all been up early, arrived and invited himself to breakfast.

"So good to see you again," said Korinna, waving him into the room as if she were the mistress of the house.

The dining room was small, and the couches could only accommodate six people reclining, which was how the Temnons insisted on taking all their meals. Early in his stay at the apartment, Damiskos had brought in a stool from the atrium, and it was a toss-up at each meal whether he or his brother would use it—it depended on who got into the dining room first and how much glaring the older generation did.

This time, Ino had contrived to get into the dining room first, and sat on the stool. Timiskos, after staring around in confusion for a moment, had gone back out to get another stool for himself. So when Olympios came in, Timiskos and Ino were perched on stools near the door, and Damiskos was sharing a couch with Varazda.

"Now," said Korinna with obvious relish, "where can we get you to sit? Oh, Damiskos, perhaps you can make room."

Myrto wasn't as good as Korinna at poisonous looks, but she was giving it her best shot.

Damiskos slid back off the couch without comment, and Varazda came too, with his usual grace, and so they were standing together behind the couch when Olympios noticed Varazda.

"Blessed Soukos!" He gave Varazda an exaggerated up-and-down look and let out a shocked laugh. "Oh, no no no, this won't do." He leaned forward to help himself to a handful of dates. "Let me be frank with you, Old Blade, as I always am with my clients. She"—jabbing a finger at Varazda—"has to go. She's a liability. Oh, yes. I've seen it before. I once defended a fellow with an impeccable character otherwise, but there was this bizarre girlfriend—"

"She's a 'he,'" said Myrto.

"—foreign, dressed funny, probably a perfectly nice girl in her way, but a liability. I couldn't get him off. He was guilty, actually—funny story about that. He was accused of staging his own kidnapping, and he'd actually done it."

"Not my idea of an impeccable character," Myrto remarked. "And I don't think you heard me. Varastes is a 'he,' not a 'she.' I mean—oh, he *is*, isn't he, darling? Not that it matters in the least either way."

Olympios looked at Myrto, taking that in, spat out a date pit, then looked back at Varazda.

"If it would help," said Varazda, deadpan, "I'd be happy to pose as a bizarre girlfriend. I didn't bring any of my gowns with me, but I can always get something ready-made in the market."

Ino gave a little yelp of laughter, and Myrto clapped her hands delightedly.

"Unnatural," Simonides muttered.

"Oh, no no no," the advocate said again. He was actually beginning to go pale now. "Did anyone see him come in?"

He rounded on Damiskos. "What were you thinking? Are you trying to ruin my reputation?"

"Immortal gods, Olympios," said Philion irritably, "this isn't about *your* reputation."

"It is for me," Olympios retorted. "I'm certainly not expecting to get rich off of this case. Everyone knows you're broke."

Philion recoiled. "Bringing my finances into it? Have you no shame?"

"It's all right," said Korinna soothingly. "Damiskos and Ino will announce their engagement, and that will make everything much better. Reputations *and* finances." She looked around with a triumphant smile. "Once his innocence is established, there will be nothing standing in the way of his political career. We all expect great things."

Damiskos was aware that he had gone still, but Varazda, beside him, had not. He had already known. Shit. He had already known. Timiskos had told him, probably, in some ham-fisted way, and of course Varazda would not exactly have believed it, but he would be worried. Anyone would be.

"The thing is," Damiskos said, putting an arm casually around Varazda's shoulders, "we're not going to do that. Sorry, Ino."

"That's all right," said Ino comfortably. "Varazda, here is your other earring."

"No no no, I'm out." Olympios grabbed another handful of dates. "I'm out unless she—he—i—"

"You know where the door is," Damiskos said.

"*Does* he, though?" Myrto mused.

"Nonsense, nonsense!" Philion turned placating, looking sick. "Of course we'll be guided by you, Olympios, old friend. We've no desire for *anyone* to lose his reputation." He laughed weakly.

"My brother told you about the fertilizer business?"

Damiskos said quietly to Varazda, while Olypios and Philion bellowed over one another.

"Incoherently, but yes. I assumed it was what you were going to tell me the other night, before we were interrupted. And it helped to make sense of what I overheard outside the window. Nione was able to fill me in on some of the history."

"Mm. It's a mess."

"I had better go, love, before they come to blows here. Besides, I have things to do. Send Timiskos to tell me when it's safe for me to return, will you? Perhaps some time when your father and his legal friend are out. In the meantime, I have to go give Helenos's old neighbourhood a look. Do you think I could borrow your sword?"

CHAPTER 9

Varazda was in a reckless mood when he finally set off for the Skalina. He went straight across the river in his Zashian finery, as he had planned. He strode into the narrow, foul-smelling streets of the slum looking like a foreign prince—gilt earrings or no—immediately drawing the eyes of shopkeepers and passersby and loungers in doorways. He didn't care. He had his knife with him, he had Dami's sword in its Pseuchaian sheath, the belt cinched tight around his waist, and even if he did not look it, he could defend himself.

He was also, in a way that he did not much want to analyze, deeply unhappy. He hadn't heard the beginning of that novel the other day. Was Eudoxia a disarmingly nice young woman with peculiar interests, trapped in a horrific home with controlling parents and needing the hero's help to escape? Had Doris been right to give him up?

That lawyer would probably have characterized Doris as a "bizarre girlfriend." But at least she wasn't something *even worse*.

Aradne had drawn Varazda a map to Helenos's lodging, based on what Dami had told him the other night. It was a very basic map, because she didn't know the neighbourhood well (Nione had never been there in her life), and at a certain point it failed him. The road dead-ended at what looked like a demolition site, and there was no obvious way forward. Varazda accepted the necessity of asking for directions.

By this time he had developed a small entourage, though they were following at a wary distance, composed of dirty children and dogs that might or might not have belonged to them. He stopped on the middle of the street and turned in a way that made his coat swing out around him, tossed back his hair, and flourished Aradne's map.

"Does one of you know the way to this place?" he demanded, pitching his voice to carry to the group of children and laying on the thickest accent that he thought was compatible with being understood.

The oldest member of the group was a thin girl with red hair and a younger sibling—or perhaps her own child—riding on her back in a sling. She came forward, eyeing Varazda's map sceptically.

"What's it say?" she asked.

"It says I am to follow this street until I come to a flight of steps beside a fountain. I am to go up the steps, and at the top find a wine shop with a sign of a crow. My destination lies across the street."

"Yeah?" The girl looked intrigued. "I know the sign of the crow."

"It is urgently important that I find it. My beloved's life may depend upon it."

Her mouth fell open. The baby on her back gurgled and kicked its feet. "I can take you there. Your map's wrong now, since last Month of Peace, when that apartment block fell down." She gestured to the pile of rubble behind him.

Varazda glanced over his shoulder at the remains of the building. He'd heard that this sort of thing happened in

Pheme: unscrupulous landlords built blocks of apartments so tall and so flimsy that they would collapse. There were laws to prevent it happening in Boukos.

After he offered the girl a flowery thanks and a copper coin, he followed her down the narrowest street he had encountered yet, overhung by rickety wooden balconies projecting from the upper stories of the buildings on either side, lines of washing hanging between them. The other children and the dogs followed, closer now, and they picked up a couple of adults: a stocky, red-cheeked young man and a small, bustling woman who seemed to be his guardian.

True to her word, the red-haired girl led Varazda around the collapsed building to the flight of stairs, which he thought he might have missed because the thing that Aradne's map called a "fountain" was a dingy yellow wall with water trickling out of a pipe into a muddy basin, choked with the fallen leaves of the only tree he had seen since crossing the river. The procession mounted the steps, picking up a trio of young women at the top who had been sitting outside the house with the tree, and whom Varazda judged to be members of a branch of Kallisto's trade. The girl with the baby seemed to be friends with them.

"He's looking for something that could save his lover's life," she informed them.

"Ooh, sounds fun!" said one of the prostitutes. She sidled up to Varazda. "What is it, handsome?"

"He hasn't said," the red-haired girl cut in officiously. "It may be a secret."

Varazda remained sternly silent. Whenever he needed to make a display of being a man, it wasn't to any of the courtiers he had known at Gudul or the diplomats in the embassy that he turned for inspiration. He could act like a Pseuchaian man at home, and often did, but when he needed to be a Zashian man, he reached back, by some instinct, to the men of his childhood on the Deshan Coast: his father and elder brothers and innumerable uncles and cousins. They were above all proud, carrying themselves as if they were always on their guard, by turns taciturn and eloquent, quick to either laughter or violence. It would have been a hard kind of man to be, but there was something satisfying about being able to imitate one, at least well enough to impress the residents of a Phemian slum.

"Here's the sign of the crow," the red-haired girl told Varazda, pointing. Again he was glad for her guidance, since the thing painted on the outside of the wine shop could to his eyes have been anything from a dog to an elephant.

"Are you going to thump One-Eyed Dolon?" one of the other children asked eagerly.

Varazda made a show of considering the question before saying gravely, "No. My business lies elsewhere." He scanned the other side of the street, looking for the door that matched Dami's description. Spotting it, he pointed. "There. Do you know who lives behind that grey door?" he asked the assembled group.

"That's Big Tio's place," one of the women said after a moment.

Of course it is, Varazda thought. He waited for someone to tell him, "You don't want to mess with Big Tio," but surprisingly no one did.

Instead, the bustling woman came forward to say, "We live there. Are you here about the young gentleman who was killed?"

"I seen who did it," said the young man with her, smiling broadly up at Varazda.

"Shh, Straton," said the woman. "He tells stories," she added apologetically to Varazda. "He can't help it. He's a good boy, though. My sister's boy. We all live in Big Tio's place. If there's anything we can do … "

"I am here about the man who was killed," said Varazda.

"*He* wasn't your lover?" one of the prostitutes asked, in a tone that suggested she had met Helenos and was ready to be unimpressed with Varazda's taste.

"No no," the red-haired girl corrected her before Varazda could speak. "He said he was here to *save* his lover, not *avenge* him." She looked anxiously up at Varazda. "Right?"

Varazda nodded sternly. "Yes. It is vital that I find the murderer."

"Oh, because your lover has been accused of the crime!" the girl guessed.

Varazda gave an even sterner nod, and it was not altogether put on.

He was treated to a flood of information from his followers, most of it quite superfluous. The prostitutes had seen Helenos often in the street and drinking at the wine shop with the badly painted crow. They couldn't say exactly when he'd arrived in the neighbourhood. They hadn't known his name. He'd never given any of them the time of day, and they hadn't thought much of that.

The children had all heard about the murder and had different accounts, each one more lurid and improbable than the last, of how the body had been found. The red-haired girl pursed her lips and propped her baby on her hip and shook her head gravely at Varazda after every new account.

Finally the young man Straton could stand it no longer, and he tugged at Varazda's sleeve.

"I seen who done it," he said again. "I seen Ruta going up the stairs."

"Ruta from our house?" said one of the prostitutes. She shook her head. "Straton, she doesn't live here any more. Maybe it was a woman who looked a little like Ruta."

Straton looked sadly at the ground. "I know Ruta," he murmured. "I seen her going up the stairs."

"Thank you," said Varazda seriously. "I will remember that."

"My sister may be able to tell you more," said Straton's aunt. "She spoke with Ora, who found the poor fellow's body."

"Would your sister be so kind as to receive me?" Varazda asked, remembering his appropriately foreign manners.

In due course he had been introduced to Straton's mother, in the ill-lit set of rooms shared by her extended family. The red-haired girl and some of her friends crammed in. The baby began to fuss, and the girl passed it off to another woman, who sat on a bed and began nursing it. One of the prostitutes tossed her a shawl to cover herself, lest she offend the Sasian's sensibilities. Varazda, who had seen plenty of babies nursed in the women's quarters at Gudul, said nothing.

He distributed more coins and heard all about the lame soldier who had quarrelled with Helenos in the street and brought him back to his room on the day he had died. Straton's mother had seen it all from her window. She tried helpfully to remember the name Helenos had called him. One-Eyed Dolon would know, someone said, as they had been outside his shop. Varazda thanked them gravely.

One-Eyed Dolon, or someone else, had obviously talked to Kontios Diophoros's men when they came to get Helenos's body, leading to Dami's arrest. Varazda considered admitting that he was there on Dami's behalf, so that they would not continue to fixate on Dami as a suspect. He decided against it because he wanted to hear as honest an account as possible of what had happened.

"And did he have any other visitors?" Varazda asked.

"No," said Straton's mother, "not that I saw."

"Yes, there was!" a boy spoke up. "A man with a beard and—" He gestured wildly around his head. "—crazy hair. Grey, like. I was throwing out slops first thing in the morning when I seen him, talking with the fellow who died, and they went inside together."

"First thing in the morning, Tono?" said the red-haired girl. "That's no help. He wasn't killed first thing in the morning."

"I know, he just said was there any other visitors, and there was. So." The boy looked sulky.

"Thank you," said Varazda, digging out another coin. "I must know of every detail, no matter how small."

This had the effect of opening the floodgates, and he heard about incidents days earlier, minute details of Dami's clothes and sword and exactly how he had thrown Helenos into the front of the wine shop, and a full description of the removal of Helenos's body, which was mostly an account of how difficult it was to manoeuvre a stretcher down the house's narrow staircase. Straton reiterated his story about seeing the woman named Ruta go up the stairs—"wearing her different-coloured cloak"—and it was intimated, kindly, that Straton had a fondness for Ruta and had been missing her since she went away. Someone remembered what Helenos had said to make Dami knock him down.

"It was something about a Sasian—'your Sasian whore,' or something like that."

The red-haired girl looked up sharply and met Varazda's eye with a look of dawning realization.

"What about the grey-haired man, though?" she interrupted. "Tono, are you *sure* he was here first thing in the morning?"

Tono, when pressed, wasn't sure. He could only connect the incident with his throwing out of the slops, and he didn't know whether that had been before or after the soldier passed by. He couldn't remember whether Helenos had had a swollen lip or a black eye or any other sign of having been roughed up in the street when he was speaking with the grey-haired man. He became truculent and inclined to take the whole thing back.

"You should speak to Ora, upstairs," said Straton's mother finally. "She found the young man's body."

No one wanted to accompany Varazda upstairs to speak to Ora. He gathered this was because no one very much wanted to speak to Ora. He climbed the steep stairs to the top floor of the building, noting with alarm the way that the steps sloped to one side. Was that the beginning of the building's collapse, or was it securely enough propped against the structure next door not to fall down?

There were three doors opening off the dirty landing where the stairs ended. He had been told that Ora's was the one opposite the head of the stairs, so he knocked at it. He heard muttering from inside.

"Yes? What?" The speaker sounded old and female, and as if she might have been trying to peer through the keyhole of the door.

"Good day, mother. They told me downstairs I should speak to you." Varazda tamped down his Zashian accent and let his voice return to its natural pitch, thinking it might make him sound less alarming. "Are you the one they call Ora?"

"What's it to you?"

"I want to ask you what you know about the young man on this floor who was killed this past week."

"Have they caught him yet?"

"Caught who?"

"The murderer! Thug with a sword. I saw him with my own eyes."

Varazda gave the door a sour look. "No murderer has been caught yet. That is why I've come to speak to you."

"Big Tio told me they'd caught him! I knew he was lying to me. I'm not opening this door if he's not been caught. I already told those other boys everything, why do you need to come around too?"

"I am acting on behalf of another party in the case," said Varazda, hoping that the legal-sounding language would impress her. It evidently didn't, because she snorted. He added quickly, "Did you see a bearded man with long grey hair come upstairs on that day?"

Ora was silent for some time, and when when she spoke, her voice had become fractionally more friendly, although the door remained firmly closed. "Of course. Nobody comes up here without my knowing about it. He was here in the morning, early. Chatting away with Hilaros, or whatever his name was, on the way up the stairs. And he had a bottle of wine. First thing in the morning, and he had a bottle of wine. Mind you, Hilaros, or whatever his name was, was drunk more often than not."

"Was he drunk then, do you think?"

Again she gave the question some thought. "No," she said decisively. "Not drunk, and not looking like he'd just rolled out of bed, either. Like he'd tried to spruce himself up a bit."

She was actually quite a good witness, Varazda thought, in spite of her unwillingness to open the door. It was too bad she would not be allowed to testify, being a woman.

"Thank you," he said, "this is very helpful. Do you know whether there was a woman, later that day, who came to see Helenos?"

"Eh? Yes, there was. How'd you know about that? It must have been, oh, nearly dusk. I'd my door closed that time—after that thug came up—but I looked out when I heard someone on the landing. It was one of them loose women from across the road. She knocked and knocked on his door, but I don't know if she ever went in. Of course he was dead by that time, poor bastard, so he couldn't have let her in."

"But you say she might have gone in, all the same. Did he habitually leave his door unlocked?"

"Doesn't have a lock," she replied contemptuously. She added hastily, "Mine does!"

"That must be a comfort. I understand you found Helenos's body."

"I did." She said that very quickly, and she sounded defensive. He wondered what that meant.

"How did that come about?"

"None of your business. The door was open."

"In the morning? But if—"

"It was open. I saw him on the floor, and I've seen dead men before. I went and told Big Tio, there's a dead man in the room next to mine, he was killed by a thug with a sword yesterday afternoon, get someone to come take him away."

There was much about this that did not make sense, but Varazda judged from her tone that it was time for the interview to end.

"And you leave Old Cosmo alone," she added, her tone sharpening again. "He's stone-deaf and mad as a fish pie. He'll tell you nothing at all."

"Thank you," said Varazda. "I can tell that you are a very keen observer, and I am most grateful for your help."

He bent to slip a silver nummos under the door and heard her hiss of surprise when she saw it, then nothing further. He couldn't tell if she had even picked the coin up.

He looked at the two remaining doors on the landing. One had a chalk sketch of an eye surrounded by flames and a number of unconnected Zashian characters scrawled on it. That would be Old Cosmo's. Varazda crossed the landing and tried the third door.

It opened easily onto an obviously empty room, the cold wind blowing in at the open shutters of the single small window. Varazda slipped inside and closed the door silently behind him.

It was the second time he'd searched a room belonging to Helenos Kontiades. This room was very different from the bedroom in Nione's villa that Helenos had shared with his acolyte Gelon. That had been strewn with the possessions of two men who had obviously moved in intending to stay. This room had been mostly cleared of Helenos's personal effects, though there were still rumpled sheets on the bed and a couple of empty bottles in a corner.

The cup with the residue of poison had been removed, and when Varazda sniffed at the discarded bottles, he smelled only strong, cheap wine. There was a fresh-looking, wine-coloured stain splashed across the floor. The murderer might have taken the bottle away with them, or the poison could have been put into the cup. Varazda looked for a second cup that might have suggested that Helenos and his murderer had drunk together, but there was none.

In spite of the open window and the evidence that the floor had recently been washed, a slight sour smell lingered in the room. Nepharos's Bell, unless administered very precisely, was not the kind of poison that put you to sleep gently, and Helenos's death had probably been messy. If his next-door neighbour hadn't been deaf, Helenos might have—well, probably not been saved, but at least not have died alone.

Varazda went back out onto the landing and considered a moment whether to heed Ora's directive not to bother Old Cosmo. He couldn't see any good reason to do so. He tapped lightly at the third door, mostly for form's sake.

"What?" croaked a voice from inside.

Ah. So "slightly hard of hearing" was what Ora had meant by "stone-deaf." Varazda pushed the door open and looked in. The room was filled with a bizarre collection of things: dried herbs hanging from the ceiling, jars with labels in Glifian characters lined up on shelves, broken shards of pottery, carved figures in dark wood, bundles of rags. There were even, on the desk under the window, a couple of books, one of them unrolled and held open with a pair of nameless metal implements.

The man sitting at the desk, with his back turned to Varazda, was small and thin and white-haired, his faded blue tunic hanging loose on his bony shoulders.

Varazda coughed loudly, and the man turned, looking over his shoulder. He started, then quickly straightened up and gave Varazda a look of great, almost comical, dignity.

Oh dear, Varazda thought. *He's been waiting for some emissary from the king for years, finally recognizing his brilliance and summoning him to the post of Grand High Court Madman or whatever it is—and he thinks I'm it.*

Varazda made only a slight bow, so as not to get Old Cosmo's hopes up.

"God guard your coming and your going," he said automatically. "I am investigating the death of the young man who lived next door. Can you—"

"What? Speak up!"

"I beg your pardon. The young man next door, who died. Can you tell me anything about him?"

The old man's expression changed to outrage. Varazda had been half prepared for that, and quickly took a step backward. He hadn't been prepared for Cosmo to surge up from his stool, shrieking something that might have been an incantation and brandishing one of his metal implements as if he would have hit Varazda in the head with it had he been tall enough.

Varazda backed smartly out the door and collided with another small old person, steel-grey hair in a knot on top of her head, a heavy stone loom-weight in her fist. She would have succeeded in hitting him with it if she hadn't been so astonished by his appearance that she froze.

"Who in the name of Nepharos are you?" she shrilled.

Varazda got to the head of the stairs, securing his escape route, before he tried to reason with them. Old Cosmo was still shouting rhythmic nonsense.

"We spoke a few minutes ago, mother—"

"You!" Ora cried in astonishment. "I thought you were a woman."

"Can you—can you assure your friend that I mean him no harm?"

"I don't know that! What did you do to him? I told you to stay away from him."

Old Cosmo had disappeared back into his room, still ranting, and Ora had finally lowered the loom-weight.

"I think your friend may know something about the crime," Varazda forged on.

"He knows nothing! Nothing!"

That was not very convincing, and Varazda stood a moment longer at the head of the stairs giving her a look that told her he thought so. It was a moment that he regretted, because not only did she not soften in her determination, but Old Cosmo re-emerged from his room with a long brass pipe in his hand, put it to his lips, and blew.

The pipe contained some kind of powder, which flew up in a cloud, perfectly aimed at Varazda's face, stinging his eyes and half blinding him. He staggered and slid down most of one flight of stairs before he was able to right himself and limp down the rest of the way, holding onto the wall and wiping his streaming eyes on his sleeve.

When he got to the ground floor, still barely able to see, his entourage seemed to have dispersed. The street—what he could see of it—was deserted. He remembered the fountain in the street below. He made his way sideways down the uneven stone steps, cursing under his breath, until he reached the pipe in the wall at the bottom. He gathered water in his cupped hands and splashed his face six or seven times, until his eyes felt better and his fingers were coming away streaked with black and green makeup. He scrubbed the rest off with his handkerchief and dried his face on his sleeve.

He leaned a shoulder against a dry section of the wall and

considered his options. Old Cosmo's room looked like it might well repay a thorough search, but the old man also looked like he probably didn't leave his room often, and even if he did, his protective neighbour would be watching out with her loom-weight in hand. Slipping in at night, while Cosmo was asleep, would be the only option, and that would mean searching the room in the dark without making enough noise to wake either Cosmo himself or Ora next door. It would be difficult to say the least.

He also had to admit that he wasn't entirely sure what he would be looking for. Remnants of thorn-flower? He didn't know what it looked like or smelled like. Aradne probably knew, and perhaps she could tell him enough that he would be able to bring back samples for her to verify. He didn't think he could bring her with him. Though perhaps she and Ora would get on. He wouldn't be surprised.

He looked up at a sound on the stairs, and saw a tall man with a scarred face coming down the steps. The scar sliced down the left side of his face, and his left eye was missing.

"Waiting for someone, my boy?" the man asked with an oily leer, stopping on the steps a little above Varazda.

This, Varazda thought, would be One-Eyed Dolon.

"Because if you are," One-Eyed Dolon went on without waiting for an answer, "you should know that this patch belongs to me, and I only let my girls work it."

Beautiful. Now I'm being taken for a prostitute.

"I'm sure I don't know what you mean," Varazda said, laying on the Zashian accent thick again and opening his eyes wide. "But perhaps you can help me. I am looking for a friend. He said he was staying around here. Helenos Kontiades Diophoros?"

The one-eyed man shrugged. "Never heard of him."

"He's dark and thin, about—" *About my age,* Varazda had been about to say, but that would only confuse matters.

"About thirty. He always wears one of those things that's wrapped around. A mantle. He talks a lot."

"Beard?"

"Yes," Varazda hazarded. Helenos hadn't worn a beard in the summer, but he might have grown one later. Phemians had such low standards when it came to beards, anyway—the least bit of hair on their chins apparently counted.

"Yeah, I've seen him around. He's dead."

"What?" Varazda didn't really have the energy to act devastated, so he settled for a combination of annoyance and alarm, as if Helenos might have owed him money or promised him a favour.

"Yeah, yeah, dead a week now. Killed himself, if you ask me."

"No! Please do not say so. Among my people, it is a great shame and a scandal to kill oneself. What makes you say that my friend did this?"

Dolon cast a glance back up the stairs and gave a not-so-subtle signal to someone at the top before answering. Varazda had been tucking his coat back to show off Dami's sword when he walked into the neighbourhood, but he realized now it had swung forward, concealing the sheathed blade. He looked like an easy target.

"Always up and down, that one," said Dolon. "One day he's capering about telling everyone he's had a letter from his old teacher, who's going to fix everything up for him. Next, he's drinking himself into a stupor and moaning to my girls about his lost 'prospects.' Day before he died, he's all excited again, about meeting someone." Dolon shrugged. "Speaking of meeting people—here's a couple of my friends that you ought to meet." He jerked a thumb at the two men descending the stairs above him.

"No, thank you," said Varazda.

Reaching beneath his coat, he casually drew Dami's

sword and tapped One-Eyed Dolon lightly on the chest with its point. The two men on the stairs froze.

"What in all the hells?" one of them muttered audibly.

"It's been lovely talking to you," said Varazda.

He backed away at a leisurely pace, sword extended, as Dolon stood rigid and staring. Before he reached the entrance to the narrow alley, Varazda turned, giving Dami's sword a jaunty twist and sliding it back into its sheath with a flourish. He waited until he was well out of sight of the men to break into a jog.

CHAPTER 10

To tell the truth, Varazda did understand what Aradne meant when she said she had been too frightened to treat Nione as an ordinary mortal. He wouldn't have said she seemed divine to him—it was true that he didn't have a particularly good sense of what that would be like—but he'd always found her intimidating. One of the many things that had intrigued him about Damiskos from the beginning was the fact that he was genuinely friends with her.

Varazda found himself sitting in the garden with Nione on the morning of Orante's Day. He had been there by himself, kicking his heels because he couldn't do anything until that afternoon, when she came out with a book. She looked at him for a moment, assessing, he thought, whether he wanted to be left alone or not. He didn't, so he moved over on the bench where he was sitting, although it was not strictly necessary to make room for her.

"You had a letter from home?" she said, indicating the tablet in his lap.

"Yes. Everyone is well. My younger brother is debating whether or not to ask his lover to pose as a mermaid for his new sculptural commission."

"Oh," said Nione. "That's a delicate question, isn't it? She might be flattered, but shy of having her image displayed publicly."

"I don't think that's the problem. It's that the commission is for a public toilet."

"Oh dear," said Nione. "He's very young, Ariston, isn't he?"

He'd forgotten that Dami would have told her everyone's name when he had written to her. He laughed. "Not young enough to excuse some of the things he does."

"Well, I hope you will be able to dissuade him from this one. After all, there will be other opportunities for him to carve her likeness. And how is your daughter? She must miss you."

They talked a little more, and he was reminded that she had been not only a priest but a public figure, almost like a politician, and if she wasn't precisely easy to talk to, she was good at compensating for it. She also seemed much happier than she had at Laothalia in the summer. Well, that was to be expected.

Aradne came out into the garden presently, kissed Nione lightly on the lips, and wanted to know what Varazda was doing sitting around.

"I have nothing to do but sit around," he said. "I can't carry on with the investigation until this afternoon."

"Why don't you go see Damiskos again?" Nione suggested.

He winced. "I'm not brave enough to face his family."

"Were they so hostile?"

"Well, no. They *mostly* kept themselves under control, but you knew it wouldn't last. The threat of hostility was there."

Aradne was standing at the end of the bench, leaning against Nione, who had put an arm around her waist.

"You could go," said Nione, "to show them you're not afraid of them."

"He just said he *is* afraid of them, though," Aradne protested.

Nione looked up at her. "Yes, but did you believe that?"

"Well. No."

They both looked at Varazda.

He laughed. "I'm not afraid of them—I'm afraid of their saying something about me, in front of Damiskos, that will hurt him."

"Oh," said Aradne, chastened.

"I think," said Nione, "that you are afraid of giving them the opportunity to be themselves—which they've probably already taken behind your back. I'm sorry—I don't mean to sound so harsh. I've never had a high opinion of Damiskos's parents."

Varazda was silent for a moment. Finally he said slowly, "I'm afraid of their saying something about me that's … true."

"Such as what?" said Aradne.

With Eudoxia you could hold your head up in the agora …

"That I'm not good for him. That he could live an easier life without me."

"But that's—" Aradne sputtered. She threw up her hands.

"Easier isn't necessarily better," said Nione.

"Isn't it?" Varazda shifted restlessly on the bench. "Wouldn't it be better not to have to fight for every bit of happiness? No—" He ran a hand through his hair and managed a laugh. "I don't know why I'm making this feeble argument. I know I am good for him—we're good for each other. I just … "

"You've just had enough of being insulted by his family," Nione suggested, "and you've every right to stay away. I'm sorry I pressed you on it, truly."

Varazda waved away the apology with a smile. But he

couldn't stop thinking of Ariston saying, "Have you not noticed that he's good at basically *everything*?" He didn't think Dami actually wanted to go into politics—that sounded like an idea that came from Ino's mother—but it wasn't a ridiculous one. And if it was actually something he wanted, at some time in the future? If he couldn't even get an advocate to defend him with Varazda at his side, he certainly couldn't get elected to anything.

It was at this point that Niko popped his head into the peristyle to announce the arrival of Timiskos, bearing the message that his father was out of the house for the day, along with the poisonous Simonides and Korinna, and would Varazda like to visit again?

"Of course," Varazda said smoothly. "I'll go on my way to the agora this afternoon."

It was cold in the apartment, and damp, and Damiskos's knee hurt more than it had in years. He felt restless and tired at the same time, missing his usual exercise at the Baths of Soukos and leisurely walks through the streets of Boukos before and after with Varazda. After lunch he wrapped himself in his warmest mantle and went and leaned on the rail of the balcony and looked out over the withering grass of the garden and the rooftops of the neighbours' houses. Timiskos came out to stand beside him.

"Did you deliver the message?" Damiskos asked. Timiskos had been gone since before lunch.

His brother gave him an aggrieved look. "I'm fine, how are you? Yes, I delivered the message. You know that house where he's staying belongs to Nione Kukara, the Speaker of the Maidens?"

"Ex-Speaker, and it's actually her freedwoman's house, and yes. Nione and I are old friends."

"Well, you've really been keeping me up-to-date on the details, haven't you? Sorry." Timiskos shrugged. "I just got back from Philo's, that's all. The wine shop that we went to the other night? I'm not welcome there any more, apparently. Pandares's men leaned on Philo, and told him they'd 'cause trouble' if he went on serving me. It was my usual place. I feel like a shit for getting Philo in trouble."

"It's not your fault," said Damiskos wearily. "Maybe I can write to someone at the Quartermaster's Office and see if I can get a loan until I can collect my pension."

Timiskos was giving him a strange look; Damiskos would almost have called it calculating. Then he shook his head. "If you can raise money, you should put it toward paying your bond so you can get out of this house. Don't you think?"

"Not worth it," Damiskos replied curtly. "I'll get out soon enough when the date is set for the trial. Mother and Father's debts in your name are a much more serious matter."

Timiskos shrugged. "Yeah, and you could help me with those if you could get out of the house."

Damiskos dropped his head into his hands. "You're right. I'm not thinking clearly. If I can borrow money to pay my bond, I can get out of the house, then go to the Bursar's and draw my pension—though I'm not sure how much that will be … No, Timi, it's no good. Then we'd just owe more money, and my pension won't be enough to cover Mother and Father's debt. I could sell Xanthe, if I owned her any more, which I don't—and even if the fellow in Thumia gave me back the money I gave him, it's only three hundred because he was selling her back to me cheap."

"And … you really don't have anything else you could sell?"

"No! She was the most expensive thing I owned."

"Yeah? Mm. It's too bad we can't stage a kidnapping, like that fellow Olympios was talking about."

"What?"

"You remember—he said a client of his staged his own kidnapping. I suppose it was to get the ransom money."

"Timiskos, no one could pay to ransom you—that's the whole problem."

Timiskos was giving him that strange look again. "Yeah. I guess you're right."

"Boys, boys!" Philion put his head out through the balcony doors. "Get in here. Olympios is back and says he's willing to take the case after all!"

"Oh," said Timiskos wanly, "you're home."

"Yes, yes, I met Olympios in the street and came back here directly. Come on, both of you."

Timiskos shot his brother a worried look as they followed their father into the house. "I told Pharastes … "

"I know. It can't be helped."

"Now don't get too excited, Old Blade," said Olympios, who stood with his fists on his hips in the atrium. "I'll take this case on one condition. You and your lady friend need to get married *yesterday*. By which I mean, as soon as possible."

"Do you think that will help?" said Philion eagerly.

Damiskos remembered how he had felt only a week ago: like a trapped animal, ensnared by his duty to his self-destructive family. He didn't feel that way anymore.

Olympios gave Philion an eagle-eyed look. "It's the only thing I can think of that might."

Mostly what Damiskos felt now was tired. Since no one was asking for his opinion yet, he let them continue to talk without him.

Myrto emerged from her room at the sound of the advocate's voice, with Gaia trailing behind her, hair falling down as usual.

"Wonderful news!" Philion called. "Olympios will take the case after all, as soon as Damiskos and Ino agree to marry."

"But darling," said Myrto, "they're not going to."

"Of course they are, of course they are. Hush. Gaia, bring us something to eat! Where are Korinna and—oh, they're out, I remember. It doesn't matter. Now, Olympios—come in, sit down, all of you. We've had a visit from some lackey from the Hall of Justice this morning, and the date is set for the trial. Next Xereus's Day at noon."

Olympios blanched visibly. That was only five days away.

"Gods curse them, they must have bribed someone to rush it through," he said as he sat down in the chair Philion pulled out for him. "Right! Well, I have a thought. We might be able to get a day's delay—and wring the jury's hearts a little in the process—if we do this. On Hesperion's Day in the morning, when they let you out of the house to go to the Hall of Justice, you and your fiancée make a quick stop at the Great Temple and make the marriage libation. Then beg the court to grant a delay for your wedding night. Eh?" He struck a pose as if expecting applause.

Damiskos had not taken his own seat. He had folded his arms across his chest in a way that one of his junior officers had once told him was known throughout the legion to signify trouble.

"Damiskos is a follower of Terza," said Myrto before her son could speak. "He wouldn't get married in the Great Temple. There's some very charming thing they do in their own temple—isn't there, darling? A kind of an oath or something?"

"Oh, they don't have to do that to get married," said Timiskos, chiming in for some reason. "I know lots of Terza men from the army. Besides, you can ... uh ... " He seemed to realize he was not being helpful. "You can worship Terza in the Great Temple."

"Perfect," said Olympios briskly. "So that's settled."

"No," said Damiskos, sounding angrier than he meant to, though not as angry as he felt. "It's not. We are not going to do that."

"Why not?" Philion demanded, looking up with surprise from where he had been selecting a raisin cake from the table.

"Why am I not willing to take a blasphemous oath—it's an oath for lovers, not for people marrying so they can inherit businesses in Kargania and escape murder charges. Or why am I not willing to degrade Ino and myself by entering into a marriage that could leave her a disgraced widow, just for the possibility that a jury might think it was cute?"

There was quite a long silence following this. Damiskos did not normally speak this way to his family.

"So am I to understand," said Olympios frostily, "that you reject my advice?"

"No no no," said Philion, coughing as he tried to swallow his raisin cake at the same time. "I'm sure we can come to a compromise. He needs time to get used to the idea."

"Oh," said Gaia, who had been setting out more dates on the table, "there's the door!"

And there, coming through the door, as Gaia blushed and stepped aside after opening it for him, was Varazda.

He was dressed in Pseuchaian clothes today, a dark blue tunic peeking out from under a flawlessly wrapped white mantle with a blue border, the quintessential outfit of the Pseuchaian citizen male. Damiskos had never seen Varazda wear anything like it before. He looked radiant, his eyes painted in blue, his hair up in a careless knot, the henna on his hands still fresh and red.

Olympios saw him and exploded out of his chair. "What?" he demanded, glaring around at the family. "What is *he* doing here again?"

"I have some news," said Varazda, coming across the atrium toward the seating area, clearly not realizing what he was walking into. Damiskos was on his feet and moving out around his chair toward him. "I've found another suspect."

"That was fast," said Damiskos. He reached Varazda and

leaned in to kiss his cold cheek. "I'd invite you to sit down and warm up," he murmured in Zashian, "but I don't think you're going to want to stick around."

"You've found a *what*?" Olympios strode right up to Varazda, pushing his face up threateningly close to Varazda's—which involved looking up, as Varazda was taller than him.

"A suspect," said Varazda, leaning away a little without taking a step back, as if he might have been trying to avoid the smell of Olympios's breath. "Hello again. I wasn't expecting you here. A 'suspect' means someone else who might have done the murder. Is that not the term you use here?"

Olympios's face twisted into a snarl. "Listen you, you cr—euugh," he broke off with a grunt as Damiskos grabbed him by the front of his tunic.

"That's enough," said Damiskos evenly, releasing him with only a token shove (he'd learned his lesson with Helenos).

"I *beg* your pardon?" Olympios glared at him, fiery-eyed. "I've never been so insulted. You'll rue the day. I wash my hands of all of you." He wheeled to distribute his glare evenly around the group. "I will send you a bill for my consultation."

"The hell you will!" Philion yelped. "Nepharos's balls, Damiskos, what are you playing at? And you, you painted Sasian hussy, how dare you come back here?"

Varazda's hand was gripping Damiskos's rather hard.

"Philion, don't be rude," said Myrto, cutting across the men's voices without raising her own. "I told him he was welcome back any time, and I'm delighted to see him."

"I'm not!" Philion bawled.

"I wash my hands, I absolutely *wash* my *hands*," Olympios declared.

"Oh good," said Myrto. "Then I wish you'd dry them too and get going."

"Shut up, woman, shut up! How do you expect me to pay for an advocate to defend your son if you drive Olympios away? Don't you know we've no credit left anywhere?"

"Holy God, Dami," Varazda murmured, "I'm so sorry. I wouldn't have come if I'd thought—"

"I know. Timiskos told you it was a good time. He made a mistake."

"Ye-es. He did."

Olympios was on his way to the door, Philion running after him shouting that he could bring his son and his wife to heel—"And the Sasian is as good as gone, I swear!"—while Olympios held up his hands and repeated his line about washing them.

"Honestly!" said Timiskos, finally propelling himself up from his chair. "Are you two trying to destroy this family?" He scowled at Damiskos and his mother.

"Sweetheart," said Myrto with a little laugh, "we *are* this family. Who do you think you're talking to?"

"I'm talking to my brother, and I'm talking to you, Myrto. Look, it's all very well for Damiskos to have a lover or whatever—sorry, Pharastes—it's just, this is a real situation that we're in, and I know you don't pay attention or even care, Myrto, but Damiskos, you should know better. We're not going to get out of this without help, and you're driving away the only person who can help us!"

"Get out of *what*, darling?"

"You stupid—" Timiskos managed to cut himself off before he called his stepmother something unforgivable, but only just. "Get out of this debt! This hole Father's dug us into —you and Father—you with your senseless spending and Father with his stupid real estate schemes and his gambling. I know you think it's not that bad, that something will turn up because it always does, but it *is* that bad—you've been stealing from your own children, that's how bad it is. You borrowed money in my name and now I'm being turned away from wine shops and hounded by Gorgion Pandares's thugs—you spent the money Damiskos was sending you for his horse and she got sold, and none of us has the money to pay Damiskos's bond to get him out of this house!"

"Timiskos," Damiskos spoke evenly but very, very firmly. "Calm down."

The front door slammed.

"I hope you're pleased with yourselves!" Philion roared across the atrium. "There goes our last chance to prove Damiskos's innocence and save our family name, so I hope you're all very pleased with yourselves!"

Myrto was laughing. "Save our family name? Oh, Philion, please. Your name hasn't been worth anything for decades—you know that. "

"Why are you still here?" Philion asked Varazda, looking like a child ready to stamp his foot and begin howling. "Get out of my house—shoo, shoo! We don't want you at the trial, we don't want you here, we don't want you anywhere near Damiskos."

"Sir!" Damiskos shouted.

Philion ignored him. "My son is a real man, and whatever Sasian witchcraft you worked on him to get him to think of you as anything more than a nice ass to fuck—it'll wear off. So get out."

Varazda gave Damiskos's hand, which he still held, another hard squeeze.

"I was on my way to interview a suspect," he said in Zashian. "I'll go do that. And—I'll be in touch, but obviously I won't come again myself. Sorry."

He let go of Damiskos's hand and stepped away, walking briskly across the atrium.

"Right," said Philion as the door closed behind Varazda. "Good. Might be just as well he's confined to the house," he added to no one in particular. "Gaia! Get me a clean mantle! I'm going down to the Crossed Oars."

Philion strode off, and Damiskos and his mother were left alone in the atrium.

"That's a gambling house, I guess," said Damiskos dully. "The Crossed Oars."

"I ... I think it must be. He does often complain of having lost money after he comes back from there." Myrto looked at the floor. "He didn't really do anything to you, in the way of witchcraft, did he?"

"No, of course not."

"Good. I didn't think so. Philion is so odd sometimes."

CHAPTER 11

Today Varazda was dressed for going into a philosophy school. He hadn't been yesterday, when he had first gone there; he had shown up in what he'd thought was a smart tunic and a cloak, and been told—fairly nicely, by some of the students—that you couldn't go in without a proper, old-fashioned mantle, wrapped in the approved Phemian way. As it turned out, he had learned from the same students that the person he was looking for hadn't been there but was expected today. He'd had time to acquire a mantle and learn from Nione how to wrap it; surprisingly, this seemed to be one of the few things Aradne didn't know.

He walked from the Temnons' tacky neighbourhood to the agora, trying to focus on the task at hand rather than what had just passed in Damiskos's family's apartment.

He can't go around throwing everyone across the room who calls me a "creature." It would take up all his time.

He laughed aloud, miserably. It didn't escape him that in a sense, the whole murder charge was his fault. Dami had knocked Helenos down after he said something about a "Sasian whore." Dami, bless his heart, had been defending Varazda's honour. How absurd.

Varazda arrived at the agora and looked for the squat, ancient building he'd visited the day before. He was again struck by how old and unimpressive it looked among the columns and statuary of the city's heart.

He'd heard the history of the Marble Porches of Pheme before. The building had been the meeting house of the citizens' assembly, far back in the early days of the Republic, when the city had been much smaller, and the columned porches on each side had become popular gathering places for philosophers and their pupils. Later, when Pheme grew larger and the new government buildings were built, the old meeting house was entirely turned over to the philosophers and was now used as a school. There was some hierarchy concerning the porches and the interior of the building, something about where the traditionalists gathered as opposed to the radicals; Varazda neither knew nor cared about the details. He had been told the day before that Eurydemos could be found inside the school these days, so that was where he went.

In spite of the cold weather, there were a lot of students milling on the famous porches of the building, huddled up in their mantles. Varazda got a few curious glances as he climbed the steps and wove through them to get to the doors, but no one spoke to him. Inside, his first impression was that it was surprisingly dark.

Well, perhaps it wasn't surprising, since the ancient meeting house didn't appear to have been provided with any windows, just a square skylight in the centre of the roof. It was all one large room, and if anything at all had been done to convert it from a place for public assemblies into a school in the centuries since it had made that transition, Varazda couldn't see it. The room was lined with ranked stone seating, bare and worn with age, and there were remains of some very faded frescoes on the walls, and that was all. It was viciously cold; given the choice, Varazda thought he would have preferred to stay outside on the porches after all.

There were two main groups of students inside the building. One, the larger, was ranged across the benches on the north side of the room, listening raptly to a speaker who stood at floor level, a youngish man with a mop of curly hair. As Varazda caught what the speaker was saying, he realized where this group fit into the school's hierarchy.

"And yet, Tios is thriving, in spite of the continued embargoes, in spite of having virtually abolished slavery within its walls. In spite of that? Or in part because of it?"

These were the radicals. If Varazda hadn't been here on a mission, he would have sat down with them to listen.

The other group, on the opposite steps, was much smaller, and were mostly talking among themselves or simply glowering across the floor at the radicals. Whatever Eurydemos was, he wasn't a radical, so Varazda scanned this group expecting to spot him among them, but he wasn't there. Then Varazda did spot him, sitting up at the top of the steps in the far corner of the room, recognizable by his shock of grey hair and untidily wrapped mantle, alone except for one young man.

That was unexpected. Had he been shunned by the other philosophers for the poisonous nonsense that he'd been peddling? Varazda stood looking across the long room at him for a moment, the kind of look that would have had old women in Zash reaching for their amulets against the Evil Eye. Then he crossed the floor, passing between the two groups of students, and began to climb the steps to where the philosopher sat.

The young man who had been sitting with Eurydemos popped up and jogged down the steps to meet Varazda halfway. He was tall and slender and very pretty, with soft brown hair that fell around his face and large, sleepy blue eyes.

"Have you come to speak with the master?" he asked, in

what sounded like an attempt at the manner of a palace guard.

"I have come to speak to Eurydemos, yes. Is he free?" Obviously he was free; he was sitting up here doing nothing.

The young man looked as if he didn't understand the question. "If you wish to speak to the master," he said, still in the same palace-guard manner, "you must answer this riddle. 'What lies—'"

"I beg your pardon," said Varazda flatly. "I am not going to answer a riddle. Excuse me."

He dodged around the young man, who looked crestfallen, and mounted the steps to approach Eurydemos. He was standing over Eurydemos before the philosopher looked up and recognized him with a start.

"Pharastes!" For a moment he just looked Varazda up and down with wide eyes.

"Master, he wouldn't answer the riddle," said the pretty young man, arriving at Varazda's side. "I'm sorry. I tried."

"Of course, Bion, of course."

Eurydemos patted the stone next to him, and the young man sat obediently and wrapped himself back up in the cloak that he had abandoned to accost Varazda.

"What brings you here, Pharastes? Does your ... new master ... "

"I have no master," Varazda cut him off. "I received my freedom more than seven years ago. I'm here to ask whether you visited Helenos Kontiades at his home a week ago Market Day."

Eurydemos's mouth hung open for a moment. Finally he closed it and shook himself slightly. "Sit, sit," he said, gesturing to the step beside him. Varazda remained standing. "Yes, I did visit him. He sent me a note saying he was back in Pheme, 'laying low,' as they say, out in the Skalina, and would I come see him there." Eurydemos shook his head sadly. "The poor boy was living in very squalid conditions, a very sad state for the son of a great family. I suffered such a great disappointment with regard to that boy. Boy? I should not call him a boy—he is a man, and able to make a man's choices. And he chose to lead so many of my students astray. Gelon, never my best pupil, but so eager to learn, and so talented in many ways—a gifted artist, did you know that?

"Phaia, now, his girlfriend—do you remember her? Such a brilliant and beautiful young woman—I have always said that more women should be allowed to cultivate their minds, to overcome the weakness of their femininity through rigorous training, and I never knew one of the fair sex rise to the challenge with such aplomb. And yet, he destroyed her too. What happened to her, in the end? Was she executed? Ah, no, of course not.

"But yes, I did visit Helenos. How did you know about that?"

"Were you aware that he died that night?"

"What? Died? Poor Helenos, I—" Eurydemos jumped to his feet, wobbling as he stepped on a fold of his mantle. "You don't think I had anything to do with it!"

As a reaction, it was neither particularly incriminating nor particularly exonerating. The man continued to be as annoying as he had been in the summer.

"You were seen meeting Helenos in the street," Varazda said, without sympathy. "You went up to his room with him."

"Yes, yes, I did," Eurydemos agreed readily. "We talked— I came in response to his note, as I told you—but it was only a short visit. He had no interest in hearing my new teachings —it was quite frustrating. I brought him a bottle of wine, but he did not even share it with me. Are you saying that I am under suspicion? Who suspects me?"

"I do," Varazda spat. "You were there at the right time, you have a grudge against Helenos, you brought him a bottle of wine which you did not drink with him, and later that night, after he had come home drunk, he died by poison. Tell me why I should not suspect you."

"He didn't do it!" cried the brown-haired youth, popping up beside his master. "He was with me!"

"Bion ... " Eurydemos shot him an irritated look. "That's very loyal of you, but it isn't helpful."

"Oh," said Bion, blushing. "Sorry. But I know he didn't do it, all the same," he added to Varazda.

"Shh, darling, shh," said Eurydemos. "He's right, of course. I didn't do it. I would never take the life of another man—not even my most wayward student. Blessed immortals, I would be less likely to take his life than another's—speaking in a purely hypothetical sense, since as I say, I would never take anyone's life—as I feel responsible for his errors. I would have taken great satisfaction in redirecting him to the true path. I have been making it my mission, ever since the unfortunate incidents of the summer, to set as many as I can on the true path."

"Is that why you don't let anyone speak to you until they've answered a riddle?" Varazda asked acidly.

"Yes," said Eurydemos, with a gnomic smile that made Varazda want to kick him in the head.

He'd spent a lot of time at Laothalia wanting to kick Eurydemos in the head. The man made his skin crawl. He reminded Varazda of a courtier from Gudul, an astrologer who had always sent for Varazda when he came to stay at the palace, who read poetry about him at dinner with the other courtiers, forbade him to speak when they were alone together, and routinely left him with bruises that would last a week.

"I asked Helenos the riddle, of course," Eurydemos went on, eyes half-lidded. "I said to him, 'What lies betwee—'"

"I'm sure you did," Varazda cut him off. "And I daresay he answered it, or tried to. He was after all in Pheme because you had written to him intimating that you could help him return from exile with a clean slate."

"I—what? No, I hadn't. Why would I do that?"

Varazda looked at him for a long moment. Eurydemos coloured slightly.

"Yes," he said finally, "I see. So that I could kill him. But I didn't. And I didn't write to him. You really must believe me."

"I don't. He was heard telling his neighbours about the letter he'd had from you."

Eurydemos shook his head emphatically. "They must have misunderstood. I did not write to him. I give you my word."

He could not, Varazda thought, have looked less trustworthy if he'd tried, but it seemed as if a staring contest would go nowhere.

"At what time did you visit Helenos in the Skalina?" Varazda asked finally.

"What time? Oh, it must have been … I've no idea. Bion?"

"Yes, Master?"

Eurydemos sighed. "Do you remember what time I left the house last Market Day?"

"Oh, I don't know, Master. You usually get up before I do."

"Ah. That's true. It was certainly some time in the morning, that is all I can tell you. And you say he was found dead that night?"

"He was found the following morning. No one knows exactly when he died." This was strictly true, though somewhat misleading. "What kind of wine did you bring?"

"What kind of wine? I don't know—I don't pay attention to such things. Bion?"

"Yes, Master?"

"Are you paying attention to what we're talking about at all, Bion?"

"Yes, Master."

"What kind of wine did I take to Helenos?"

"I don't know. I was asleep, remember?" This was spoken in a slightly less respectful manner, and the word "Master" was conspicuously absent.

"Yes, yes, but it's all your wine, and you know I don't know a thing about it. It was in a, let me see, a sort of pointy bottle, with a bird on the seal."

"Uh." Bion's sleepy eyes widened. "That was the Xanos red. You gave away a bottle of the Xanos red? To someone you don't even like?"

"Oh, dear," said Eurydemos, smiling, "I see I have erred."

"It's just—if my father finds out … " Bion looked uncomfortable.

What in the world was going on with these two? Varazda decided he very much did not want to know.

"So it was a bottle of expensive red wine with a bird on the seal," he said. "And you left it, unopened, with Helenos."

There had been no bottle like that in Helenos's room that he'd seen, but then the room had been cleared of everything valuable. Did that argue that the valuable bottle of wine had been full, or at least partially full, when the room was cleared, and had been taken away? If it had been empty, would it have been left there with the other rubbish?

Or, of course, it had been poisoned, and it had been removed by the family's lawyer to be used as evidence in court. Yet again Varazda found himself cursing Pheme and its ridiculous lack of a public watch or official investigative body.

"What size was the bottle?"

"About like this," Bion supplied, unprompted, holding up his hands. About what Varazda would have expected—certainly not a size that *he* could have finished off in one sitting, but some men could drink a great deal more than he could. Living with Dami for a month would have taught him that, if he hadn't already known it.

"Poor boy," Eurydemos said, shaking his head. "I don't suppose … Is there any indication that he might have taken his own life?"

That was a possibility that had occurred to Varazda even before One-Eyed Dolon raised it. It would explain why the neighbour Ora had said that the door was open in the morning when she found the body, yet had been closed after Damiskos left, when she imagined Helenos was already dead. If Helenos had really been counting on help from Eurydemos, which had not materialized, perhaps he'd been left in a desperate state of mind.

"What do you think?" Varazda turned the question back on the philosopher. "Was he crushed when you refused to help him?"

"No, not crushed—quite angry, really. And I wouldn't say I refused to help him—I wouldn't say that at all. I offered him the most precious kind of help at my disposal. I offered to set him right, to—"

"Yes," said Varazda. "So you think you left him angry but not despondent." It didn't signify; anger could as easily be the outward sign of despair as tears. He had seen that enough times back at Gudul.

"I really must impress upon you my total innocence in this matter," Eurydemos went on. "I went to see the young man only to help him—yes, to help him—bearing a gift in a spirit of forgiveness, and I left after he showed his disinterest in changing his ways and was rude to me. You must tell your master—"

"I. Do. Not. Have. A. Master."

"Oh, I do beg your pardon. Your … employer?" He spoke as if using a euphemism to humour someone.

Varazda wanted to kick him in the head with a new vehemence. There probably wasn't enough play in the stupid mantle he was wearing to allow it.

"I am investigating Helenos Kontiades's death as a private citizen because I have a personal interest in seeing justice done in this case."

"Oh, I see. How noble. I heartily approve." Now he sounded as if he were praising a pet for learning a new trick.

It wouldn't help Dami's case if it came out that Varazda had been going around threatening other suspects, so he restrained himself, with a huge effort, from saying, *Of course, if it turns out I can pin this crime on you, it will give me the greatest pleasure.*

He turned and descended the steps without taking his leave of Eurydemos or his whatever-he-was Bion. As he passed back between the rows of seats to the entrance, he heard one of the radical philosopher's students asking a question.

"But in Eurydemos's Ideal Republic, slavery is not abolished, is it?"

"No," the curly-haired philosopher replied. "Interesting, isn't it? Makes one think the Ideal Republic might not be so ideal after all."

CHAPTER 12

"I don't know what was going on there," said Varazda that evening in Aradne's dining room, "and I don't want to know. At first I thought he was Eurydemos's student, then I thought he was his slave, then they started talking about Eurydemos taking some wine that belonged to Bion, and what would happen when Bion's father found out—*I don't want to know.*"

"I can tell you," said Nione, "unless you really mean that."

Varazda sighed dramatically. "I do mean it, but you'd better tell me all the same."

"Bion is the son of a very wealthy freedman from Kos. The family spends most of their time on a private island now, but they bought Bion a house in town. Eurydemos went there for a party in Euthalion Month and just never left."

"Ugh," said Aradne, perfectly encapsulating Varazda's feelings.

"Is this very widely known, then?" he asked.

"No, I only come to know it by chance," said Nione. "I don't have anything to do with Eurydemos myself, after what happened in the summer, but I still am in touch with one of his sisters. She told me he has more or less given up teaching—closed the school in Boukos altogether—and has repudiated all his former ideas."

"All except the idea of being a sponging jackass, apparently," said Aradne.

"The school in Boukos was closed by the government, not by Eurydemos," Varazda added.

Nione laughed. "His family has always tended to cooperate with his myth-making. I did myself, for a time. Do you think he did murder Helenos?"

Varazda ran a hand through his hair. "I'm not sure," he hedged. "I'm going to have to do some more searching. I wish I could find that wine bottle."

"What can I do to help?" said Aradne, in a tone that would not take "Nothing" for an answer.

Varazda looked up at her. "How are you with cranky old women?"

She made a face. "Not marvellous. You mean you need someone to keep the neighbour at bay so you can have another look for the wine bottle."

"Or you could help me deal with the possibly volatile old alchemist, or whatever he is, and find out what sorts of poison he keeps on hand."

"Oooh, that sounds more fun."

"I can't tell whether you're serious or not."

"I'm half-serious," Aradne admitted. "Now for the old woman, Nione would be able to take care of her better than I would, but she can't show her face in a neighbourhood like the Skalina."

"I'm afraid not," said Nione. "Too many people recognize me."

Varazda had known Nione was an important person in Pheme, but it hadn't occurred to him that she would be known on sight by enough people that she couldn't pass unremarked in such a big city. The idea was rather staggering.

"I'll come with you," said Aradne resolutely. "Do we go in the front door, or under cover of darkness? Do we need to do our fortune teller impressions again?"

Varazda opened his mouth to say that that had given him an interesting idea, then closed it when he saw Nione's expression.

"That would hardly help if everyone in the neighbourhood knows him already," she said rather severely. "Do be careful, both of you. Varazda, it sounds as if you may have made yourself enemies at the wine shop as well as among Helenos's neighbours."

Aradne waved a hand. "Don't worry, love. Pharastes is a professional. He knows what he's doing."

Varazda and Aradne went back to the Skalina the following morning. He was dressed discreetly in black today and armed with more copper coins as well as Dami's sword. She had wrapped her hair in a turban of violently purple cloth and wore a red gown draped very low in the front and every piece of jewellery both she and Nione owned. It wasn't an awful lot of jewellery.

"You're sure Nione doesn't mind you doing this," Varazda said, as they took their seats in the ferry across the river—the faster option for reaching the north bank than taking the bridges further east.

"We talked it over last night," Aradne said, arranging her skirt on the seat, "and she agreed that it was a good plan. Tch, look at this—I *clank* when I move. Oh, don't give me that look, I know, this would be an average weekday for you."

"I didn't bring much jewellery with me," he said sadly. "I didn't know I would have so many occasions to dress up."

"By the way," she said, "how did it go with Damiskos's family yesterday?"

"Ghastly." He rolled his eyes. "I don't want to talk about it." He contradicted himself immediately by adding, "The father returned unexpectedly, with the advocate, who has now definitively dropped the case—understandably, since Dami very nearly knocked him down. Then his father called me various names. You know. About what you would expect."

After a moment Aradne said, "Nione's already been speaking to a lawyer she knows. She thinks he'll be willing to help."

Varazda nodded. "Thanks."

"Pretty sure you know you don't deserve to be called names either, right?"

"Right," said Varazda, smiling. "I do know that."

They made their way up through the grubby streets of the Skalina, sleepy and near-deserted in the cold morning sun. Aradne took Varazda's arm and gruffly forbade him to tease her about it.

"It's just because these streets are uneven, and this stupid gown is too long."

When they reached the ruined apartment building blocking the road, Varazda saw the red-haired girl from the other day, sweeping the front steps of a nearby house.

"Hello!" she called out, waving. "It's you. You're back."

He bowed.

"You made a conquest," Aradne whispered.

"Shush."

Since they had stopped, the girl left her broom in the doorway and came down into the street.

"I do not know your name," said Varazda. "I am Varazda son of Nahaz, and my companion is … " He hesitated a moment, wondering if he should tell her Aradne's real name. "Zora the Seer."

"I'm Simoe," said the girl. She looked narrowly at Aradne. "Are you sure about her? Don't get fooled, sir. There's a lot of people who pretend to be seers but aren't. And between you and me, she looks fake."

Varazda and Aradne glanced at one another and both burst out laughing.

"All right," said Varazda, toning down his accent and his grand manner without dropping them altogether—he didn't want to disappoint the girl. "What can we do to make her look more real?"

Simoe gasped. "Soukos! She really *is* fake. Are you—you're still looking for the killer, aren't you? Because the soldier, the one everyone thinks did it—he's your lover. I knew it! And she's helping you? Well, she'd look more like a real seer if she was dirtier."

Varazda looked at Aradne, who shrugged. "It's for a good cause," she said. "Nione will understand."

They thanked Simoe and spent some time dragging the hem of Nione's red gown through the muddy basin of the fountain on the corner and disarranging the purple turban. Then they went on up the stairs to the street above.

It was easy to get in the window of Helenos's old room, even in broad daylight. It was on the top floor, and the buildings here were so close together on all sides—the dead-end alley behind this block was barely shoulder-width—that all Varazda had to do was find one of the neighbouring buildings with access to the roof, jump across to the roof of Helenos's building, and swing down to unlatch the shutters on Helenos's window. Compared to the production involved in finding and getting to Dami's window a few nights ago, it was child's play.

As he swung down through the window, he heard Zora the Seer speaking in a loud voice to Old Cosmo next door.

"The spiiiiiirits have a messsssage for youuuuuuu!"

Helenos's room was in exactly the same state as Varazda had last seen it. This time, he took it apart methodically. He found a purse with two copper coins in it stuffed between the mattress and the bedframe, and a jar which smelled strongly of vinegar under the bed. He studied the empty wine bottles on the floor, and found he'd been right to think none of them had a bird on it. He searched the cupboard, and when he found that the shelves could be removed, he pulled them all out—not because he expected to find anything by doing this, but because he couldn't think what else to do.

"What do you want?" he heard Ora demanding. "Who in the hells are you?"

Old Cosmo gabbled something unintelligible, and Aradne announced, "I am Zzzzzzora the Ssssssseeer! The spiiiiirits—"

"Oh, no you don't! We don't want any witchcraft around here! Get out!"

The shelf at the bottom of the cupboard had stuck for a moment but now popped out suddenly, and something that had been stuck behind it clunked to the cupboard floor. Varazda reached down to snatch it up, and looked toward the still-open window.

"Get out, I tell you!"

"Ow! Take your hands—"

Varazda dove for the door and opened it. Aradne was in much the same situation he had been in two days ago: backing toward the stairs while Old Cosmo waved his arms and capered furiously in his doorway and Ora shouted epithets and brandished her loom-weight.

"You again!" the old woman shrieked, seeing Varazda.

He shot out an arm to catch Aradne as she stepped on the hem of her too-long gown and teetered at the top of the stairs. Old Cosmo dove back into his room, and Varazda knew what was coming next.

"Quick!" he told Aradne. "Down the stairs—turn your back on them!"

"I couldn't get—a look—in his room," she panted as they plunged down the stairs.

"Cosmo, no!" Ora shouted in alarm.

Something sailed past Varazda's shoulder and smashed against the wall, scattering fragments all down the steps. It was a wine bottle.

They ran down the steps, dodging shards of pottery, while above them Ora yelled, "You can't throw that!"

"Go on," Varazda told Aradne suddenly, turning back. He realized what he had just seen on the stairs.

"Are you mad?" Aradne yelped.

He sprang back up a couple of steps and snatched one of the shards of wine bottle before plunging back down after her.

"What's going on up there?" a man's voice boomed up from below.

Varazda leaned over the railing to look down. A huge man in a dirty tunic stood in the bottom of the stairwell, looking up. Beside him was Simoe, with her baby on her back again. She waved tentatively.

"It's my friends that I told you about," she said to the big man.

"I see. Old Cosmo and Ora giving you trouble up there?"

"Er—" The shouting from the top floor seemed to have ceased. "Yes, some trouble, but we're all right."

Varazda and Aradne managed to descend the rest of the stairs with dignity, and no loom-weights or other projectiles came flying after them. The big man was standing by the door to the street when they arrived, listening with a look of scepticism while Simoe told him how Zora the Seer was using her powers to uncover the truth about Helenos's murder.

"Well, I can solve the mystery for you without consulting the spirits," he said with a grin. "Sorry about Old Cosmo, though. He's a real piece of work. Lived here since my father's day, and he always pays his rent—I don't know where he gets the money, and I don't much want to—or I'd have had him out a long while ago. Do you know, when your boy Hilaros was lying dead up there, Old Cosmo goes into his room and takes away the bottle of wine he'd been drinking before he died—*and drinks the dregs himself.* Can you believe that?"

"No!" said Simoe. "Did he get sick?"

Big Tio—this was presumably Big Tio, the landlord—shook his head. "He was fine. Scampering about chanting weird nonsense like usual. So it wasn't the wine that killed your boy, was it? The spirits tell you that, Madam Seer?"

Aradne straightened her turban and gazed at the ceiling as if in deep thought—or a trance, or something, Varazda wasn't sure. "I see a jar," she said vaguely. "With liquid … there is something floating."

"Oooh," said Simoe, "what do you think that could be?"

Big Tio was looking startled. "Well, I'll be. You're right—it was the pickles."

"The pickles?" Varazda repeated.

"Demos, the pickle-seller at the Rhina Market. He drinks at the Crow across the street, and I saw him get into a fight—well, more like an argument, I guess—with your Hilaros … huh, that wasn't his name, was it?"

"Helenos," Varazda supplied. "And he was no friend of mine."

Big Tio laughed harshly. "Didn't seem like he would've had many friends, if you ask me. Anyway, it was Demos with the pickles, mark my words. Well—you don't have to listen to me, do you? You've got the spirits telling you what's what." He looked impressed.

"Did you get anything?" Simoe asked, when they were back out in the street. "Old Cosmo didn't hurt you, did he? Or Ora?"

"We're all right," said Aradne, "but by all the gods, it was a near thing. I appreciated the rescue," she added to Varazda.

"We got a couple of things," said Varazda. "Aside from the tip about the pickles."

"You don't set any store by that, do you?" said Aradne.

"Not really, no, but there was an empty pickle-jar in the room. And I suppose vinegar might be strong enough to mask the smell of the poison. Maybe. But no—I was talking about these."

He withdrew the two things that he had managed to tuck into his sash in the course of fleeing down the stairs: a folded writing tablet and a piece of pottery.

"That's what you went back to grab on the stairs," said Aradne. "A bit of the wine bottle he threw at us?"

The fragment of pottery was stamped with a delicate seal in the shape of a bird.

"It's a bit of the wine bottle that Old Cosmo took from Helenos's room—the one, apparently, that Helenos had been drinking from before he died." At least it was probably that bottle. It was certainly the bottle that Eurydemos had brought to Helenos that morning, and it had certainly been in Old Cosmo's room.

Aradne seized Varazda's wrist and brought the fragment to her nose to take a deep sniff. "It just smells like wine."

"Well, yes. As we would expect, if it's true that Old Cosmo drank off the remaining wine and felt fine."

"Oh, yeah. Right. What's the other thing? A letter! That looks more promising."

"What does it say?" Simoe asked.

Varazda slipped the piece of wine bottle back into his

sash and flipped open the writing tablet that he'd found in Helenos's cupboard.

"Yes," he said after a moment. "This is more promising. This is proof that someone has been lying to me."

The letter began: *To my once-beloved pupil Helenos, from your sometime master, Eurydemos, greetings.*

CHAPTER 13

"We can't possibly accept money from your ex-girl-friend!" Philion cried. "Think how that would look! It's out of the question. You're staying here."

"How can you even think of heaping further disgrace on your family at a time like this?" Korinna murmured.

"Sir," said Damiskos, pointedly addressing himself only to his father, "you have misunderstood the situation. Nione Kukara is a former Maiden of the Sacred Loom, and she has not offered me any money—I'm sure she is as sensible as you are of the impropriety of that. She has secured my release on bail using her authority as a former Maiden."

"Well!" said Korinna, and then couldn't seem to follow it up with anything.

Philion subsided into his chair, nonplussed. "Well, all right then." He rallied a little. "Let's rub Kontios Diophoros's nose in it, show him we have friends in high places."

"That strikes me as distasteful, sir. The man has recently lost his son."

Philion shrugged. "Well, parade about the city a bit, anyway. Show them you're free to go where you like. But you don't need to go stay at this Maiden's house, do you?"

"It's her freedwoman's house. And I do intend to go there, sir. She has invited me. I will probably stay the night, as it is late already."

"Oh," said his father, now looking simply confused. "Myrto!" he bawled finally, in the direction of his wife's dressing room. "Tell Gaia there'll be one less for dinner!"

"Philion, surely—" Korinna began as Damiskos turned on his heel and left the atrium.

The guard was already gone from the downstairs door when Damiskos exited the house for the first time in more than a week. He was in such a good mood that he couldn't even feel disappointed at missing the opportunity to flourish Nione's court document in anyone else's face.

He walked all the way to Aradne's house—refreshingly, it was mostly downhill—and made it there by the twelfth hour. The girl at the door recognized him, and was about to go tearing off into the house to announce him, but he put his finger to his lips, and she indulged him and just pointed him in the direction of the dining room, letting him walk quietly in and open the door himself.

Varazda was sitting cross-legged on his couch, the way he sometimes did, and Damiskos thought he looked tired. He was deep in conversation with Nione. It was Aradne—reclining on her own couch, with little gold flower clips in her hair—who was the first one to look up and see Damiskos.

"Pharastes ... " she said in a singsong tone.

Varazda looked up, frowning, and saw Damiskos. He gave an adorable yelp of surprise.

"Dami! How did you— Don't tell me you climbed out a window?"

"No, of course not. Nione exerted her influence to get me released from house arrest."

"I would have done it sooner," said Nione, "but it took me several days to contact the proper authorities and have the document drawn up. I didn't tell you what I was doing, Varazda, because I didn't want to get your hopes up."

By this time Varazda had sprung up from his couch, run across the dining room, and was in Damiskos's arms. Damiskos realized that he was holding onto Varazda so tightly that he might be making it difficult for Varazda to breathe, and he made an effort to relax. Then he noticed that Varazda was holding onto him just as tightly.

"When you have a moment," said Aradne dryly, "do come have something to eat."

"At first I couldn't see my way out of it," Damiskos said, later that night as they lay facing each other on Varazda's bed in Aradne's house. "You have to drop everything when it's your family, you know? And it wasn't as if they were asking anything of me that I couldn't do.

"They never actually asked all that much of me. They didn't need to—I was ambitious in my own right, and successful in the career I'd chosen. I gave them reason to be proud of me. And of course they took advantage, they were always wanting me to send them money and come to parties where I could introduce them to people, but none of that was much trouble. It wasn't anything worse than embarrassing.

"Even after I was injured, they could trade on my former rank and my record, and it seemed to make them happy—and, to be fair, my mother certainly realized how hard it was for me to have my career cut short, and was sympathetic—and neither of them ever made me feel like I'd let them down, particularly, I'll give them that. But I think that might have been mostly because they didn't quite realize that I wasn't going to go on and cover myself with glory working for the Quartermaster's Office."

He fell silent. Varazda was stroking his hair, something that he didn't ordinarily do.

"How's the—how's everyone at home?" Damiskos asked.

"Worried about you."

"Oh."

He hadn't expected that, and it made him feel guilty. What had he thought—that their lives had been going on as normal with Varazda away in Pheme trying to save him from a murder charge?

"They know about the murder?"

"Yes, I told them. I didn't explain the business with Ino and your family. Ari would just have lectured me about making sure I'm satisfying you in bed."

"He'd *what*?"

"I mean, no, that's certainly not something he would do."

"I'll shake him until his teeth rattle, the little brat."

Varazda laughed. "You manage to make that sounds utterly unthreatening."

"It's important to know how to be unthreatening when you're, you know—" He gestured at himself. "—and a civilian. I, uh, could stand to get better at that, apparently."

"It might help you attract fewer murder charges, yes." Varazda was silent for a moment, still stroking Damiskos's hair. "Did he—Helenos—did he say something about me?"

"Mm." He should have known Varazda would have worked that out.

"That's what made you knock him down."

"Yes. But don't think that makes you my 'weakness' or something."

"Ah. If you say so."

"I do."

Varazda rearranged himself on the bed, leaning on one elbow. "You were talking about your family's situation, and I want to understand that better."

"Of course." He sighed. "Well, it's only in the last few

years, since my father started gambling, that things have become as bad as they are. They're not just asking us for money any more—they're taking it. They used Timiskos's name to borrow from people who wouldn't lend to them."

"They *what*?"

"They ran up debts in their son's name. They spent the money I'd been sending them for Xanthe, too, but that seems pretty minor by comparison. Look, I know none of that's right. But I also know they're doing it because they're desperate—even if they wouldn't say it or don't even know it themselves. I got my father to stop betting on the races, but now Timiskos says he's going to gambling houses instead, and it's not like in Boukos where all those places are legal— some of them are run by people you really don't want to owe money to. So if there was something I could do to really help them …

"But I know this was never that. It's obviously a nightmare—you can tell just from the way Ino's mother talks about it. They had got her engaged to this ex-archon who's just been charged with profiteering during a time of emergency—I mean they got her engaged to him before the evidence came out and he was charged, but really, everyone knew for *years*, even before he was elected, that he was corrupt. And I think—they haven't said, because of course they wouldn't—that *they* knew very well, because they were up to their necks in something with him. They've obviously had a financial catastrophe themselves, sold their house in town and moved in with my parents, before they decamp to their country place I guess. It's not a villa, it's just a house in the mountains, and Ino hates it up there.

"So the thing with the shit … " He rolled over onto his back and passed a hand over his eyes, laughing ruefully. "Terza, it's almost too perfect, isn't it? The absurdity of it. Ino has this inheritance that her parents won't let her touch unless she marries, and they picked me for the honour of going to Kargania with her and getting rich selling fertilizer, in order to—as they imagine—restore the fortunes of her parents and mine."

"Can they do that? Keep her from touching her inheritance like that."

"I suppose so. She would need her father's permission to inherit."

"In Boukos, she wouldn't. I wonder what the law is in the colony where the will was made."

"Hah. I never thought about that. I assumed the law would be the same as in Pheme, but you're right—it could be different. They're doing things differently in the colonies, especially since Tios declared its independence."

"That's what I was thinking. Though it may not matter—she's here, and so ... " He shrugged. "I don't know which law applies."

"Neither do I." Damiskos rolled onto his side again. "I'm sorry—to be here with you, finally, and talking about all this ... But it's been so hard to work out where my duty lies in all of this. Or whether 'duty' is even the right word. I wish I'd had you by my side through it all. But in a way I did—if that makes sense."

"Mm. I think so, but tell me."

Damiskos smiled. "You've taught me so much about love. I don't think I would have understood, before you, that saying 'yes' to my parents over this—sacrificing my happiness for something that wouldn't really be good for any of us—might be dutiful, but it wouldn't be loving. You taught me about happiness, too. You make me actually believe in it."

Varazda smiled back at him in the dark. "So ... you said no?"

Damiskos felt cold. Had he not actually said that? "Repeatedly."

"I would have understood, if you had felt you had to say 'yes.' Your family has to come first."

"I still don't know what's best to do for them."

"I wasn't finished," said Varazda gently. "I would have understood, but I would have fought for you. They may be your family, but they're not mine. And they don't deserve you."

He spoke with that silky ferocity that was so much a part of him, and all Damiskos could say in response was, "I want to live the rest of my life with you."

"I'd like you to," said Varazda simply. "I love you. It may be true that I knew about love before I met you, and I knew how to find happiness and hang onto it. But you—you open me up, like the sun opens up a flower. I love you so much."

It hung in the dark between them, the simplicity of it. They both wanted the same thing.

After a long moment, Damiskos rolled over onto Varazda, bracing himself on his forearms, letting just enough of his weight settle onto Varazda's slender body.

"I want," Damiskos whispered, "to spend all night getting you off. If it's all right with you."

Varazda shivered slightly. "It's not going to take all night, First Spear."

Varazda fell asleep in the middle of a fairly incoherent sentence about how he was not going to fall asleep, and Damiskos lay looking at him in the moonlight that filtered through the shutters. He was sleeping with his face mashed into the pillow, his hair strewn over his back. Damiskos pulled the covers up over them because the room was cold.

It was almost like being back in their own bed in Boukos. Almost. But that bed was there, waiting for them, in the haven of Varazda's home.

He rolled over to lie on his back, linking his fingers behind his head and listening to Varazda's quiet breathing.

Maybe—the thought popped into his head from nowhere—they could adopt another child. That could be nice. When Remi was a little older, after Ariston and Kallisto moved out, or whatever they were going to do, and there'd be extra room in the house ...

He remembered that he still stood accused of murdering Helenos, and there were four days until his trial.

They had talked over dinner, Varazda and Aradne telling Damiskos everything they had learned in their investigation.

Right. So Eurydemos was the obvious suspect. He'd written a letter inviting Helenos back to Pheme, full of fulsome rhetoric about citizens of the Ideal Republic and vague promises that he could get the charges against Helenos dismissed using his great influence. He had lied to Varazda about the letter's existence, and anyway didn't seem to have much influence left, in Pheme or anywhere. He'd brought the bottle of wine that Helenos had been drinking when he died.

But the bottle of wine didn't seem to have been poisoned. Helenos's neighbour had finished it off and suffered no ill effects.

Helenos's neighbour had to be considered a plausible suspect himself, and it was too bad, as Aradne had reported, that she hadn't been able to carry off her fortune teller act long enough to ask him if he had any powdered thorn-flower on hand to complete a spell, which had been her plan.

There was also this rather thin story about the pickle-seller, and a possibly unreliable witness who said he'd seen a courtesan visiting Helenos in the evening.

Damiskos thought about the state Helenos had been in that day when they met in the street. Stinking and unwashed, drunkenly flirting with Damiskos with an air of mocking self-disgust. It was by no means implausible that he had killed himself. Poison was perhaps an odd way to do it, but the fact that it was a poison used judicially in Boukos was suggestive. It seemed like something that a philosopher at the end of his rope might very well do.

It would be hard to convince Varazda of this. For one thing, Varazda seemed very determined to find a murderer to offer to the judge in place of Damiskos. And Zashians never really understood about suicide, that for Pseuchaians it wasn't always a choice of sordid desperation, but could be a dignified exit, the last way to do the honourable thing. If Helenos had killed himself, even in such a strange and inconvenient way, Damiskos was inclined to think he had finally done something decent.

He thought again about how Helenos had behaved when they met in the Skalina. *How unexpected, and yet how fitting...*

Damiskos turned on his side and shook Varazda's shoulder gently. "Varazda, I've just remembered something."

Varazda stirred and peered up from the pillow, and Damiskos immediately felt like an idiot.

"Mmm?"

"Oh, uh. Sorry. It's nothing."

"Hm?"

It wasn't nothing—it might even have been important—but Damiskos couldn't think about it at that moment. Varazda had rolled onto his back, sweeping his hair out of his face and stretching under the covers with a sound that was somewhere between a sigh and a purr.

"Did I fall asleep? I wasn't going to fall asleep. I left you unsatisfied." Once he would have said that with some kind of defensive anger that masked real embarrassment. Now it was very nearly a joke.

Damiskos leaned over and kissed him, long and deep. "You could never leave me satisfied," he murmured against Varazda's lips, "because there is no such thing as enough of you."

Varazda gave a gratified little snort.

"Mind you," Damiskos added, drawing away slightly, "there probably is such a thing as too much of me."

Varazda responded by hooking a leg around Damiskos and tugging him over again so that their hips met. He gave a little slither against Damiskos, sleepily uncoordinated—for him—and half-aroused.

Still Damiskos hesitated, wondering if he should offer to let Varazda go back to sleep.

"I'm all right, actually," Damiskos admitted. "I took myself in hand, after you fell asleep."

"Mmm. I'm sorry to have missed that." His hips made a tight, irresistable undulation, and Damiskos was instantly hard again. "Didn't do a very good job, though, did you?"

"I—" He stopped when Varazda put his fingers to his lips.

"Don't start. Apologizing for your virility, or whatever you were going to do."

"What if I say I wasn't going to do that?"

Varazda leaned his forehead against Damiskos's. "Then I'd say we're making progress." He slid his knee between Damiskos's thighs and nudged. "Sit up."

"Mm?"

"Up. That direction. Good job."

Varazda had slithered off the bed, pulling some of the covers with him, and took a moment arranging himself on his knees on the floor, tucking the blanket under him and wrapping it around his shoulders, so that he looked quite cosy down there. Damiskos looked at him for a moment. The cold air of the room felt bracing against his hot skin. He pushed back the remaining blanket and slid himself over to sit on the edge of the bed.

"Be gentle with yourself, all right?" he said, his voice rough with a mixture of desire and affection.

Varazda nodded. His hands moved up Damiskos's thighs, fingertips stroking and teasing the curls of hair. Damiskos leaned back on his hands and let Varazda spread his legs wider, cup his balls, his thumbs moving over the sensitive skin. He let his head fall back, eyes closed, and groaned as Varazda's tongue flicked over his skin and Varazda's fingers curled around the base of his cock.

The room was utterly silent around them, and Varazda was the only source of warmth. Damiskos hauled one hand off the bed, shifting his weight onto the other, and plunged his fingers into Varazda's silky hair.

Varazda looked up at him, his eyes black in the moonlight, his lips swollen and red. Damiskos couldn't suppress a thread of anxiety, willing Varazda to keep within his limits. But he did, licking and touching with a cautious assurance.

Damiskos felt as if he were offering himself like a gift: his sex and his pleasure, entirely at Varazda's disposal. It was like some astronomical pattern, he thought dreamily: his pleasure sliding into Varazda's, which circled back on itself, and around and around like a dance of planets. And now the blanket around Varazda's shoulders had fallen away and parted in the middle as Varazda reached down to touch himself. Damiskos watched that, Varazda's right hand sliding between his white thighs, while his left was wrapped around Damiskos's cock and his mouth on the tip had become softer, clumsily hungry.

Damiskos held on only a few moments longer before he reached down to cup Varazda's jaw and gently tip his head back. Varazda let himself be held there, open-mouthed and ecstatic, while they both came.

When the spell was broken, Varazda began to giggle.

"Oh, Terza!" Damiskos let go of him.

"I'm a mess," Varazda observed happily.

"You are—I'm sorry."

"No, you're not."

Damiskos took Varazda's face in his hands and leaned down to kiss him softly. He thought of the first time he had kissed Varazda, on the beach at Laothalia, how tense Varazda had been, how much he had allowed himself to surrender since then.

"I love you," he whispered.

"I love you too," said Varazda.

CHAPTER 14

"Why did you wake me last night, anyway?" Varazda asked as he was fastening the ties of his trousers. "There was something you wanted to tell me, wasn't there?"

"Oh." Dami sat amid the bedclothes, still naked and rumpled, and at least part of the reason Varazda put his question now was to keep him from getting up and dressing and composing himself for the day. "I remembered something Helenos said. He mentioned seeing someone else, Giontes, as if Giontes was connected in his mind with me. Was he one of the students from the summer?"

Varazda nodded. "The tall one. He was released along with Helenos, because there wasn't enough evidence to try him."

"So he'd also be in hiding if he was in Pheme. Damn."

"Quite. But we could try to track him down." Varazda pulled the shirt over his head and tugged out his hair. "You're thinking he might have been in a position to forge the letter from Eurydemos."

Dami shrugged. "It's a possibility, right?"

"It would certainly be worth looking into."

"What do you think of the, er, eccentric neighbours as

suspects?" Dami pushed the covers aside and swung his legs out of bed. The room was bright with sunlight, and Varazda spent a moment enjoying the view.

"Right," he said, businesslike again as Dami reached for his tunic. "It has occurred to me that if Cosmo was the one who poisoned the wine in the cup, he would have known very well that the wine in the bottle was safe to drink."

"That's true."

"The trouble is, having met him, I'm inclined to think he's just a confused angry person, who would have been more likely to drink the wine because he didn't think it through than because he knew it was safe. If you follow me."

"Sort of? You're saying he's too obvious a suspect, so you don't think he did it."

"Well, something like that."

Damiskos sighed. "You're probably right. Honestly, I think Helenos probably killed himself."

"That shit? He didn't have the decency. I think we were *meant* to think he killed himself—drinking alone out of a single, poisoned cup, just like a philosopher probably would do—and that it was the murderer's bad luck you were around to be suspected, because if you hadn't been, the thing might not have been investigated at all."

"You mean if I hadn't been around, *you* wouldn't have got involved."

"Exactly."

They finished dressing—even with his head-start, Varazda took a lot longer to finish than Dami, who lay back on the bed in his clothes and watched with a smile on his lips. Then Varazda broached another subject that had been on his mind and that he thought ought to be discussed privately rather than in front of Aradne and Nione.

"Dami, your brother, Timiskos. How … how are things between the two of you?"

"Eh?" Dami looked surprised. "I don't know. Good, I

suppose. He's ten years younger than I, so we were never close in that way, but I've always tried to look out for him."

"I remember what that was like," Varazda said, smiling as he put in his earrings. "From the other side, I mean. I had several much older brothers, when I was a boy."

"Yeah?"

He turned to see Dami giving him a curiously soft look, and he realized it was because he never talked about his childhood.

"Four of them. I'll tell you about them sometime. What I remember, which isn't a lot." Right now he wanted to talk about Timiskos. "It was different for me, though. I wasn't illegitimate—I was the son of my father's favourite wife, who was younger than my eldest brother."

"Timiskos isn't illegitimate," Dami said after a moment, when it must have been clear to him that Varazda wasn't going to say any more. He pushed himself up to sitting again and ran a hand through his hair. "He's my father's legitimate son by his second marriage."

Varazda took a moment trying to think that through. If Dami had been born ten years before Timiskos, and the woman their father was married to now was the one who had given birth to Dami—and it was hard to believe, given how alike they looked, that she wasn't—then ...

"So," he said finally, "are *you* the illegitimate one?"

"No! No, look, it's very simple. My father has been married three times, twice to my mother."

"What?"

"My parents were married before I was born—*well* before, thank you—and when I was eight, they divorced. It was because my father wanted to marry his much younger mistress—or I think more because her parents wanted him to marry her. So my mother and I went to live in a house that he bought us, and he was paying our expenses, so we didn't have to go back to her family. They lived on their estate in the middle of nowhere, and Mother wanted me to be able to go to a good school and all that. At this point my father was ... well, he wasn't really rich, he'd already had to sell the villa, but he *thought* he was rich and that he could afford this.

"He couldn't, of course. This was the point where he started dabbling in real estate and haemorrhaging money because he has no idea how to do business. He was on the brink of bankruptcy, no longer on good terms with his second wife, and he decided he had to choose only one woman to support. So he divorced Timiskos's mother—Timi was two at the time—and remarried my mother. Sold the big city house he inherited from his parents and moved in with us. Timiskos came to live with us a couple of months later, because his mother's family wouldn't let her keep him."

"I see."

"Look, if you're thinking 'that's ridiculous,' yes. It's ridiculous. And if you're thinking it's hard on Timiskos, yes, that too. He's not the bastard, and my mother has always treated him as her own son, but ... she wasn't all that interested in raising another child when he came along. So, as I say, I've always tried to look out for him. As far as I could. Why were you asking about Timiskos in the first place?"

"Oh, just wondering." He weighed for a moment whether to go on. "You know he told me to come to your parents' apartment the other day when their advocate was there."

"Yes. That was an accident. Father was out but came back unexpectedly with Olympios."

"I see," said Varazda. "I didn't realize that."

Dami sighed. "I think it was an accident. He doesn't dislike you, but I think he's ... confused by us?"

Varazda nodded. "Right. He thinks you should want all this other stuff that your parents and Ino's parents are trying to dangle in front of you—the marriage and the Karganian business and the political career—and he doesn't understand why you're not interested."

"Exactly. Divine Terza, the political career, though—I'd forgotten that was part of the plan." He shuddered. "Can you imagine me as a politician?"

"Um … "

Dami gave him a stern look. "No, you can't, because it's unimaginable. I would hate it."

"Then you shan't have it." Varazda made a little flinging motion, as if tossing away the whole idea.

He came and sat on the bed next to Dami, wanting suddenly to feel him near, to feel secure in his presence. Everything Varazda had said last night, when he had sounded so sure of himself and what he wanted, that had all been true. But it didn't mean his worries had gone away entirely. You really did have to fight for every bit of happiness.

"He landed on his feet, didn't he?" said Dami, looking around the palatial atrium of Bion's father's house.

"I guess so," said Varazda.

The slave who had let them in returned, followed by Eurydemos, wild-haired and messily mantled as usual.

"Ah!" he exclaimed, coming toward Varazda. "It is you—I thought it might be, when the girl announced 'A Sasian.' And in your more accustomed garb, I see. It suits you far better than our Pseuchaian raiment, I must say."

Varazda gave him a brief, unfriendly smile. *Also makes it easier to kick you in the head.*

"Ah!" Eurydemos was saying again, as he spotted Damiskos. "We meet again! Damiskos from the Quartermaster's Office, I believe? Are you also investigating poor Helenos's demise? Don't tell me he's suspected of having stolen some army rations or something!"

"No, not exactly." Dami rubbed his chin and did his thing where he pretended to be much more rough-around-the-edges than he actually was. "The thing is, I happened to see Helenos on the day of his death—like you, I hear—and I've been charged in connection. So I'm interested in finding out what really happened."

Eurydemos blanched and took a step backward. "Immortal gods. I knew that you and Helenos had a quarrel, but *murder?*"

"No, you see, I didn't kill him. That's why we're looking into the whole thing."

Eurydemos's gaze flicked from Dami to Varazda. "You ... two ... are ... ah. There you are, Bion!"

The young man with the sleepy eyes had come out of a hallway into the atrium. He looked much less like Eurydemos's slave today, and more like the young master of the house, dressed in a sumptuous red tunic and the kind of elaborate sandals that Ariston and his friends favoured. His curly hair was slicked back in a way that made him look older and less decorative, and he carried a basket.

"I thought we were going out," he said, looking discontentedly at Eurydemos.

"Patience, my dear boy. Now, let me see." He addressed Dami. "You are here to find out what I know, but I can assure you—"

"Do you want me to ask them the riddle?" Bion whispered loudly.

"Shh!"

"I found the letter you wrote to Helenos," said Varazda.

Eurydemos stared at him. "You *what?*"

Bion was staring at Eurydemos. "You what?"

"It was in his room," said Varazda. He produced the letter from the folds of his sash and held it open for Eurydemos to see.

Eurydemos peered at it for a moment, then recoiled. "That's—that's not my writing!"

"Isn't it?" said Bion, leaning in to look at it himself. "It's very like your writing, Master."

"I didn't write it!" Eurydemos cried, swatting at the young man. "You don't even know how to read."

"I—I—" Bion looked pathetically hurt.

"It is a little like my writing," said Eurydemos, "but only as if someone with a passing familiarity with my hand attempted to imitate it."

"It sounds like something you'd write," said Varazda. He flipped the tablet around to read from it. "'No man of your talents would be permitted to be exiled from the Ideal Republic ... '"

"Oh, no no no—I would never say such a thing, not now. Once, I grant you, I might have held such a view, but—"

"Master doesn't believe in the Ideal Republic any more," Bion spoke up again, sounding proud.

"Don't interrupt, darling. You see, I have repudiated my past teachings. They were subject to dangerous misinterpretation in the wrong hands. And Helenos's, I am sorry to say, were very much the wrong hands. I did hope, when he wrote to me, that he might be rescued from his errors, but he ... he did seem more interested in what I might do to help him. If he had received this letter, that would explain much. But who wrote it?"

There was an uncomfortable silence. Then Bion said, slowly, "They could think that you wrote it as a trick, Master. Because, well, you and I know that you've re—repoo—uh, what you said, but Helenos wouldn't know it. So if you wanted him to come see you, you would probably write to him like your old self, wouldn't you?"

"Shut *up*, you stupid clod!" Eurydemos hissed. "You imbecile, you useless piece of—"

"That's enough," Damiskos rapped out in his First Spear of the Second Koryphos voice. When Eurydemos froze, mouth snapping shut, Damiskos addressed Bion, at an ordinary volume. "I don't believe we've met. My name is Damiskos Temnon."

"Oh, um. Bion Doliades. Pleased to, um."

"This is your house, Bion?"

"My dad's. Well, sort of mine."

"Right. And how long have you known Eurydemos?"

"I fail to see what—" Eurydemos tried unsuccessfully to interrupt.

"Not very long. Just, maybe, a couple of months." He added, proudly, "He's letting me help him with his new teaching."

"Yeah?" said Dami sceptically. He cocked an eyebrow at Eurydemos.

"It represents a complete departure from my former path," said Eurydemos. "So you see, for me to write to my former pupil in such a style … " He gestured at the tablet in Varazda's hands. "Unthinkable."

"Let's see a specimen of your handwriting to compare," said Varazda, not so much because he thought this would prove anything as because he wanted to keep this conversation going, to make Eurydemos uncomfortable for as long as possible.

"Ah, yes. Bion, fetch me a tablet and stylus, and I will write something to show these suspicious—"

"Don't you think I should find something you already wrote, Master? That way you couldn't try to change your writing or, you know … "

"I'm not going to try to change my writing!" the philosopher yelped.

"Yes, I know, I know, but they might *think* you did."

"That's well thought of, Bion," said Varazda. "Thank you."

Bion flashed a nervous smile and took off into the house, thrusting his basket into Eurydemos's hands before he left.

"Divine Emanations," Eurydemos muttered.

"He's looking out for you," Dami remarked. "That's good of him."

That was much more polite than what Varazda had wanted to say, and he wondered how Dami had managed it.

"You have an imperfect understanding of me, I realize that," said Eurydemos smoothly. "You remember who I was in my old life—"

"It was only a couple of months ago," Varazda remarked dryly.

"Yes, yes, but I have emerged as a butterfly from a chrysalis since then—the change has been total. Am I sorry for the harm done by the man I was? Yes, yes I am. But am I in a position to do as much good now as I did ill then? Yes, resoundingly yes. As I said to Helenos, on that fateful day, 'Philosophy has led us astray—we must abandon Philosophy like a sinking ship. The spar to which we must cling now is the Search for Truth.'"

"Isn't that," said Dami, "the same thing?"

Eurydemos chuckled indulgently. "I see how you could think that. But no. That is a simplistic view. It can be summed up in the riddle which I like to pose to seekers of Truth who come to me: 'What lies—'"

"Here you go, master!" Bion came loping back into the atrium, brandishing a tablet. He moved in a way that made Varazda wonder if he was some kind of athlete, maybe a runner. "Here, look."

He opened the new tablet and set it on a little marble table in the middle of the atrium. Varazda laid the letter to Helenos open beside it. He scanned the two pages of writing.

"Ooh, they're very close, aren't they?" said Bion, bending over the table beside Varazda.

"Nonsense!" Eurydemos scoffed, gesturing at the tablets

but not really looking at them. "What would you even know about it? He really doesn't know how to read—and before you protest, yes, I *have* tried to teach him, as have others before me. He's impervious to instruction."

Bion had looked up from the tablets and his sleepy blue eyes met Varazda's unexpectedly at close quarters. He looked apologetic, as if perhaps he knew Varazda wanted to tell him he deserved better than this—as if he might be about to beg Varazda not to.

"I just … " he said in a small voice, "I can look at the shape of the letters, and see whether they're the same—look, here. These ones are different."

He pointed with a long, slender finger, and Varazda, following the gesture, saw that Bion was right. Eurydemos, damn his eyes, might be telling the truth. The handwriting was very similar, but it was not identical. Some letters, in fact, were quite different; perhaps they had not occurred in the text the letter-writer was copying from.

Varazda straightened up. "He's lucky to have you looking out for him," he said to Bion. "I don't think I would have seen that on my own."

Not least because he hadn't *wanted* to see it. It would have suited him very well for the letter to have been written by Eurydemos.

"What wouldn't you have seen?" Eurydemos crowded Bion out of the way to stare anxiously at the tablets.

"Oh, but look," said Bion, warming to his subject, "these two words look different, but they're both ones that you wrote, Master! That's interesting, isn't it?"

Eurydemos looked at Bion as if he was contemplating the philosophical ramifications of biting him.

"Here's another one," Bion went on, oblivious. "Sometimes you write the big sigma like this, and sometimes like this."

"Bion," said Eurydemos in a martyred tone, "are you suggesting that you think I did write this letter?"

"No, Master. You said you didn't write it, and you wouldn't lie."

"Of course not, of course not," said Eurydemos impatiently. "More importantly, the man I am now would never have written such a letter. I told Helenos so at the time—I said, 'I have consigned all my former teachings to the abyss of Primordial Chaos, so how could I have written such a thing?'"

He paused, mouth open, and looked up at Varazda as if to see whether Varazda had noticed what he just said. Varazda just raised his eyebrows.

"Oh, Master," said Bion despairingly, "but you told him you didn't know about the letter, before."

"You *cretin*!" Eurydemos roared at him. "You—"

Dami's hand landed heavily on Eurydemos's shoulder, and the philosopher—Seeker of Truth, whatever he was—made a strangled noise and looked fearfully back at Dami.

"Eurydemos," said Dami evenly, "you're a turd. You're a liar and a grifter and a waste of space. If you speak one more word of insult against your inexplicably loyal boyfriend, I'll hurt you."

"You *are* hurting me," said Eurydemos, wriggling under Dami's grip.

Dami just rolled his eyes. "Varazda, will you give me that letter?" Varazda passed it to him, and Dami held it in front of Eurydemos. "Look carefully at the writing. Can you think of any of your former students who might have written this?"

"No! None of them. Any of them. I don't know. Gelon—Gelon could have done it. He's always been good at copying things. Pictures and so on."

"You know Gelon is dead," said Varazda.

"What? Him too?" Eurydemos looked around wildly. Dami had let go of him but still stood threateningly close.

"No," said Varazda dryly, "he wasn't murdered—he did a murder, remember? He killed a prominent Boukossian aristocrat. He was executed for it."

"Oh. Oh, yes. I do recall now. Of course."

"I thought you said … " Bion began, then gave up with a sad shrug.

"So, as it wasn't Gelon who wrote the letter," Varazda persisted, "and you claim that it wasn't you—can you think who else it might have been?"

"I don't know! Why should any of my students do such a thing?"

"What about Phaia?" Dami suggested. "She was Helenos's girlfriend, and he didn't exactly do well by her."

"She is imprisoned on Choros Rock," Eurydemos reminded him pityingly.

"Yeah? How sure are we of that?"

"As a matter of fact," said Eurydemos, "my sister just returned from a pilgrimage there. I had sent her with a copy of my most recent treatise for the poor girl—I thought she might find it edifying—and she reported that Phaia received it with thanks." He looked smug. "An entirely changed character—unlike poor Helenos."

"What about Giontes?" Dami prompted.

"Who?"

Dami rolled his eyes. "He was one of your students. Tall fellow."

"Oh, him! No. Not very promising at all, I am sorry to say. Though from a very good family. His late father served a term as Third Archon, I believe."

"When did your sister visit Choros Rock?" Varazda asked.

"Oh, it was … " Eurydemos waved a hand airily. "Bion?"

"Yes, Master? Last week. Last week Moon's Day was when she came to see us—you, I mean. I remember because we had eels for dinner, and we'd got them that morning in—"

"Yes, yes. This is the sort of thing he fills his head with, you see." Eurydemos caught the look Dami was giving him and blanched. "Yes, well. As for the letter. It was probably … "

"Yes?" Dami prompted.

"It was Lysandros Stesanos." Eurydemos said it with the air of a dramatic revelation, as if the name had been wrung from him under torture.

"Who's that?" said Dami.

Eurydemos gave him a scornful look. "You don't know who Lysandros Stesanos is?"

"No. That's why I asked."

"He's a philosopher," said Bion, who had gone still at the mention of the name.

Eurydemos waved a hand. "Young firebrand at the Marble Porches—popular among the radical set. His ideas of course are utter … disastrous … what can one even say?" He didn't appear to know.

"And you think he had some reason to want to bring Helenos Kontiades back to Pheme and kill him?" Varazda prompted.

"Oh, to frame me, of course."

"I see. He bears you a grudge, does he?"

Eurydemos gave a harsh laugh. "I can only assume so."

"That's … vague," said Varazda. "Can you tell us a bit more?"

"Why should I?" Eurydemos turned peevish.

"Because they want to find out who killed this other fellow," said Bion. "And right now they still think it might have been you. And … I was just thinking … Lysandros wouldn't have been able to copy your writing, would he? Because you didn't send him that letter after all. Did you?"

"What? No, no, of course I didn't send him *that* letter, darling. But I did, later, send him other letters."

"Other letters?"

"Yes—purely about philosophy, nothing that you would have been able to understand or need have concerned yourself with."

"But," said Bion, "you told me you weren't going to write to him at all, after Sosia found that first letter and read it to me. And … I don't believe you, that you only wrote to him about philosophy. You don't even believe in philosophy any more. I think you wrote to him about his thighs and his glistening whatever, like in the letter Sosia found. I may be stupid, but I'm not that stupid."

For a moment Eurydemos looked winded. Then he rallied, as apparently he always did. "You are entirely, entirely mistaken, my dearest boy. I will explain everything." Glancing around, he said haughtily, "I feel it deeply inappropriate for this conversation to have witnesses."

"Sure," said Dami easily. He turned to Bion. "Want us to escort him out?"

"Oh," said Bion, looking a little surprised. "Yes. Would you?"

CHAPTER 15

"I COULD WISH," said Nione's lawyer, wiping his fingers delicately on his napkin, "that you had not gone and found that out. It weakens the case against our principal suspect considerably. But, as I do in fact prefer to see justice done, I must own that it was the right thing to do."

"Thank you," said Damiskos dryly.

He liked this man. Chariton was his name, and he was worlds apart from the aggressive buffoon Olympios. He was an older man, white-haired and thin, with skin as dark as Nione's. They had met him over lunch at Aradne's house.

"So then," he said. "Our most promising suspect vanishes in the face of your thorough investigation, and what are we left with? Remind me, if you will." He turned to Varazda.

Varazda ticked off items on his hennaed fingers. "There's the pickle-seller, the strange neighbours, some philosopher suspected by Eurydemos on very questionable grounds—and the possibility that Helenos killed himself."

Chariton nodded. "In other words, nothing. It doesn't matter. My task is to defend Damiskos, not assign the blame elsewhere—though it is always nice to be able to do that. I must commend you both for the work you have done to make sense of this thing. However, I believe our defence—and it will be a strong one—must hinge on the unlikelihood that Damiskos, a man of impressive military background, who routinely carries a sword and was doing so at the time, should resort to poison if he wished to kill the deceased."

Damiskos shot Varazda a wry look. It was almost exactly what he had said himself, but he didn't feel like saying "I told you so."

Varazda looked like he wouldn't much care to hear "I told you so," but he nodded at Chariton and said, "That makes sense."

"Of course we will also emphasize that Damiskos had no reason to wish to kill the deceased—we will need to tread a little carefully there, as I understand there is a complex history, which, by the way, I will need to understand much better than I do at present. Additionally, and perhaps most importantly, we will want to bring witnesses to Damiskos's good character. Nione will be able to fill that role admirably—her status as a former Maiden allows her to testify, of course—and I presume we may find a few of your fellow soldiers in the city who will do as well?"

"Oh. Yes, I expect so. I can give you some names. But what about the letter that Varazda found? It may not incriminate Eurydemos, but it's relevant, surely. Someone wrote to Helenos to lure him back to Pheme under false pretences—isn't it likely that the same person killed him? I know we don't know who that was, but it would help my case to show that there was something like that going on, wouldn't it?"

Varazda was already shaking his head.

"I'm afraid we can't introduce the letter," said Chariton.

"Why not?"

"I'm not entirely happy about the circumstances under which it was found."

"I climbed in a window," Varazda elaborated. "After having already been chased out of the building once. And I'm your weird eunuch boyfriend. You don't want me testifying —if I'm even allowed to. The other lawyer was offensive about it, but it doesn't mean he was wrong. I'm a liability."

"Varazda!" said Damiskos miserably. "No, you—"

Chariton cut him off. "I would *by no means* characterize you as a liability. Is that what the family advocate said? That *is* offensive. You are obviously not a liability—you are the one who has been working to find the true perpetrator of the crime. You have uncovered a great deal of useful information. If you are a citizen of the Pseuchaian League, and a freedman —which I believe you are?—then you *would* be permitted to testify. However, as you have realized, your connection to the accused, combined with the irregular manner in which you obtained the evidence, makes me feel that we should leave it out."

"Sorry," said Varazda, looking at Damiskos. "If I'd known what it was when I found it, I'd have put it back so someone impartial could have found it later. As it was, I hoped I could get Eurydemos to confess with it, so the whole thing would be moot."

"Right," said Damiskos. "Yeah. I wish that had worked."

Dami spent most of the afternoon working on his defence with Chariton. Varazda milled about the house, waiting to see if he could be of use, but there were lots of other people to be sent on errands, all of them better qualified than he by virtue of knowing their way around the city.

He might have gone out himself, chasing down one of the other, increasingly unlikely suspects, but he thought about how he would have felt if he'd had to have the kind of conversations Dami was having with Chariton all afternoon —trawling through his past trying to think of people who could say nice things about him and dark secrets that might be used to the advantage of the other side—and he thought he would stay close by.

He was rewarded, when Chariton left, by Dami coming out into the atrium, rolling his shoulders, and saying, "Gods, that was exhausting. Want to go for a swim?"

They went to the baths in Dami's old neighbourhood, where they saw several men Dami knew. Dami introduced Varazda casually, and his acquaintances were all friendly—obviously curious but not in an overt way, nothing that Varazda found at all offensive. After their swim they walked through the city, past the local temple of Terza, a long, low building with green-painted columns and Zashian-looking statues in the porch. There was a much more Pseuchaian frieze of scorpions and leaves across the top. They crossed a long bridge, five arches leaping over the slow surge of the Phira, with statues of stern river-goddesses standing at attention on the parapets at either end.

In the middle of the bridge, Dami pulled Varazda over to the parapet, and they stood side-by-side looking out. The sun was beginning to set over the harbour, apricot- and lemon-coloured light gleaming on the water and making the sleek shapes of boats look black. Dami tucked his arm around Varazda, and they stood like that for a while, not speaking.

"Do you think it's beautiful?" said Varazda at length. "The city, I mean."

"Beautiful?" Dami repeated, as if it was not a word that had occurred to him.

"I do," said Varazda. "So many people in one place, living together, like parts of a whole. I was surprised to find it so beautiful."

Dami looked at him for a moment. "You continue to surprise me, you know that?"

Varazda frowned at him. "Oh yes? Well, I suppose that's a good thing."

"Is this your first time seeing Pheme?"

"Yes."

Dami *tsk*ed. "I wish it was a better occasion. Come on," he said after another silence. "I'll take you to my favourite restaurant. It's on the island."

The island in the middle of the Phira, at the heart of Pheme, was another surprise. It was mostly a sacred site, grassy humps of hills capped with stones that were supposed to have been part of something-or-other—Dami was frankly vague on the details—and around the edge a very old retaining wall with a broad walkway on top, and small, strangely rustic shops on the land side, all showing stains on their front walls from previous seasons of high water.

"They're built too close to the river," Dami explained. "But you're not allowed to build any further up the hill, and the water only rises high enough to really flood them out every ten years or so. Here we are."

They had arrived at one of the most rustic-looking of all the shop-fronts on the island, a wooden building so weathered it looked to Varazda like something that belonged in a derelict shipyard, but with braids of garlic hanging in the low windows and a delicious smell of fried fish curling out the open door. Varazda had to duck to step inside.

The interior of the restaurant was cozy, an herb-scented fog filling the air, the tables plain and freshly scrubbed and the benches mostly full. At the back, louvred doors opened out onto a small terrace, nestled at the foot of the green sacred hill in the island's centre. Dami found a table for them outside, and ordered the only thing that the restaurant sold, which was indeed fried fish, greasy and delicately seasoned, with fresh white bread and salty olives and a bottle of pungently resinated white wine.

"Do you know," Dami said, as they ate, "this is the first time I have taken you out to dinner?"

"What? No, we've … Hm. I suppose you could be right."

They had been out to dinner several times in their month

together in Boukos, but of course that had always been at restaurants that Varazda had suggested, where they might see people he knew, and he would recommend the best dishes to Dami. More often than not he had paid for their meals, too, without thinking about it, and Dami had never made a fuss about that.

"Well," said Varazda, "thank you. You should do it again some time."

"I'd like that," said Dami dryly.

Their meal finished and wine drunk, they walked around to the north side of the island, looking across at the lights of the city's north shore.

Dami's mind must have returned to their investigation, because he said thoughtfully, "Eurydemos's sister saw Phaia on Choros Rock, but that was some time after the murder—do you think it's possible Phaia left and went back?"

Varazda considered that for a moment and shook his head. "No. If she got out, why would she go back? She wasn't to know Eurydemos's sister would be visiting with a patronizing 'present' to give her an alibi."

"Oh." Dami winced. "No, you're right. And if she did make it to Pheme, it's easy enough to get lost here—just like Helenos did."

"I don't know why they bother to exile people at all, honestly." He was silent for a moment. "I wonder if she really did repent? I was surprised to hear she didn't throw the book in Eurydemos's sister's face with a cutting remark."

Dami laughed. "You have to remember these people worshipped at Eurydemos's shrine at one time—perhaps she thought he'd actually written something worth reading."

"When I went to the Marble Porches to look for him," Varazda said, as the thought occurred to him, "I heard one of the radicals talking. Arguing that slavery should be abolished." It felt a little shocking actually to say it. Like suggesting one might dispense with hunger, or darkness at night, or some other inconvenient but basic fact of life. "That's a philosophy I think I ... well. I'd like to hear more of it."

Dami looked at him, and his expression was hard to read in the dark. "Yeah," he said finally. "I always used to think the best you can do is be kind personally, if you have to own slaves—you know, be a good master, because we can't do without slaves altogether. If you own a big farm or a mine or something, how else are you going to get the work done?"

"You used to think that."

"Yeah. I didn't know anybody who'd actually been in that position and freed all their slaves."

"But now Nione has."

"I know."

"Because she's in love with a freed slave." Varazda poked him with an elbow. "Hey, so are you!"

"I know," said Dami seriously. "So if you want to go listen to the radicals, invite some to dinner, whatever—it's not much, but I'll do whatever I can."

"Thanks," said Varazda, slightly surprised. "I wasn't even thinking of anything so concrete. I've a ways to go before I can really make sense of the proposition that slavery could be abolished. Of course I know it's wrong—but I only know that from the inside. It's wrong to *be* a slave ... it's a wrong state to be in—you feel that, especially if you were born free. But to think of its being wrong from the outside?" He spread his hands. "I don't think I know where to begin with that."

Dami had his arm around Varazda's waist already, and now he drew him closer. "Let's go to the Marble Porches when all this is over, and see what we think."

"How much exactly do your parents owe?" Varazda asked that night. He was already under the covers, and Damiskos was getting undressed.

"Continuing our habit of extremely romantic conversations at bedtime, I see," said Damiskos.

"I have to play to type sometimes, First Spear."

"Right." He sat on the edge of the bed and stretched. "Two thousand that I know of. That's the money they borrowed in Timiskos's name. I'll be able to pay off the rest when I can draw on my pension and—"

"I'll pay it. Don't even think about selling your horse. That is what you were thinking about, I know it."

"But—where are you going to get the money for that?"

"From the treasurers at the temple of Kerialos—that's where I have my money. It'll only take a couple of days for them to contact their counterparts in Boukos. They're very efficient. It was Chereia who put me onto them."

He was relating all this as if it were incidental details instead of a revelation. Damiskos looked down at him. He lay with his hands tucked comfortably behind his head, wearing his warm pyjamas, made of a soft blue-and-white check fabric.

"You have money in the treasury of Kerialos," Damiskos said. "Two thousand nummoi."

Varazda's eyebrows went up. "A great deal more than that. I thought you knew this was part of the package."

"What was?"

"That I'm rich. Were you just thinking that I live beyond my means? I don't—I'm actually quite careful with my money. But I do have a lot of it."

Damiskos thought about the careless way that Varazda seemed to live, working here and there at different jobs, guests coming and going at his table, his house always a mess, his gorgeous clothes flung over pieces of furniture. He did not live lavishly, but he also did not give the impression of someone who had enough money saved to be able to casually pay off his lover's family's debts.

"Where—how?" was all Damiskos could manage.

"Where did it come from, you mean? When I was freed, I had a lot of very valuable jewellery, and I sold it. Most of it was given to me by men I didn't care to remember. I put all the cash in the treasury, in case I was ever out of work, but I never have been. People pay me anywhere from fifty nummoi to a couple of gold tyroi for an evening's dancing, and there's the money from the school and the shop, and I get a retainer from the Basileon and occasional sums and gifts and things from the embassy."

"I see," said Damiskos. "This was all out in the open, wasn't it? I could have figured this out."

"I wasn't keeping a secret of it, no. Were you worried that I couldn't afford to keep you?"

"What? No! Divine Terza, I—"

"I'm joking, Dami. The point is, I can afford to pay your brother's debts, and we'll be fine. And yes, I am expecting you to get work in Boukos. Marzana's said he has work for you to do with the watch."

"Chereia has said she'd hire me in the sweet shop, too. But in all seriousness, I could see myself working with Marzana. I also thought ... I might teach swordsmanship somewhere?"

"You could use my school! What a good idea. You'd be brilliant. Though I might have to insist that you tone down your, er, magnetism if you can."

"My what?"

"You're very *attractive* when you fight, First Spear." Varazda was blushing. "I should know."

"Hm," said Damiskos. "I guess you should."

CHAPTER 16

"You will not be surprised to learn that Demos the pickle-seller was a dead end," said Varazda, flopping down into a chair in Aradne's atrium the following day.

"What?" said Aradne, looking over from where she was arranging a large vase of autumn foliage on a table. "You mean my message from the spirit world led you *astray*?"

"Believe it or not. I found the man, and he remembered arguing with Helenos at the wine shop, but that was *after* he sold Helenos pickles, not before—the argument was about whether or not Helenos had given him a debased coin when he paid for the pickles. And Demos was at a meeting of the Rhina Market merchants on the evening Helenos died, where he spoke at length—about the problem of debased coinage, as it happens—and was remembered by several other merchants. And frankly I couldn't imagine someone so obviously devoted to the art of pickling using poisoned pickles to murder someone. Are they still busy in there?" He nodded toward the door of the office where Dami and Chariton had been working.

"As far as I know. I've told them if they don't come out

for lunch at seven bells, I'm going in and dragging them out."

The pickle-seller was not the only dead end Varazda encountered that day. He also failed entirely to track down the exiled student Giontes, even with all the resources of Aradne's household at his disposal. He found students at the Marble Porches who remembered him vaguely, but said they hadn't seen him in months and didn't know why. He also learned, discouragingly, that plenty of people had access to documents written by Eurydemos, because he was a voluminous letter-writer and well known for writing his own correspondence rather than using a secretary, and for frequently using parchment or paper for things that other people would have scribbled in the less permanent wax of a tablet. That was particularly annoying to hear, and it was another mark against the authenticity of the letter to Helenos, which had been written on a tablet.

And then, that evening, Giontes turned up on Aradne's doorstep. He'd heard that someone was asking around for him at the Marble Porches. Varazda had left an address for anyone to contact him if they remembered or learned anything, and Giontes had come plainly hoping there would be money in it for him. Unlike Helenos, it seemed, he had been entirely cut off by his noble family. He was alarmed when he recognized Dami and Varazda and realized that he was in Aradne and Nione's house, but by then it was too late for him to get away.

"Of course I was a different man back then," he said earnestly.

"There's a lot of that going around," said Dami.

"I, er—yes?"

"Eurydemos said more or less the same thing," Varazda explained. "Though it *has* only been a couple of months."

"Ah, you've been in touch with the master, have you?" Giontes didn't appear to know what to say about that. "And, er, Helenos?"

"Helenos is dead."

The colour drained out of Giontes's face, and he murmured an oath. "They got him so quickly?"

"Not executed," said Varazda. "Murdered."

"Oh." Giontes looked relieved. "Oh, I see."

His story, which he eventually told, was that he had fled to Pyria with Helenos after escaping from Boukos. They had split up once there, but he had known where to find Helenos, so that when a messenger arrived looking for Helenos, Giontes had taken the letter to Helenos himself, apparently as an excuse to renew the acquaintance. He could say nothing about where the message had come from, just that it had been delivered by a girl, and Helenos had seemed pleased by its contents. Boasting that his fortunes were about to improve, he had invited Giontes to return with him to Pheme, which Giontes had done, but he had been waiting in vain for the promised word from Helenos since they parted on the docks.

They were up very early on the day set for the beginning of the trial. Varazda had not been able to sleep much, but for Dami this was a perfectly ordinary time to be up. He was acting as though it were an ordinary morning, too, and Varazda did his best to play along.

"We will have to try to keep you away from my family as much as we can," Dami said.

He ran the comb gently through Varazda's hair, and

Varazda shivered at the tingling sensation that this sent across his scalp and down his neck.

"Mm. Yes, of course."

"Did I hurt you?" Dami's hands stilled.

"No, no, quite the opposite. Carry on—if you want to."

Dami chuckled and resumed combing. Varazda's hair was freshly washed and still damp, and the combing was a practical necessity as well as a pleasure. Varazda wished he could have enjoyed it a little more.

"I'm sorry we weren't able to continue the investigation," Dami said. "I'd like to have known who did kill Helenos."

Varazda closed his eyes and let his head fall back. "Maybe you were right. Maybe he did it himself."

They had spent the previous day rounding up witnesses for Chariton: one of Dami's fellow officers from the Second Koryphos; two of the men he had commanded, who were eager to testify to his good character; the new Quartermaster, who had taken over from Dami after his brief tenure in the role. One of Chariton's clerks had gone back to the Skalina and found a couple of reasonable-looking people who had witnessed the altercation with Helenos in the street and could testify that it looked like a minor squabble, not a prelude to murder. Varazda had wanted to go on that mission himself, but he had to acknowledge that he was becoming too well known in that corner of the city to do an effective job.

Chariton, meanwhile, had been busy selecting the jurors for the trial. There would be twenty of them. He was cautiously optimistic that they would be sympathetic; over dinner he'd given an account of some of the worse candidates that he had been able to eliminate. There had been a man who spat every time he said the word "Sasia," and another who was well known for a satirical poem he had written on the subject of "unmanly lusts." Varazda had tried not to look too openly pained at the thought that Chariton was having to object to jurors because of him. If it hadn't been for him, no one would have looked at Dami and thought *unmanly* or *Sasian-lover*.

It was nice that Chariton didn't think he was a liability, but Varazda wasn't sure he agreed. Still, he was doing his best to look respectable. He had borrowed the blue-and-white mantle from Nione again; it was laid out on the bed next to Dami's military cloak, a gorgeous red garment that Varazda had never seen him wear.

"I'm going to get you to do this all the time," he said, leaning back on his hands as Dami drew the comb carefully through his hair. "But if there are tangles, you don't have to be so gentle."

Dami snorted. "Easy for you to say."

Varazda wasn't sure quite what that meant, but he smiled. He pictured Dami with someone he really did have to treat gently, instead of just someone he liked to be gentle with. A baby, for instance. He could see that so clearly, all of a sudden: Dami cradling a tiny baby, holding it against his shoulder, trying to get it to go to sleep, the way Varazda had done sometimes with Remi when she was tiny and the wet-nurse had gone home or fallen asleep herself.

He sat up too abruptly, causing the comb to tug at his hair and Dami to draw an audible breath.

It had never bothered him very much that he couldn't father children. It was supposed to be the big tragedy of his life, but he really didn't care particularly. He had built himself a family—he *was* Remi's parent, legally as well as in his heart. Dami should have that too, he thought. It would be wrong for him not to. Varazda wished he could have given that to him.

They finished dressing and went out into the main receiving room of the house to meet Chariton. Aradne and Nione were there already, although it was still very early. It was cold, and the lawyer was warming himself over the brazier, still wearing his heavy cloak. His face looked strained, but he smiled as he turned to see Dami and Varazda enter.

Timiskos and Ino arrived before breakfast, having, as they reported, sneaked out of the Temnons' apartment separately and met up in the street.

"I know we can't do anything to help," Timiskos said, "but we thought, you know, friendly faces and all that."

In fact, Varazda thought Timiskos seemed to be looking for an opportunity to talk to his brother alone, but wasn't quite bold enough to ask for it outright. He never got it, because Dami immediately introduced him to Aradne, and said, "If you're thinking of redecorating your new house, my brother might have some ideas for you. He's just done some work for my mother that she was very happy with."

Aradne began peppering him with surprisingly technical questions about ornamental mouldings and east-facing windows, which he did his best to answer.

"I don't think you'll be convicted," Ino told Damiskos. "You have a very honest manner. I think the jurors will believe you when you say you didn't do it."

Dami smiled. "I hope you're right. I expect you are—I think it will all turn out well." There was a moment's awkward silence, then he said, "When this is all over, you will have to tell us where your stepson's silver shop is, so I can buy one of those bracelets with the snail on it for Varazda."

"We don't sell those in the shop," she said, "but I can do you one as a special order." She turned to Varazda. "Would you rather a snail or one of those bugs that are good luck in Gylphos?"

Over breakfast everyone tried to talk about things that had nothing to do with the trial or the murder. This meant that there were frequent awkward pauses in the conversation. Chariton had brought his notes with him into the dining room but was trying not to look at them. He broke into the conversation unexpectedly when Ino was telling Nione and Aradne about her inheritance in the colonies.

"But of course," she was saying, "my father won't let me accept it."

"Did I not hear you say that you are a widow?" said Chariton.

Ino looked at him. "Yes. My husband died six years ago."

"Then you do not need your father's permission to inherit." He shook his head sadly. "I do not understand why this is not more widely known. You would, of course, have needed your father's consent to inherit if you had never married, and while your husband was alive, you would have needed *his* consent. However, after his death that power does not of necessity pass back to your father. Your husband could have left it to someone in his will, even to your father. Did he?"

"No."

"Then you have unimpeded power to accept any inheritance in your name."

"I ... " Ino started. She stopped, and stared down at her hands. "I do, do I?"

"Even property in the colonies?" said Aradne.

"Especially property in the colonies," said Chariton. "There any woman can inherit property—married or unmarried."

"It's a new law," Nione added. "First introduced in Tios, when they declared independence. But it was a local custom already, I think."

"You were right," said Dami, looking at Varazda with a smile.

"Well, I don't know about 'right.' It was just a guess." He was pleased, all the same.

"So what do you think?" Aradne was saying. "Do you

want to move to Kargania and run a, uh—you know—business?"

"I don't want to live in Kargania," said Ino after a moment, looking thoughtfully into the distance. "At least, I don't think I do. But if I can inherit the business, I can sell it." She looked at Chariton. "That's right, isn't it?"

"Of course. If you own it, you are at liberty to sell it."

"Or," said Nione, "you could hire a local overseer to help you run it, so you didn't have to live out there. That way, if the business does increase in value—from what you were saying, it's mostly potential now—you can sell it later for a much greater sum. That's what I would do."

Aradne chuckled. "You two had better talk business for a bit. Come, Timiskos—tell me more about what I should do with the mosaic in the foyer. Are tiles worth the extra expense, or are pebbles more hard-wearing, would you say?"

CHAPTER 17

THEY ALL WALKED to the agora together, accompanied by two women and a man from Nione's household—or Aradne's household. Damiskos wasn't quite sure which they belonged to, technically. Perhaps it didn't matter very much, except on payday, now that they were all free.

The day was bitterly cold, and everyone huddled in their cloaks and walked briskly without talking. Damiskos thought nostalgically of the sedan-chairs that were everywhere for hire in Boukos.

When they arrived at the Hall of Justice, their party had to split up. Varazda kissed Damiskos on the cheek with cold lips, and stood in the porch with the women while Damiskos followed Chariton through the pleaders' door into the court. Damiskos glanced back for a final, comforting look before stepping inside. Varazda's eyes met Damiskos's, and he smiled.

"Have you attended many trials before?" Chariton asked, as they walked through the chilly hallways of the court.

"Only military tribunals. I don't know if they're the same."

"Neither do I. What will happen is that the prosecutor's

advocate will present his case first, then I ours—that is, the truth. The prosecutor will then call his witnesses. I assume they will consist mostly of the people in the Skalina who saw you and Helenos quarrel in the street, but they may also attempt to raise other suspicions about you—they may have assembled some people to speak to less-than-flattering incidents from your past, in an effort to blacken your character."

"They've had a lot longer to work on the case than you have," said Damiskos. "I'm sorry about that."

"As I understand it, it is not your fault. In any case, I am not especially concerned about what they may have dug up. After our witnesses have spoken, the jury will vote, and, in the case of a guilty verdict, the judge would deliver a verdict —in your case, of course, not."

Damiskos smiled. He appreciated the lawyer's straightforward confidence. He couldn't quite share it, but that was not Chariton's fault.

<hr />

There were marble benches at the back of the courtroom, behind a balustrade, for female spectators. The men had to stand, but at least they would have a view of the proceedings. Since they were there early and the space was not close to filling up, Varazda came into the women's section with Nione and Aradne and their attendants and sat down.

Of course the place was grander than its equivalent in Boukos, with a soaring ceiling and columns down the sides. But it was cold and cheerless, painted in austere shades of dark red and green.

"Chariton is very good," Nione said, touching Varazda's arm. "I have every confidence in him."

"I know," said Varazda. "We can't thank you enough for getting him."

"Of course." She gave his arm a squeeze. "I'd say, 'Don't worry,' but that's asking too much, isn't it?"

He smiled wryly.

He was trying not to worry. He knew Nione's lawyer was good, and Dami's case was strong. Rationally, he knew he should have felt confident in the outcome of the trial. But he felt instead a kind of formless dread, like a premonition that had nothing to do with rational cause and effect.

Perhaps it was just that he'd wanted to find the murderer, and hadn't, and that made him uneasy.

A shadow fell across his lap, cast by someone standing in front of the next row of seats. He looked up to see the older woman from the Temnons' apartment: Ino's mother. The servant with the falling-down hair was beside her, looking like she would rather be anywhere else.

"What do you think you're doing here?" Korinna hissed at her daughter, in a voice that made Varazda think of Remi's pet goose when she was mad. "I told you to stay home, you were forbidden from leaving the house, and instead you are consorting with *that*—" She jabbed a finger at Varazda.

"We have all come to support Damiskos," said Nione sternly. "Our friend, who is wrongly accused. Are you a relation of Ino's?"

Korinna stared fiery-eyed at Nione, whom Varazda suspected of knowing exactly who she was. "I am her mother, and I am ordering her to come with me. Gaia—you'll escort her home."

"I—I—" The servant glanced around miserably.

"I'd like to stay here," said Ino, looking at the floor. "I think I'll stay here."

"As for you," Korinna said, turning back to Varazda, "have you no decency? Do you want all the world to know about Damiskos's sordid weakness? Do you want it known that he jilted my daughter for a Sasian catamite?" She actually did stick her neck out like an angry goose as she said that.

Aradne, of course, was on her feet by this time. "You don't dare speak to my friend like that, you stupid sack of—"

"Shh!' said Nione commandingly. She stood, towering over Korinna herself, and from the look on the older woman's face, Varazda thought she'd recognized the former Speaker of the Maidens now. "Creating a spectacle at this point will serve none of us. Do you wish your daughter's name to be linked with *two* convicted criminals?"

"Sosikles Phostikos hasn't been convicted yet," Korinna protested weakly.

Myrto, who had been speaking in the aisle with her husband and stepson, now followed Korinna into the women's section.

"Oh, Varastes, don't you look adorable in that mantle!" she exclaimed. "Gaia, are you all right? You look as though you're about to faint. Sit down, girl."

"Did you know about this?" Korinna demanded of Myrto, flinging out an arm to indicate Varazda. "Did you arrange this to humiliate me and my daughter?"

"Immortal gods," said Myrto, looking at Ino, who by this point was rocking in her seat and clutching at the skirt of her gown. "I can't see what Varastes sitting in the women's section—if that's what you're talking about—has to do with your daughter. I daresay he can if he wants to. I know if I had something where people said I wasn't 'really a man'—you know, if I *was* a man—I'd certainly take advantage of it to get myself a seat." She laughed.

"I could go perch on the railing," Varazda suggested archly. He got to his feet. "Ino, would you like to come with me and get a drink of water?" He held out a hand to her.

She took his hand and pulled herself to her feet, and they went out together to find a drinking-fountain in the porch. Varazda took a long drink himself.

"Thank you," she said, drying her hands on her gown. "I feel better. It isn't … " she began after they had stood there a moment longer. She frowned down at the stones of the porch. "It isn't always like this, being you, is it?"

"You mean, people being rude?"

She nodded.

"No, it isn't."

"Good, I'm glad. It isn't always like this being me, either."

He wanted to say it shouldn't *ever* be like this, but he had a feeling that she knew that. They ventured back into the courtroom, to find that the other women had sorted themselves out, with Korinna sitting several rows away from Nione and Aradne, who were saving an empty seat for Ino.

It was as he was standing at the rail of the women's section, waiting for Ino to take her seat, that he looked over the crowd in front of him and saw Eurydemos at the front of the courtroom. He was talking to a tall man whom Nione had pointed out earlier as the advocate acting on behalf of Helenos's family.

"I think it is time for me to go," he said apologetically to Aradne and Nione.

"What?" said Aradne. "No! That bitch won't say anything. I'll stop her myself."

"Shh," said Nione. "He just means go stand among the men."

"Oh," said Aradne. "Right. Well, good luck."

"Thanks," said Varazda.

He wove through the men gathered on the floor of the court, passing Damiskos's father, who gave him a dirty look, and Ino's father, who was staring at the floor and didn't see him. He wanted to get close to the front not only so that Dami could see him, but so that Eurydemos could too. That absolute shit. It hadn't been bad enough that he had failed to be provably the murderer himself, but now he was going to show up here and attempt to pin it on Dami? He would rue the day.

A young slave slithered past Varazda near the front of the assembly, to stop breathlessly before the tall advocate.

"Here, sir! I got it!" He dug a small object out of the bag he carried and held it out, panting and bracing his other hand on his knee.

"You fool," the tall advocate spat. "Put that away and keep it safe!"

Eurydemos was looking curiously at the thing the slave held. "What is that?" he asked.

The advocate pushed the slave's hand away, and the slave, stumbling and straightening up, shoved the object back into his bag.

"It's an important piece of evidence," said the advocate loftily. With a casual cruelty he clouted the slave on the side of the head with the back of his hand. "Keep it safe, I said."

Varazda watched the slave creep up the steps of the dais to the spot by the back wall where other members of the prosecutor's party were standing.

The thing the slave had held out to the advocate was a lump of tarnished silver in the shape of a scorpion. Varazda had caught a clear glimpse of it, and the image hung before his eyes. He had seen it somewhere before, and in another moment he remembered where.

※

"He was sitting at the back with the women for a little while," said Chariton, craning his neck to see the back of the room. "But no, he is certainly not there now. He is hard to miss, isn't he?"

"Yeah," said Damiskos.

The lawyer gave him one of his wry smiles. "I hope," he said, looking back out at the assembly, "that he did not take the words of your family's legal advisor too much to heart and fears to compromise your case with his presence."

Damiskos shook his head and said he was sure not, but he wasn't sure at all. Varazda was very secure in his own identity and unafraid of appearing eccentric, but Damiskos didn't know how much that extended to their relationship, or how worried Varazda was about this trial. He might have decided he would be better out of the courtroom than in.

There were benches for the jury on the dais at the front of the room, but the parties to the case were expected to stand throughout. Damiskos tried not to lean too obviously on his cane, not because he cared who saw it but because his defence depended on the claim that he could have killed Helenos in any way he liked without using poison, and he wanted to look the part.

Aside from Eurydemos, the witnesses on the opposite side of the dais included a couple of people Damiskos vaguely recognized from the Skalina, and a clerk from the Quartermaster's Office, an incompetent fellow with whom Damiskos had been lenient for longer than he deserved before giving up and letting him get himself dismissed.

"If that philosopher really intends to speak for the opposite side," Chariton was saying, "I will produce that letter he claims he didn't write, and be damned to him. I'll send Tiko to my office for the letter now."

"But, er, we're pretty sure Eurydemos *didn't* write it." And he thought they had all agreed that the less said about Varazda climbing in windows the better.

"That doesn't matter. If he has a motive for trying to incriminate you, that will discredit him." Chariton's brow furrowed as he looked around the courtroom again. "Where has your friend *gone*?"

"Probably to find a public toilet," said Damiskos, who was getting tired of having this conversation with his lawyer.

Varazda did not reappear before the ceremonial lighting

of the torches at the front of the courtroom and the reading out of the invocations that began the trial. But as the jurors were taking their seats, a boy passed a note to Chariton, which he passed on to Damiskos. It read: *Gone to find real murderer. Back soon. Will send someone to help with E. – V*

Chariton gave Damiskos a worried look but refrained from saying anything. Damiskos just smiled.

The advocate acting for Helenos's family was an orator named Eulios. "All style and no substance," was how Chariton had characterized him. But he was famous for winning several high-profile cases, and even Damiskos had heard of him.

He was a tall, hawk-nosed man with intense dark eyes, his mantle flawlessly wrapped, his hair slicked back.

"My friends," he began in a ringing voice, "the act that brings us here today is among the most wasteful acts imaginable. Wasteful? You may ask yourselves why I use that word. I say 'wasteful' because a citizen was killed who was not only the son of one of the Republic's leading men, not only a man in the prime of life, not only … "

Damiskos made an effort not to listen to this part. It was all a bit basic: if you'd ever fought on a battlefield, you had probably thought through most of this many times over. You'd cut short someone's life. They had a family who would be diminished by their loss; they'd had a path in life that they would now not walk, and you didn't know but that it might have included great things, better things than you would ever do. They might have been a wonderful person, or they might have been a piece of shit. They might have been a piece of shit who would have gone on to change and become a good person, except that you'd killed them. That was about the best that you could have hoped for with Helenos, and you never knew—these things were in the hands of the gods—but Damiskos personally doubted it.

The advocate moved on from describing Helenos's potential for greatness, briefly admitted that during his life Helenos had not entirely lived up to that potential and had in fact been in unofficial exile and hiding in the slums at the time of his death, then moved on to describing Damiskos.

"Here we have a young man of the same age as Helenos Diophoros, like him of a good family, like him full of potential. Where Helenos Diophoros devoted himself to philosophy, Damiskos Temnon chose a military career. He distinguished himself quickly." And so on, until, voice rising in volume as he described the triumphs of Damiskos's career, he stopped, looked around at his audience, and said, "You are now asking yourselves, 'For which side does this man think he is acting? Has he forgotten that he is here to make the case *against* Damiskos Temnon?' No, my friends, I have not forgotten."

"Trying to take the wind out of my sails," Chariton muttered. When Damiskos glanced at him, he saw that he was smiling, rather wolfishly.

"I wish merely to paint for you a picture of the heights from which Damiskos Temnon fell. For fall he did."

Pious Zashians often carried strings of beads to count while they prayed. Yazata had a set that he brought out sometimes. Varazda, who was not particularly pious himself, had bought Damiskos a string of blue and white glass beads at a Zashian stall in the market a couple of weeks ago. "I suppose there's some sort of prayer to Terza you can say with them," he'd said, somewhere between shy and arch.

There wasn't, really; you could repeat the epithets of Terza, but there weren't as many of them as there were beads on the string, so you had to start over, and then there weren't enough beads to finish. But the beads were smooth and cool to the touch, and Damiskos wished he had them with him now. He would have focussed on the feeling of the beads running through his fingers and let the advocate's words fade into meaninglessness. At least he would have tried to.

" ... devastating defeat ... "

" ... captive in the hands of a vicious Sasian ... "

" ... tortured for ... "

Here Eulios was mercifully short on details, and Damiskos did not have to listen to a description of exactly what Abadoka's men had done to him. He was already feeling the beginning of that sensation of floating free of his body, which was not a good sign. He tightened his grip on the handle of his cane.

" ... left permanently lame, his brilliant career in ruins, relegated to an ignominious job procuring supply contracts for the legions."

Damiskos opened his eyes. "It wasn't that bad," he said through clenched teeth.

"Oh, he's just alienated all the merchants on the jury," Chariton whispered back. "And I made sure there were plenty."

"Returning to Pheme, he found the woman he had once been engaged to marry lost to him, unhappily tied to a lowly tradesman."

"Keep going," Chariton whispered gleefully.

"That's not even true," Damiskos whispered back. "I had no idea she was married until the other week, and they were very happy."

"Why he moved out of his wealthy family's home to live in a shabby rented room in the squalor of the Skalina Hill, one can only speculate. Was it shame on his part, or were they embarrassed to acknowledge him as their son after his spectacular fall?"

"Where was your place?" Chariton asked. "Not in the Skalina."

"No, the Vallina."

"Shabby?"

"Not really."

"He had always been devoted to the cult of Terza, into

which he had been initiated as a youth, but now his religion became increasingly important to him—it became the consuming passion of his life, taking the place of everything else that had been stripped from him."

Chariton shot Damiskos a slightly wary look. "Is that true?"

"N-no. Not the way he makes it sound." Perhaps it was just as well he didn't have the prayer beads.

Eulios went on, offering more inaccurate details about Damiskos's life and making more vague speculations. He represented Damiskos as possibly being in debt, as erratic in his work and disliked by his colleagues, a pitiable wreck. What surprised Damiskos, listening to it, was how little of it convinced him now. A couple of months ago, he thought he would have agreed with the advocate's general characterization, even if not with some of the details. He had thought of himself as a wreck and a shadow of his former self. Now, he could see that was never what he had been. His job had not been very enjoyable, but he had worked at it conscientiously and taken pride in his work. He had exercised, recovered full use of his less-injured knee, and kept up his skill with a sword, during a period when getting out of bed every morning had felt like the hardest thing he'd ever done.

Then Eulios came to the week at Nione's villa. He leaned heavily on the absurdity of the fish-sauce-factory-owning former Maiden of the Sacred Loom. ("Another mistake," Chariton muttered wolfishly.) He characterized Helenos and his fellow students as misguided patriots, seeking to restore the greatness of the Republic but hampered by naïveté and infighting. He hinted coyly at a romantic rivalry between Helenos and Damiskos, then went on to describe their political differences with reasonable accuracy. Where Helenos had been a passionate if slightly too ruthless lover of Pheme, Damiskos was a bitter apostate, disillusioned with the Republic for which he had suffered so much for so little reward, preferring Sasia and Sasians to Pheme and Phemians, and slavishly devoted to his religion, which, as everyone knew, itself had roots on Sasian soil.

Eulios was a skilled orator, Damiskos had to admit, and this part of his speech was strangely convincing. Perhaps it was because he had taken care to admit some of the good qualities of this "Damiskos Temnon" character he was building, and to allow that his "Helenos Diophoros" character had had his flaws. It wasn't the truth, but it was a story that Damiskos could imagine having been true.

He wondered where Varazda was and what he was doing.

CHAPTER 18

Varazda was leaving the Marble Porches and wondering what was the fastest way to the Skalina. He chose what looked like the straightest street heading north, hitched up his mantle, and set off at a jog.

He had chosen well, for once, and the street let him out at the riverbank near a pier with boats for hire. After a slightly hair-raising ride across the strong current of the river, he arrived on the opposite bank and headed up into the slum. He paced himself well and arrived only mildly out of breath at the corner with the brothel and the wineshop and Big Tio's apartment building. Big Tio himself was down at the Hall of Justice in his cleanest tunic with his greasy hair tied back, waiting to testify to his theory about the pickle-seller and the story of the mad neighbour who drank the leftover wine. Varazda felt a momentary pang, wondering if he should have been there himself, to speak to the finding of the letter in Helenos's room. But they had agreed that it was better not to go into details about climbing in windows if they could avoid it.

In any case, right now he thought he could be more useful here. He knocked on the downstairs door that he thought he remembered entering when he came here the first time.

"Come in!" a woman's voice called.

He opened the door on the room where the young man Straton lived with his mother and aunt. The two women were there, and a baby whom he recognized after a moment as Simoe's was crawling on the floor.

It took the women a moment to recognize him. "Oh, it's you! Did you find the murderer?"

"Not yet, but I hope to, very soon. Is Straton here?"

"Straton?" said his aunt, jumping to her feet. "Why? He didn't do anything! Did he?"

"No, no, nothing like that," said Varazda soothingly. "But I believe he saw something."

"Oh, he tells stories!" the aunt protested. "He can't help it, poor boy. He means well, you know."

Straton's mother got to her feet. "He doesn't tell stories, Sister," she said quietly. "He doesn't always understand what he sees, but he is very good at remembering things, and he never lies." To Varazda she said, "He's out in the courtyard. I'll get him. Sister, look to Doros, will you?"

The baby was crawling industriously toward the front door in a bid for escape. Without thinking, Varazda bent and scooped him up. He was one of those sturdy, solidly built babies, and came up off the floor with his limbs all pulled in tight to his body. Very different from Remi at the same age, who had been softer and smaller and somehow floppier.

"Oh, thank you," said Straton's mother, surprised.

"Not at all." Varazda got out of the way so she could go out the door into the hallway, where he heard her calling for her son. The aunt made no move to take the baby, so Varazda propped him on his hip and went on holding him.

The young man with the rosy cheeks came in promptly and had no difficulty recognizing Varazda in his Pseuchaian outfit. He was very amused by the sight of Varazda holding the baby. The women, Varazda observed, were also amused but trying to hide it.

"Straton," he said, "I wanted to ask you about the woman you saw coming to visit the man who was killed."

Straton nodded. "Ruta."

"Yes. She is a friend of yours?"

"Um." Straton looked sadly at his hands. "No, she's not my friend. I don't think she's my friend any more. She used to like me, we had fun together, but now she doesn't talk to me. Maybe I did something wrong." He shot Varazda a hopeful look, as if looking for reassurance that it wasn't his fault.

"She didn't stop speaking to you," said Straton's aunt. "She *left*."

"Shh," said the mother.

"Straton," said Varazda, "how did you know it was Ruta when you saw her on the stairs?"

"Her cloak," he said promptly. "She has a cloak with different-coloured squares."

"Plaid," the aunt supplied. "She's from Kargania, and she wears a plaid cloak. Beautiful blonde girl. I think she came here as someone's mistress, and then he left her, and what was the poor girl to do?" She *tsk*ed, and her sister shushed her again.

"Thank you, Straton," said Varazda, then paused for a moment to extricate his mantle from the baby's grip before it came unwrapped and fell in a heap on the floor. "So ... Ruta didn't speak to you this time either?"

Straton shook his head.

"And did you see her face?"

He shook his head again. The women gasped. Then Straton himself frowned.

"Do you think maybe it wasn't her?" he asked Varazda. "Do you think maybe it was someone else wearing her cloak?"

"I think maybe," said Varazda.

"I told you he doesn't lie," said Straton's mother.

"You said Ruta went away," Varazda pursued, flicking his hair out of reach of the baby's fists. "Do you know where?"

They all shook their heads, but after a moment the aunt said tentatively, "That place … what is it called? Where they all go to repent. The convent."

"Choros Rock?" Varazda supplied.

"That's it! I heard the girls across the street talking. I think she went there."

"My honourable colleague is asking you to believe that Damiskos Temnon, a man with an exemplary military record and well known for his integrity, met Helenos Diophoros in the street, quarrelled with him, did not at any time draw his sword, but rather assisted Helenos back to his lodging, where he proceeded to poison him using an unusual and slow-acting substance which would have ensured—since we know that Damiskos left the scene immediately—that he was not there to witness Helenos's death. Nor even, in fact, to be sure that Helenos did die, which he might well not have done, had he, for instance, possessed an especially strong constitution which afforded him some immunity to the poison.

"All of this, my friends, is very strange. Yet my colleague has offered no compelling reason why these strange things might have come to pass. He has spoken of a rivalry between Helenos Diophoros and Damiskos Temnon. On what basis they may have been rivals, he does not say. I submit that this is because he does not know, and I urge you to dismiss this baseless speculation.

"My colleague has described Damiskos to you as a man beset by loneliness, bereft of love. In fact, he has a devoted lover, a Sasian-born citizen of Boukos, with whom he has been living. He came to Pheme two weeks ago to attend to family matters in the city in advance of a permanent move to Boukos. After his arrest, his lover followed him to Pheme and has since worked tirelessly to secure evidence of what really happened to Helenos Diophoros. In due course you will hear what he has uncovered.

"It is conventional, when speaking of male lovers, to cite examples of legendary heroes whose love spurred them to martial feats and acts of courage. I will not do that. What I think of when I see these two together is the love that I bear for my wife, to whom I have been married forty years. I think of the love my daughter bears her new husband. I think that these two have been blessed by the gods to have found each other, and I think that they know it.

"Varazda—that's his name—it's a little difficult to pronounce, so he goes by 'Pharastes' in Boukos, but his name is Varazda. He has endured hardships that could have broken a lesser spirit. He was born an aristocrat in Sasia, but lost his family along with his freedom at a young age. Fate brought him to Boukos, where he was freed, but it was his own determination that built the life he enjoys there today, as a respected citizen and head of his household. He is, I dare say, entirely worthy of Damiskos Temnon, whose virtues I have already described to you—as, indeed, has my esteemed colleague.

"So when you hear that the cause of the quarrel between Damiskos and Helenos Diophoros on the day of Helenos's death was an insult offered by Helenos to Damiskos's lover, Varazda, well—you will understand as I do why Damiskos laid hands on him. It was a particularly coarse insult—I am not going to repeat it, but when I imagine a man saying such a thing to me about my wife ... I am not a young man, and it has been many years since I traded blows with anyone, but you can be sure that with such provocation, I would.

"We need seek no further for the motive behind this

altercation. There is no mystery here, no hidden motive. Helenos bore Damiskos a grudge for thwarting his plans—his *treasonous* plans, let it not be forgotten—Helenos insulted Varazda, whom Damiskos loves, and Damiskos hit him. That, my friends, is all there is to it.

"Well, except that Helenos died by poison later that day. Now, Helenos was a young man who had made many enemies. He was in hiding in Pheme, afraid to be tried for his crimes on Phemian soil. Several people were seen visiting him in the course of that day. He boasted to neighbours of a letter received from his former master, the philosopher Eurydemos, and his hopes for a return to his studies. Eurydemos was seen entering his lodging-house that day, but, by his own testimony, he disappointed Helenos's hopes. He was not able to help Helenos escape justice for his crimes. One can imagine that Helenos must have been left despondent after this blow, and indeed he was seen to be drinking heavily while the sun was still high, around the ninth hour. We know that the bottle of wine from which he drank was not itself poisoned. One of his neighbours drank the remainder and suffered no ill effects. You will hear more about that shortly.

"It may be that someone who visited Helenos that day sat down to drink with him, and poisoned only the cup intended for the victim. Damiskos, recall, did not sit down to drink with Helenos—he was not in the house long enough, as several neighbours can testify. Or it may be that the poison belonged to Helenos himself, and that he drank it voluntarily.

"My colleague places great significance on a silver object which was found in Helenos's room. He has told us that it is the stopper of a flask, and that this flask must have contained the poison which killed Helenos. Either of these things may be true—it *may* be a stopper from a flask, or it may be a game piece or a good-luck charm. The flask, if there was a flask, *may* have contained poison, or it may have contained perfume. What is certain is that the silver object, whatever it was, has no connection to my client. He had never seen it before my colleague waved it in front of us a short time ago, he never possessed the flask—if there was a flask—to which it belongs. He did not, in fact, enter Helenos's room. It is an interesting fact that the scorpion design on the silver object —and I will have to take your word for it that it is a scorpion, as from this distance to my eyes it looks more like a lobster—that this design is one found occasionally in cult statues of the god Terza, whom my client worships. That is an interesting fact, but it proves nothing."

While Chariton was still speaking, Damiskos noticed an olive-skinned young man with a mop of black curls making his way rather clumsily through the assembly, to arrive breathless at the base of the dais on Damiskos's side. He wasn't anyone Damiskos knew. He wore the carelessly wrapped mantle that Damiskos had come to associate with philosophers, though he managed to make it look almost elegant. He stood there watching the proceeding with fierce attention.

The women at the brothel across the street were vague about Ruta, and Varazda wasn't sure if it was because they didn't trust him or they genuinely hadn't known her very well. He was beginning to form a picture of her: a woman alone and friendless in a foreign country, doing what she could to survive. He hoped she'd found the peace or clarity or whatever it was she sought at the island convent. He hoped she was not in fact dead.

The prostitutes weren't sure, or wouldn't say, where Ruta had gone, but when Varazda suggested that it might have been Choros Rock, they admitted that they thought that was true.

"She used to talk about it," one of them said, toying with the string of glass beads she wore. "She's very religious."

"You wouldn't have thought," said another, "that she'd have wanted to go to a Phemian convent, would you? Being Karganian. But she did tell me that's where she was going."

He asked if they knew where Ruta had lived when she was in Pheme. At first they didn't want to tell him that either, and he gathered that was because she had not moved out permanently but was expected back. That was exactly what he had hoped to hear, so he waited patiently for more. Finally the woman with the beads mentioned a room above a sandal-maker. It was just up the hill, she said, near the new armoury.

Trying not to appear ominously eager, Varazda forced himself to linger a few more minutes, diverting the conversation into other channels, although he was itching to be off, his mind straying to what was going on back at the Hall of Justice, whether Dami had got his note, how hurt he must feel that Varazda wasn't there if he hadn't.

Had the advocate for Helenos's family produced the damned scorpion stopper yet? Had he tried to make a connection with the cult of Terza? It was only by chance that Varazda even knew about that; he remembered Marzana and Chereia's elder son pedantically listing all the cult symbols of Terza one night over dinner, and Remi asking what a scorpion was. But Sorgana was full of trivia about religion. Maybe this wasn't the sort of thing that most people knew about.

Finally Varazda excused himself casually and left the brothel. He hurried up the hill, further into the warren of the Skalina, looking for a sandal-maker's shop across from an armoury.

It took him longer than he would have liked to find it, and when he did, he was not entirely sure he could find his way back. The armoury, a forbidding building bristling with armed guards, looked out of place in the neighbourhood. The shop was closed, only the painting of sandals above the shuttered window alerting him to its identity. But that suited him well enough. It was a small, squat building, without even a full second storey; Ruta must have lived in the attic.

If time had allowed, he would have tried to talk to the neighbours, find out what they knew about the sandal-maker's tenant. Had they seen her recently, going about in her distinctive checked cloak, pretending not to know them? Or had she given the key to her room to a friend, who had been staying there in her stead?

He didn't have time for that. He satisfied himself that the sandal-maker's property looked empty, and went around the back to find the wall that edged the small paved yard. It was not much overlooked by the surrounding buildings, which were also low shacks unlike the ramshackle towers down the hill. The top of the wall was toothy with jagged shards of pottery. Varazda rolled his eyes at them and sloughed off his mantle. He folded up the thick wool cloth, tossed it over the pottery teeth so that he could grab hold of them, and swung himself up. One of the shards cracked under his hand, and he wobbled, but caught himself in a crouch on the narrow lip of the wall. He swivelled to perch sideways, hanging onto the opposite edge with one hand, contemplating his options.

He could attempt to shuffle cautiously over the teeth to the other side, but perhaps not without cutting himself on the way over, and he didn't even have the slight protection that would have been afforded by trousers. It just seemed like an opening for some kind of bad eunuch joke. He settled for planting his hands as well as he could on the opposite side of the wall and doing a slow backflip over into the paved yard.

He landed beautifully, and wished he'd had some sort of audience. He was thirty; he couldn't always do that as well as he'd been able to when he was eighteen.

He was also freezing cold in his short tunic, but he

couldn't stop to rewrap the stupid mantle now. He tugged it down off the wall and hid it in a wheelbarrow in the yard before trying the back door of the sandal-maker's house. It was unlocked.

He slipped into a dim, leather-scented workshop, and found the stairs leading up to a trap-door in the ceiling. This was not locked, either; perhaps there had been no need for Ruta to lend anyone her key after all.

Before pushing the trap door up, Varazda cast his gaze over the room below. It was very tidy, with no pieces of leather left out on the counter, no tools lying ready for the day's work. It looked as though the sandal-maker had left for something more than a day off. Varazda pushed open the attic door and went through.

The room above the shop had a few pieces of simple furniture: an unmade bed, a chest with its lid flung open, a small table littered with nutshells and fruit peels. Clothes—a blue gown and a stained white scarf—were draped over a wicker chair with a red leather cushion. When Varazda moved these, he found underneath an oilcloth travelling bag, tied shut. He tugged it open and withdrew a small silver flask.

It was an ugly object, moulded in the shape of a woman's head, with beetles for earrings. The scorpion stopper had been a sort of headdress, holding up a veil—the flask was now closed with a wad of cloth, somewhat stained with its dark brown contents. No doubt Sorgana could have told him who the head was supposed to represent; it had the look of some unpleasant Pseuchaian goddess. Varazda sniffed it cautiously. He didn't know what thorn-flower smelled like, but whatever was in the flask certainly stank, and that was good enough for him.

If she had chosen to keep her poison in something unobtrusive, she could have left the whole damn flask of it in Helenos's room and it wouldn't have helped lead Varazda to her. But he remembered this thing because it was so ugly. He had last seen it at Nione's villa in the summer, when he was searching for the stolen documents in Phaia's room.

She should have been an obvious suspect from the beginning. He knew she was ruthless and vengeful, and that she felt betrayed by Helenos. For that matter, she *had* been betrayed; he'd been her lover, and she thought he believed in their common cause, but he hadn't. He'd left her to her fate and escaped from justice himself. That she would come after him, lure him with a forged letter supposedly from their old master, and murder him with the same poison that had been used to execute their old associate Gelon, was entirely to be expected. It was just that everyone had been so sure she was confined to an inescapable prison on Choros Rock.

But Choros Rock wasn't really a prison; it was a temple complex and a convent, and it should have occurred to someone that a woman like Phaia would not have much trouble talking her way out of a place like that. There were any number of ways she might have done it: pretending to be repentant to win herself more liberties; befriending the lonely Ruta and telling her some sad story to get her to offer the use of her lodging, perhaps even assist her escape. And someone —maybe Ruta, maybe another woman who had looked more like Phaia—had posed as her when Eurydemos's sister had visited.

He replaced the ghastly flask in the oilcloth bag, retied it, and returned it to its home under the pile of clothes. Glancing over the table, he saw a folded tablet amid the debris, and gingerly brushed aside a couple of nutshells to flip it open.

Helenos Kontiades Diophoros to Eurydemos, greetings.

I was surprised to receive your letter, my former master, but since you seem desirous of a reunion, I will not deny you. I wonder how you found out my current residence. I will travel to

Pheme in a week, if the wind is favourable, and you will hear from me when I arrive.

It was exactly the kind of letter one would expect Helenos to write, its arrogance masking his desperation, expressing no affection for his former master, no apology for the way he had betrayed and tried to supplant him (not that Eurydemos hadn't deserved it), no gratitude for the forgiveness which Eurydemos was apparently willing to extend. Varazda wondered how Eurydemos would have reacted if he had actually received it.

Phaia's forged letter had ended with an innocuous-sounding phrase about sending a reply by the messenger who had delivered it, which was how she had ensured she would receive this letter herself. Perhaps she'd already been in Pheme by that time. When Helenos wrote to tell Eurydemos of his arrival, he would presumably have sent that letter to the Marble Porches, but Phaia must have found a way to intercept it and learn where Helenos was staying. That wouldn't have been difficult either. Varazda could think of several different ways he might have done it himself.

He closed the letter, flicked the nutshells back to their prior place, and was heading for the trap-door when he heard the sound of a door opening and closing in the shop below. He paused for a moment, glancing around the attic room, then he headed for the window.

CHAPTER 19

The curly-haired philosopher type came up the steps to speak to Chariton during the recess after his speech was finished and before the witnesses were presented.

"My name is Lysandros," he said. "I understand Eurydemos is speaking as a witness against you? I would be delighted to help discredit him for you. Your friend Pharastes sent me."

"You teach at the Marble Porches?" said Damiskos.

Lysandros shot him an interesting look. "I teach in a lot of places. Wine shops, mostly. But also the Marble Porches. I was there just now—that's where your friend found me."

"What would you say, to discredit Eurydemos?" Chariton asked.

"It would depend what he says himself. I am good at thinking on my feet." The philosopher had a wolfish smile rather like Chariton's own.

He also looked young enough to be Chariton's grandson. Chariton gave him a stern look. "I am not prepared to let you speak as a witness if I do not know what you are going to say."

"I think I know what he's going to say," said Damiskos.

"He's going to say that Eurydemos is a washed-up charlatan with a grudge against me for helping to destroy his career."

"I thought I might lean a little more on his intellectual bankruptcy," said Lysandros. "I'm not sure he actually holds grudges, as such. He's too far up his own ass."

"That … yeah. That rings true."

"But I know all about his Great Disillusionment, and I know you had something to do with it. I can certainly say that. Also, if he tries to ask that fucking stupid riddle, I know the answer to that, which will take the wind out of his sails."

"I think we should let him testify," said Damiskos to the lawyer. "But it's up to you."

"Why not?" said Chariton. "If nothing else, it will give Varazda more time to find whatever it is he's looking for."

"That's what I was thinking. I, er, appreciated what you said about him—about us. In your speech."

Chariton gave him a rather sad look. "It was all true. We lawyers don't have a reputation for frankness, but I meant every word of that."

"I, um. I thought you did. Thank you."

"It was a splendid speech," said the philosopher enthusiastically. "Convinced me."

"You were not present to hear the opposing speech," Chariton pointed out.

"No. But I got the gist of it from hearing yours. What was the story about the silver scorpion, or lobster, or whatever it is?"

"They found it at the scene," said Damiskos. "He was holding it when he died. We didn't know about it until their advocate brought it out at the end of his speech. He tried to make the case that it's mine because scorpions appear in images of Terza." Damiskos shrugged. "Which they do, sometimes."

"More likely to be one of those things of the Daughters of Night, don't you think?" said Lysandros. "Bug earrings and scorpion jewellery and so on. I've never seen one done in silver, but I suppose if you were morbid and rich, why not?"

Chariton pursed his lips. "I should have thought of that," he muttered.

"Don't worry," said Damiskos. "Your speech was great. Really."

A gong and an announcement from a court official signalled the return to the proceedings, the jury filed back into their seats, and the audience quieted and composed themselves again to listen.

"Kontios Diophoros, you may now summon your witnesses!"

Helenos's father stood up briefly and waved a hand at his advocate, giving him formal permission to proceed on his behalf.

The first few witnesses were predictable. A man who had seen Damiskos knock Helenos down in the street described what he had seen, which accorded well with what Damiskos remembered himself, and one of the neighbours from the building testified to seeing Damiskos go upstairs with Helenos, adding that he had not seen either of them come down, because he'd been on his way out himself. He referred to Helenos as "that nasty young fellow on the fourth floor," and began to advance his own theory that Helenos had been blackmailing Damiskos before Eulios cut him off and called his next witness.

The next witness was Damiskos's former subordinate from the Quartermaster's Office. He began his testimony by stepping on his mantle and nearly falling on his face as he got up from his seat, and it went downhill from there. He actually drew laughter from the audience for his attempt to describe Damiskos as a bad superior officer.

Among the rest, Damiskos thought he caught the sound of his father's laughter, and looked out to see him indeed grinning broadly. Timiskos, who had been standing with him at the beginning of the trial, was nowhere to be seen.

The slaves who had actually come to remove Helenos's body from his rented room could not testify, of course, but someone seemed to have thought of that at the time, and a freedman from the household had gone with them. He stood up to give an account of the finding of the silver scorpion, which had not been in Helenos's hand, as Eulios had implied, but lying concealed under his body. The object itself was passed around to the jurors, and a discussion about the differences between scorpions and lobsters ensued, to the advocate's obvious impatience.

"But are lobsters a symbol of Terza? That's what I want to know."

It went on for some time, and was never really settled to anyone's satisfaction.

Eurydemos was the final witness for the Diophoros family. The advocate, obviously rattled by the long scorpion/lobster digression, introduced him as, "The famous philosopher and Damiskos Temnon's former master," whereupon Eurydemos interrupted him with an indulgent laugh.

"Oh, no. Damiskos Temnon was never a pupil of mine. No, no. Nor would I characterize my reputation today as 'fame.'" He gave a martyred sort of sigh. "I would rather characterize it as 'infamy.' My students have deserted me—and how should they not, when I have repudiated my own teachings? I no longer teach—I lead. Helenos Kontiades was one of my pupils, a fact which I lament. Had he never sat at my feet, he might never have devoted himself to the unworthy cause which he chose … "

"What in the hells is he doing?" Chariton hissed. "Is he using this trial as an opportunity to commit public suicide?"

"I don't think," said Lysandros dryly, "that I'll need to say anything to discredit him."

The Diophoros advocate tried to intervene, to redirect

Eurydemos to something, anything relevant. Eurydemos treated him as if he were a student asking interesting but rather dim-witted questions. He debated definitions, quibbled about phrasing, went off on long tangents about abstract concepts. He dismissed Damiskos as a blockhead and rhapsodized about Varazda's beauty. He discussed the merits of suicide and seemed—it was hard to tell—to come down on the "pro" side.

"He is," muttered Chariton furiously. "He's going to stab himself or—poison himself—in front of my court. I'll—I'll defile his corpse."

"I think," said Lysandros soothingly, "you don't have to worry about that. I think he's of the opinion that suicide is a good option for people who aren't him."

Damiskos had to press a fist to his lips to keep from laughing.

In the end, the advocate Eulios rallied enough to shut Eurydemos up definitively, in the middle of posing the riddle that Lysandros had predicted.

"*Wisdom*," Lysandros whispered, cocking an eyebrow. "That's the answer. No, I don't know what it's supposed to mean, either."

"It was very good of you to come," said Chariton, looking weak with relief, "but I do not think there was much in his testimony—if you can call it that—that needs to be refuted. Nor that you could discredit him much more than he has already done himself."

Lysandros nodded, with his wolfish smile. "You probably don't need more than one philosopher testifying at your trial. I might get up there and start blathering about slavery, myself."

"Slavery?" said Damiskos.

"I'm a radical. I want to see slavery abolished."

"Oh, good for you." He was about to ask some question, or perhaps share some anecdote about the household of freed slaves in which he had lived for the past month, before he remembered that he was still on trial for murder.

"It's our turn to present evidence," said Chariton. "And, as you may recall, that means it's your turn to speak."

"Oh," said Damiskos, who had forgotten. "Oh, right."

He had been standing still for so long that his leg was incredibly stiff, and he had to lean heavily on his cane as he walked out to the middle of the dais.

"Uh, hello," he said, looking at the jurors on their benches. "I'm Damiskos Philiades. Well, you know that, I suppose."

Divine Terza, he was going to sound like he was trying to win them over with a display of folksy likeableness. He had to pull himself together.

"I want to, er, to thank Master Chariton for all the kind things he said about me—and Eulios, you said kind things as well, though I do understand that was strategic—and Chariton, thanks for what you said about Varazda. He's ... he's my whole life, and it's nice to hear that other people have noticed what a good person he is. That's—obviously not—I just wanted to say that."

He cleared his throat. "On the afternoon of Xereus's Day, the 18th of Eighth Month, I arrived in Pheme from Boukos. The crossing was uneventful, and we docked around the seventh hour. I had made the trip in order to see my family and to transact some business preparatory to relocating permanently to Boukos. My first objective was to secure possession of my horse, who had been stabled on the Tetrina but had recently been moved to a location outside the city in Thumia. Accordingly I proceeded to Thumia, taking a route which led me through the neighbourhood of the Skalina Hill ... "

Varazda crouched behind the wood pile in the sandal-maker's yard, trying to rewrap his mantle quickly and discreetly. He had stayed on the roof of the house long enough to hear the sound of footsteps going up the stairs inside, and catch a glimpse of a plaid cloak through the window, then he'd descended to the yard. He wasn't exactly trapped—there was no back gate, but he could get over the wall if he had to, or slip out through the shop while Phaia was upstairs—but getting himself off the property was not the main problem here.

He looked down at the mantle, thinking it looked as sloppy as any philosopher's. That gave him an idea.

He ran lightly across the yard, eased open the back door and crept across the deserted shop. He could hear Phaia moving around upstairs as he unbolted the front door and slipped out. He took off down the street.

In a few minutes he was back, forcing himself to walk as he approached the shop so that he would not appear out of breath, and knocked soundly on the door. He had to repeat the knock several times before the door opened a crack and a white face with familiar dark eyes peered out.

"The shop is closed. Tono is gone to visit his mother. Go a—" That was when she recognized him.

"Phaia?" he said.

She opened the door wide in order to stare scornfully at him. "You!"

"Pharastes," he supplied.

"I remember!" she snarled. "You don't think I'd forget *you*? You're the snake who was spying for the Basileon, who seduced that soldier and ruined our plans. We could have restored the glory of Pheme if it hadn't been for you."

He'd had no idea she had such a high opinion of his achievements; it was honestly rather flattering.

"People change," he said, looking at her levelly.

If he hadn't known who would answer the door, he might

not have recognized Phaia. Her black hair had been cut military-short and only just begun to grow out. Probably that was part of the regime at the convent, but it must have helped her impersonate the blonde Ruta by pulling up the hood of her plaid cloak. The short hair almost suited her.

"What do you want with me?" she demanded.

He raised his eyebrows. "I could want to return you to Choros Rock, couldn't I? If I were still the *snake* you think me, if I still worked for the Basileon."

"You don't." She looked sceptical.

"I've come to warn you. Eurydemos sent me."

"He didn't." She frowned. "Did he?"

"Well, in a manner of speaking." Varazda smiled, as if fondly. "He asked me to find you, but he had no idea where to look. That's why it has taken me so long."

"Why would Eurydemos ask *you* to find *me*?" But she was looking less sceptical now.

"He saw you come out of Helenos's place, the day Helenos died. Oh, did you know Helenos was dead?" She said nothing, and he forged on. "Eurydemos wants me to warn you that you may be under suspicion. For murdering Helenos."

She looked at him for a long moment, dark eyes narrowed. He could imagine what she was thinking. Eurydemos might well have been near Helenos's lodging that evening; he had met with Helenos earlier in the day, and perhaps he'd come back, still hoping to persuade his wayward pupil to embrace his new teaching. And if he had seen her, and then found Helenos's body, or learned of Helenos's death, nothing was more likely than that he would try in some cockeyed and belated way to protect her, whether he thought she had done it or not. The only part that was unlikely …

"I know what you're thinking," said Varazda dryly. "Why should he send me? What am I even doing here, in Pheme?

Dressed like this?" He spread his arms, displaying his sloppy mantle.

Phaia's smile was slow and sly. "You and Eurydemos. He always did like you. So the soldier, he was just a means to an end?"

"I felt sure you would understand."

She tossed back her head with a laugh, as if charmed. "Oh, you've no idea! Here." She swung the door open and stepped back, waving him through. "You'd better come in."

He entered the sandal-maker's shop, looking around as if the place were new to him.

"The shopkeeper's away," Phaia explained, shutting the door behind him. "He's renting me the upstairs room."

"Eurydemos was surprised to see you in Pheme," Varazda said. "He had sent his sister to Choros Rock with a gift for you only a few days earlier, and she said that she had delivered it to you. I suppose that wasn't really you?"

Phaia laughed. "Of course not. We all look the same in those veils—that was what made it so easy to get away. I made a 'friend,' a barbarian whore, who offered to trade places with me when she heard my *sad story*."

Varazda chuckled appreciatively. "We should have known that Choros Rock could not hold you."

"You should have. Tell me—what did Eurydemos see?"

"What there was to see, which wasn't much, I suppose. He guessed that you were visiting Helenos for purely ... er, sentimental reasons."

"He what?" Phaia looked angry.

"Well, he knew that there was something between you and Helenos. He assumed that Helenos would have been behind your escape from Choros Rock, but I said I thought you could have done that on your own."

Phaia gave him a long, considering look. "You were right," she said. "Come upstairs and help me pack my things.

I am going to heed my old master's advice, one last time, and leave the city."

"Good," he said. "I think that's wisest."

He followed her up the stairs. There were two ways he could see this going. She might have more sense than to let herself be goaded into boasting that she had killed Helenos all by herself—but that was only the easier option.

In the upstairs apartment, Phaia began gathering things up from the chair and table. She took the oilskin bag over to the bed and began rummaging through it, with her back to Varazda. She looked over her shoulder. "Pass me those cups on the table, will you? Help me finish off this bottle that I have here—it's too little to take, and too good to waste."

He plucked a pair of dirty cups from the table and handed them over. She turned her back on him again to fill them.

"It's an awful place, Choros Rock," she said. "Full of small-minded, religious women, atoning for things that they imagine they have done wrong. I have never liked the company of other women." She turned with the full cups in her hands and walked over to where Varazda sat. She set both cups back on the table and picked up a discarded cloth from the floor. "Eurydemos must have known that it wouldn't suit me."

He looked at the two cups, which had been placed side-by-side. He wondered if this was exactly how she had done it with Helenos. He picked up the cup nearest him and cradled it.

"He said that he thought it was a waste for you to be imprisoned in such a place, as if you were just like other women."

She nodded with a smile of satisfaction. She picked up the other cup and pretended to drink; her lips weren't even wet when she set it down. He pretended not to notice.

"So, Helenos is dead?" she said, as if she'd just remembered that she wasn't supposed to know this.

"He didn't escape justice after all."

"Justice?" she repeated, surprised. "Yes ... I suppose it was justice, wasn't it."

She turned to take a scroll down from the windowsill. When she turned back, Varazda had emptied his cup, all except for a dark sludge in the bottom.

"Delicious," he said, lowering it from his lips.

Phaia picked up her own cup, smiling, then fumbled it, letting it slip through her fingers to shatter on the floor. Its contents splashed out.

"How clumsy of me," she remarked. "And that's the last of the bottle. Ah, well. How did he die?"

"Helenos? Suicide. I suppose you might have had something to do with that."

"What?" She whirled to look at him sharply.

"Well, you obviously didn't patch things up with him when you met—you didn't even seem concerned to hear that he's dead—so I suppose you must have quarrelled. Perhaps that's what drove him to it."

She tossed her head with a laugh. "Helenos didn't have the courage to kill himself, and he certainly wouldn't have done it over me. He liked having me at his side—and in his bed, though he was never able to think of anything exciting to do with me when he had me there—because it gave him status. Eurydemos's brilliant girl student. Everyone wanted me, and he had me—but he didn't care about me. I never thought he did. I just thought he cared about our cause."

"Your cause," Varazda repeated slowly. "The one where you wanted Pheme to go to war with Zash again?"

She took a step toward him, looking up into his face, fiery-eyed. "We could *destroy* you."

He looked back at her, eyebrows raised. "I'm a citizen of Boukos."

"You're a poison," she hissed. "An infection. You don't belong among Pseuchaians." She glanced down, with a flicker of satisfaction, at the cup he was still holding. "You deserve the same fate that Helenos met. If only the gods would allow me to bring it down on Eurydemos too."

"Oh? What fate did Helenos meet?"

"I killed him!" she said impatiently. "I told him we would drink together, from the bottle that our former master had brought him—drink to the glory of Pheme and the ruin of the Ideal Republic. I poured the wine and watched him drink. I watched him die, too. It didn't take long."

The silence that followed was broken by the sound of liquid dripping onto the floor. Phaia looked sharply over at the chair with its red leather cushion, which had briefly disguised the wine that Varazda had poured out onto it, and that was now dripping down through the wicker.

"You—didn't drink."

"No, I didn't."

She flew at him, with no clear plan except maybe to sink her teeth into him. He dodged, keeping hold of the wine-cup with its telltale residue of poison. He circled around to the stairs and ran down a few steps before vaulting over the railing into the shop below.

She pounded after him, grabbed an awl from the sandal-maker's workbench, and lunged again. He twisted away, causing the point of the awl to catch in the folds of his mantle. He jerked at the fabric, and the whole thing fell off him and pitched her forward. She shrieked. He caught her, pinning her arms to her sides. That was when the door opened, and three of the guards from the armoury down the street burst in.

The speeches in Damiskos's defence were finally finished. There had been a lot of them, some very eloquent; one of Damiskos's former standard-bearers had a gift for storytelling, and gave a long, suspenseful account of a battle in which Damiskos had distinguished himself. It didn't have an awful lot to do with the case, but the jury and the audience seemed to enjoy it. Big Tio talked nervously about his pickle-seller theory, and several other men from the Skalina spoke, saying that they'd seen Damiskos leave Big Tio's house very shortly after he had entered it, that Helenos had provoked Damiskos in the street with some rude remarks, and that the conflict between the two had not looked serious.

Finally Nione walked up to the dais from the women's seats, to gasps and murmuring from the assembly, and said a lot of very nice things that Damiskos found hard to listen to.

The court official began to pronounce the solemn formula calling on the jurors to cast their votes, and a commotion from the door of the room interrupted him.

Damiskos looked up. He remembered Varazda walking out of Nione's house to tell Helenos that he didn't have hostages any more.

And there he was, marching into the courtroom, looking tired and triumphant, without his mantle, his hair falling down, carrying a wine-cup in one hand and something silver in the other. Behind him came several armed guards, escorting a short-haired woman whom Damiskos recognized after a moment.

"He did it!" said Chariton with wonder. "He did, didn't he?"

"Well," said Lysandros, with a gleam in his eye, "this is exciting."

It became much more exciting in a moment, when Phaia tried to bolt past the guards, who failed to catch her. But someone stepped out of the women's section at the back of the court and seized her around the waist. It was Aradne. She lifted Phaia off her feet as she hauled her back up the aisle, shrieking and clawing. Several more guards jogged down to assist, and Aradne turned her prisoner over to them, but not before pausing to look Phaia in the face and say something to her. Damiskos was too far away to hear what it was, but from Aradne's expression, it was not hard to get a general idea.

CHAPTER 20

Varazda's testimony was brief and (deliberately, Damiskos thought) undramatic. He explained that he had sought out Phaia because he remembered her owning a flask matching the stopper that had been found with Helenos's body, and he knew that she had once been Helenos's mistress and bore him a grudge. He recounted how, when he arrived on her doorstep, she had invited him in and then tried to poison him using the same technique she'd used on Helenos, eventually going so far as to boast about how she had done it. Damiskos could tell there was a lot he was leaving out.

As businesslike as Varazda tried to make his account, it was still some time before the court settled down enough for the magistrate to finish pronouncing the address to the jury. By that time their unanimous vote of *Not Guilty* probably felt like an anti-climax to much of the assembly. To Damiskos it felt like the lifting of a weight that had started to feel familiar. It wasn't that he'd thought he would be found guilty, exactly; he just somehow hadn't believed that the trial would ever be over.

And it wasn't—at least, not for the court officials, who

had to deal with the new charge being brought by Kontios Diophoros against Phaia, who was shouting at Eurydemos that she wished she had killed him too. Eulios the advocate descended on Varazda, making sure to secure his testimony for the new prosecution. Damiskos and his supporters were rather unceremoniously told that they were free to go.

"Congratulations," said Lysandros, shaking Damiskos's hand. "Glad you didn't need my help after all!"

"Don't go," said Chariton to the philosopher. "I want to talk to you. Damiskos, congratulations."

"No, I—it's all your doing. Thank you. From the bottom of my heart. I wouldn't have expected a murder trial to be so ... so ... Well, listening to you and the others say such nice things about me—" He felt like a fool now, saying this. Of course Chariton had said all those things, but he'd had to. He had been trying to convince the jury that Damiskos was innocent. "I know you had to defend my character, but you didn't have to say what you did about Varazda. My parents' advocate didn't want him mentioned at all. So ... thank you."

Chariton nodded. "It was an honour," he said. Then he gave Damiskos a brief, dignified hug.

Damiskos looked for his family, but couldn't see them in the crowd. He saw Aradne and Nione working their way up toward the dais, but his former standard-bearer had come up to congratulate him, so he waved to them with a smile.

"Damiskos!" he heard someone shout, as he was speaking to Tio the landlord. It was Ino, standing below the dais and waving urgently.

"Excuse me," he said to Tio.

Ino shoved aside a captain from the Sixth Colonial, who had been waiting to speak to Damiskos.

"Damiskos! You have to come. Your brother is in trouble."

Instantly she had all his attention. "What kind of trouble?"

"I don't know. Your parents are outside—your mother's crying. One of Timiskos's friends came to tell them that something has happened."

"Something" could only be that Timiskos's debt had been called in, and the creditors weren't taking no for an answer. But Damiskos had given Timiskos a sum of money the day before, and assured him that there was more coming, enough to pay the full amount.

"Right." Damiskos nodded. "I'm on my way."

He looked over at Varazda on the other side of the dais, still deep in conversation with Eulios.

Chariton touched his shoulder. "I'll tell him where you've gone," he said.

Damiskos retrieved his sword, which he had left with the guards at the entrance to the courtroom, and made his way back out through the back passage to the porch. By the time he got there—most of a day spent on his feet had taken its toll, and he was not moving very fast—Aradne and Nione seemed to have found out what was going on from Ino, and caught up to him.

"If there is anything we can do to help ... " said Nione.

"Where did they go?" Varazda asked, rhetorically, as he stood on the empty steps of the Hall of Justice with Chariton and the radical philosopher who was still, for some reason, hanging around.

"I know only that it was something to do with Damiskos's brother," Chariton supplied apologetically. "Perhaps they went to the family home."

"Right."

"Do you know where that is?"

"Um … roughly."

He made an effort to pull himself together. He *did* know where the Temnons' apartment was; he had found his way there from Aradne's house multiple times, once after dark. He didn't entirely know where the Hall of Justice was in relation to Aradne's house, but that was not an insurmountable problem. It was just that he was very tired, and, if he was honest, he had been looking forward to falling into Dami's arms and perhaps being lifted off his feet and swung around in a celebratory embrace.

Instead, there was another long slog from the agora back up the Goulina Hill, to arrive at the familiar barbershop, shuttered now in the deepening twilight. In front of the door at the side that led to the Temnons' apartment, several porters were busy piling furniture into a wagon. Varazda recognized one of the wicker chairs from Timiskos's tasteful seating area, and one of the potted trees was carried down after it.

"They're taking the furniture?" Varazda said out loud, puzzled. "But we told Timiskos the money was coming."

Chariton looked away, embarrassed. Wealthy Pseuchaians always seemed to think debt was somehow in poor taste.

Varazda spotted Damiskos's father sitting with his head in his hands on the barbershop doorstep. Varazda approached.

Philion Temnon looked up. His face looked empty, forlorn. "Varasdes. Gods. This is all my fault."

"What is your fault?" Varazda found he had folded his arms sternly as he stood looking down at Damiskos's father.

"They took Timi. I never imagined it would come to this. The debts … these gangsters, they threaten all kinds of things, but I thought they never followed through."

Philion dropped his head into his hands again. Dami's mother came down the stairs from the apartment, followed by her maid, who was in tears.

"Mistress, all your nice things!"

"Shh-shh, Gaia, we can always get new things—don't worry about that. Oh, Varasta! I'm so glad to see you. Damiskos has gone to get a horse … "

That was when Dami himself rode up. Varazda had never seen him on a horse before, and couldn't help admiring the sight even under the circumstances.

"Darling," Dami said when he had dismounted, "I'm so glad you caught up with us. I wish I hadn't had to—" And he broke off to seize Varazda and do the lifting in his arms and swinging around that Varazda had imagined, following it with one of his most devastating kisses. "I'm so proud of you. No, that doesn't even come close. Sometimes I can't believe you're real."

He set Varazda on his feet and said, in Zashian, "I have to go get Timi. The message we received was confused, but it seems he might have been taken down to the Lower Goulina docks. Do you want to wait here or come with me?"

"I want to come with you, of course."

Dami nodded. He mounted the hired horse again and held out a hand to pull Varazda up behind him.

They rode fast through the deserted streets and arrived at the river docks in the pitch dark. They could see some shuffling activity and the faint light of a muffled lantern down at one end of the dock.

"You stay mounted," Dami whispered, sliding down off the horse.

Varazda could just make out Dami approaching the end of the pier, and another figure coming up it to meet him. The lantern-light gleamed on the newcomer's bright red hair, but he had a scarf pulled over the lower half of his face and was otherwise just a dark shape.

"Stand down," said Dami evenly. The light caught the edge of his sword blade. "I've come for Timiskos."

There was a moment's tense pause. "Just, uh, just a second," said the redhead nervously.

Dami cocked his head, lowering his sword a fraction. "Soukios?"

"Oh gods," moaned another figure who had come up behind the redhead, "it's the brother, isn't it? Soukios, show yourself, you dumbfuck, before he kills us all!"

Dami had lowered his sword entirely but did not sheathe it. "I'm not currently planning on killing anybody," he said, "but I'd like to know what's going on. Where's Timiskos?"

The redhead, Soukios, had pulled down his scarf, and the other young man had unmuffled the lantern. They were joined cautiously by a couple of others who had been lurking on the pier.

"Uh, the thing is, he's not here," said Soukios. "We were —it was—the whole plan went sideways."

"The plan," Dami repeated. "Which was?"

"Just, you know, to scare his—your—parents. You weren't supposed to show up. You were supposed to be busy being, uh, being tried for murder? That's why we were going to do it now."

"You were staging a kidnapping," Dami interpreted. He gave an angry sigh. "I know where he got that idea."

"Yeah, but then, see," one of the other young men cut in, "Pandares's men came to take away your parents' stuff, and I guess they thought there was a ransom to be had, so they … they took him off us."

"So what you're saying is your pretend kidnapping gave the real gangsters ideas."

"Yeah. Basically, yeah."

"We didn't put up much of a fight," Soukios admitted. "But we were going after them, to, uh … " He gestured uncertainly.

"Where have they gone?" Dami prompted.

"We think they're at Philo's. He has a back room that he lets them use—I mean, he doesn't have much of a choice, with the way things are. But we think they've gone there."

Dami must have been giving them a sceptical look, because the redhead added hastily, "There's a river door, we were looking for a boat to get to it, but we've had no luck."

"Right," said Dami, turning back toward where Varazda was waiting. He slid his sword back into its sheath. "We're going in the front door."

Philo's was the wine shop where Damiskos had been drinking with his brother the afternoon before he was arrested. It was quite close; they didn't really need the horse, but Varazda seemed tired, and Damiskos was glad to be able to let him ride.

"Not that it wasn't a terrible plan," Varazda said, as they arrived at the lit front of the wine shop, "but it did work. Your parents seemed quite shaken."

"They'll bounce back," said Damiskos wryly. "But yeah, I know what you mean. Right, we'll have to play this by ear since we don't know what we're going to find in there. I'll go in first—"

"Perhaps both of us should go in quietly and order something at the bar to get our bearings," Varazda suggested.

"Divine Terza. Yes, of course. And I'm supposed to be the tactician."

"Yes, dear," said Varazda, patting his shoulder, "but I'm the spy."

They tied their horse and entered the wine shop casually. They went to the counter and ordered drinks. Damiskos spotted the door to the back room, almost hidden behind a huge guard, who stood leaning against the doorpost, cleaning his nails with the point of a knife. He hadn't been there the last time Damiskos had visited the wine shop with his brother, and from the looks that the waiters gave him as they had to step around him, his presence was not exactly welcome.

"Want me to distract him?" Varazda asked, inclining his head minutely toward the guard.

Damiskos hesitated. "How? I don't want you to have to do anything you don't like."

Varazda smiled warmly. "Just a bit of light flirting. I like the 'mistaken identity' gambit myself—you know, pretend to have taken them for someone you know, and see where it goes from there."

Damiskos nodded. "Understood."

Varazda picked up his drink and sauntered over to the guard, loosening his hair and shaking it out with a nicely judged nonchalance, as if he might not have been aware of all the eyes in the bar swivelling toward him. Damiskos watched him strike up a conversation with the guard and draw him gradually away from the door, asking some question that required the big man to walk out toward the front of the shop, pointing and gesturing as if giving him directions.

Damiskos wasted no time in slipping behind the counter and through the door that the man had been guarding. He closed it noiselessly behind him. He was in a narrow, paved passage, with a heavily barred gate onto an alley to his right, and opposite him another door. To his left was a blank wall. He drew his sword and banged on the door with the pommel.

A skinny, scowling young man in a dirty mariner's cap opened the door and jumped back with alarm when he saw Damiskos. Behind him three other men stood and sat around a wooden table. Through an arch in the far wall Damiskos could make out other figures. The rooms were dark, with small windows, lit only by a couple of tapers on the walls. He could not immediately spot Timiskos.

That meant he needed to give Timiskos the opportunity to spot him.

"I'm here for my brother," he announced, stepping inside the room, sword up.

"Damiskos?" There was a scuffle from the back room. "Let me go!"

"Let him go," Damiskos agreed.

"Who's gonna make us?" asked a deep voice from the other side of the table.

"Why do you clowns always ask that?" Damiskos growled.

He strode forward, parrying a knife-strike from a bearded man who emerged from the shadows to his left.

"Damiskos, don't!" Timiskos called out. "There are too many of them!" He grunted as someone punched him. Damiskos could see him now through the archway, between a big redhead and another skinny blond sailor, who were both holding onto him.

The man in front of Damiskos swung an infantry-style short sword. Damiskos dodged, bringing his own blade down on the man's sword-arm. It wasn't a severe enough cut to disable him, but it did cause him to lose his grip on his sword. Damiskos caught the hilt and wrenched it out of his hand.

Fighting in the dark was not ideal, and the numbers were certainly against him. But he had two swords, and they were in an enclosed space—a disadvantage to his opponents, but not to him. He'd had a lot of practice recently fighting in an enclosed space.

His main problem was that, in the heart of Pheme and freshly acquitted of murder, he could not afford to kill anyone.

The owner of the deep voice came around from behind

the table, casually hefting a small wooden bench as if it were made of wicker. Damiskos avoided a knife-strike from his immediate opponent, flipped both swords in his hands and dealt him a pair of solid blows with the flats of the blades. The man staggered, dazed, and Damiskos smashed the hilt of his borrowed sword into his nose. Deep Voice swung the bench at Damiskos's head.

Damiskos caught the edge of the bench on its way down against the blades of his swords, but as he was braced like this, the skinny blond who had opened the door darted in, his knife aimed at Damiskos's stomach. Damiskos sidestepped neatly so that the bench came down on the knife-wielder's head. The blond went sprawling, and the man whose nose Damiskos had already broken tripped over him.

The man with the bench swore in a loud rumble and swung again, but Damiskos had used the confusion to slip past him and duck under the table. Dropping his borrowed sword (it was an inferior weapon, weighted all wrong), he pushed the table up behind him, making a couple of cups slide down to crash on the floor. He gripped one leg of the table and swung it around like a shield to catch another impact from the bench.

In front of him, Timiskos had wrenched free from one of his captors and was reaching for the man's sword.

"Guda!" someone shouted at a very young man standing frozen in the corner facing Damiskos. "What in the name of Nepharos are you doing? Attack him!"

Guda, who was well illuminated because he was standing under one of the tapers, looked sick. Damiskos looked him in the eye and shook his head firmly. The young man stayed where he was.

Timiskos had secured the sword, but his other captor had got him firmly by the upper arms now, so all he could do was wave the blade in short, ineffectual arcs. Damiskos manoeuvred his table to block a knife-strike in one direction and another swing of the wooden bench in the other. Then he pushed back, smashing the table into the bench-wielder with his whole weight against it. The man went down—barely—with a crash and a startled bellow. Damiskos just managed to catch his balance and right himself while hanging onto the table-leg.

The red-haired man holding Timiskos had got him to drop the sword, and from somewhere in the room behind them a new figure emerged: a well-groomed man in a clean mantle, whose face Damiskos could not see clearly.

In a ringing voice, but sounding slightly bored, he said, "Just kill him."

The man whose sword Timiskos had taken glanced at his boss and then shrugged. He reached down to pick up the dropped sword. Damiskos was still several paces away, with Timiskos and the man holding him blocking his way, and the terrified Guda edging out of his corner, knife in hand.

"My brother will kill you!" Timiskos yelled in defiance as the sailor raised his weapon.

A cold, wet breeze blew through from the back room. The door to the river had opened at some point, while everyone had been distracted.

The man in the mantle gave a choking grunt and grabbed at his neck. There was a rope around it, and behind him, streaming water and pulling the garrotte tight against his throat, was Varazda.

His eye makeup made dark streaks down his face, his wet hair was plastered to his bare shoulders, and his tunic clung to him in sodden folds. In the flickering light of the tapers, he looked like an angry river-nymph risen up to claim her prey. That may have been what flashed through the mind of the man about to stab Timiskos, because he let out a shriek, stumbled backward into the outer room, and crashed into Guda.

Damiskos leapt forward, knocking the red-bearded man

holding Timiskos on the side of the head. He staggered and loosed his hold, and Damiskos grabbed his brother's arm.

The bench-swinging giant was on his feet by this time, and had seized Damiskos's abandoned table in both hands. He hefted it over his head as if he intended to throw it. The man Varazda was strangling gave an indignant gurgle. Damiskos had time to wonder whether Varazda had ever actually strangled anyone before—he was doing a pretty good job. Then Varazda heaved the man up and out the doorway, into the river.

One of the underlings laughed in a sputtering guffaw. Someone was yelling at the giant to put down the table, for the love of Nepharos; someone else tried to take the table away from him, and got it dropped on his foot instead. Their boss, flailing in the water below the doorstep, was shouting, "Get—me—out—of this—you sons of goat-fuckers!"

Damiskos reached for Varazda's hand, and herding Timiskos between them they made for the outer door, unbarred the gate in the passage, and emerged on the street in front of the wine shop.

"Where did you—how did you—gods, I'm so sorry," Timiskos was gasping as they hurried away.

Damiskos unfastened his cloak and slung it around Varazda's shoulders.

"Got to get you warm," he said.

"Thanks," said Varazda, who was visibly shivering.

"It's not really the weather for swimming."

Not to mention that Varazda must have spent much of the day running around the city finding evidence for Damiskos's trial, and he'd been exhausted before he ended up in the river. Damiskos had seen men die under similar circumstances if they didn't warm up quickly enough.

"Didn't mean to go swimming," Varazda admitted. "Was creeping along a ledge—back of the building—fell in."

Timiskos was still trying to ask how they had found him

or why they had come for him, and apologizing over and over. Damiskos shushed him. There were footsteps behind them, and shouting voices. They were being followed.

"Like your cloak," said Varazda, tugging the thick fabric up under his chin. "Always wanted to be wrapped up in one of these."

"Who's that?" Timiskos asked suddenly, pointing.

A couple of figures were coming purposefully down a flight of steps from a street above, heading toward them.

"Damiskos?" one of the figures called, just as someone else arrived at the top of the steps with a lantern. "Pharastes? Is that you?"

The two people approaching were the boy Niko from Nione's household and the philosopher Lysandros. The person with the lantern was Aradne.

"We found them!" she yelled triumphantly over her shoulder.

Nione had the use of the private carriages of the Maidens' House, and she and Aradne had found out where everyone had gone, driven over to the Temnons' building, and followed Damiskos and Varazda's trail. They were all inside the carriage by the time the men from the wine shop caught up with them. Aradne was ordering Varazda to strip off his wet tunic. Out the window, Damiskos could see their pursuers recognize the Maidens' carriage and fall back nervously. Aradne gave an order to the driver, and the carriage rolled sedately up the street.

They returned to Damiskos's parents' house, and from there an assortment of people whom Damiskos was too tired to catalogue rode back with them to Aradne's. Varazda, warmed up and snuggled in Damiskos's cloak, fell asleep on the way there, with his head on Damiskos's shoulder.

Damiskos was prepared to let him sleep, and would have tried to carry him into the house if necessary—though he knew he wouldn't have been able to do it—but when they arrived, Varazda woke up looking quite alert, and even when they had retired to their room and got under the covers, he did not immediately shut his eyes. Damiskos pulled him close.

"I wish you could have heard the way Chariton talked about you today," Damiskos said.

Varazda snorted. "I'd rather have heard how he talked about you."

"Oh, well. You'd have liked the other advocate's speech too. It was a fiction, but you'd have appreciated the ingenuity of it."

"Hm. Maybe. In all seriousness … I was surprised to hear that Chariton mentioned me. I suppose the reaction of your family's advocate affected me more than I liked to pretend. I'm afraid I *was* beginning to think of myself as a liability."

"My whole family's reaction was shameful," said Damiskos. "I am sorry you had to put up with any of it."

"You did an admirable job of shielding me from them—but of course, since I noticed that's what you were doing, in a way it only made me feel worse. That's not a criticism, just … "

"I know." He squeezed Varazda's bare shoulders. "And I know you don't suffer torments every time someone is casually cruel, but that's only because you're used to it, and it's no use for me to say, 'You shouldn't have to be,' because … "

"Stop it before you tie yourself into an *actual* knot," said Varazda, laughing. "You know, I think you've been right about your family all along. You love them, but you have to love them from a distance. It doesn't have to be as far away as Zash, but it does probably have to be a little further than the Vallina Hill."

"Like Boukos?"

"I think Boukos will be perfect."

Damiskos smiled wryly. "I hope so. I mean, I don't want you to have to ... I don't want them to be your burden too."

"I do," said Varazda simply. "And I've an idea about that, too. Tell me what you think."

CHAPTER 21

Everyone was at Aradne's house the following morning. Some of them, indeed, seemed not to have left: the philosopher Lysandros was there, in the mantle he'd worn yesterday, chatting with Aradne, and Chariton emerged from one of the guest rooms, rubbing sleep out of his eyes.

Varazda retold the story of his investigation, why he had known the significance of the silver scorpion—everyone, for some reason, kept interrupting to say, "If it wasn't a lobster!" and roar with laughter—and how he had tracked down Phaia, once over breakfast, and again when Dami's parents arrived shortly afterward.

The latter telling involved introducing a lot of background information about what had happened at Laothalia, in order to explain how the various parties were related to one another and who held grudges against whom. In the end, it amounted to Varazda, Dami, and Aradne giving a more or less complete account of the events of the summer, absent a few of the more confidential and private details.

"Do you mean to say," said Dami's mother, "that that ridiculous philosopher who spoke at the trial was a suspect?"

"A very credible suspect," said Nione.

"We all hoped he'd done it," said Aradne.

"And he spoke for the prosecution?" said Philion, wide-eyed. "The nerve of the man!"

"Don't you think," said Ino, when there was a pause in the conversation, "that in a way he *did* do it?"

"No, dear, you see—" Myrto started.

"I know what you mean," said Varazda. "I think you're right. One of his students killed another one, over a disagreement that, if it wasn't exactly philosophical, was pretty close to it. He should bear some responsibility."

"He won't," Lysandros intoned. "But I don't need to tell you that."

"I thought it was a romantic entanglement?" said Timiskos. "With the two students."

"They were lovers," said Varazda, "but I think that was incidental. They seemed to regard each other mostly as trophies. He was the rising star, and she was the only female student—they thought they were going to go on to great things together. It just turned out they didn't have the same idea of what those great things were, and she couldn't forgive him for that."

"We don't hold with any of that," said Philion stiffly. "War with Sasia. Phemian, uh, uh, whatever it was." He glanced at Dami. "You know that, don't you, son?"

"Yes, sir." Dami smiled and looked at the floor. "Yes, sir, I know that."

"You're tremendously brave to have done all that climbing in windows and hunting down suspects," said Myrto to Varazda. "I feel faint just thinking about it."

Dami draped an arm around Varazda's shoulders and grinned. "You don't know the half of it, Mother."

"Has he told you about the time Pharastes freed the hostages at Laothalia?" asked Aradne.

He hadn't, so then that story had to be told, in a way that made Varazda's role sound much more heroic and much less like it had been a matter of luck and dramatic timing than the way he remembered it. He listened with half his attention.

He didn't know if he would go so far as to say that Timiskos's cock-eyed staged kidnapping scheme had *worked*, but maybe it was the combination of the threat to their son with the loss of most of their possessions. Maybe, he thought charitably, they had been more worried about Dami's trial than they had let on, and everything coming to a head on a single day ... Whatever it was, they had clearly reached some kind of realization about their behaviour that had eluded them before.

Philion had said several times the night before, "This was all my fault." He'd even said something, in Varazda's hearing, about wanting to stop gambling but not knowing how. Myrto was being elaborately nice to everyone, especially Timiskos, and had explained proudly that morning how he was going to start a business decorating houses. Philion had looked as if the idea didn't thrill him as much as it apparently did his wife, but he too was making an effort.

Dami's father had been darting awkward glances at Varazda ever since arriving, as if he might feel he ought to say something but didn't know what. Finally, in part because he simply didn't want to hear whatever the man might come up with, Varazda spared him the trouble.

"Will you come walk in the garden with me, sir?" he said.

Philion looked startled, then faintly alarmed, then tried to cover it all with a breezy attitude. "Of course, of course."

"I'd like to make you an offer," Varazda said as soon as they were out the door into the chilly peristyle surrounding Aradne's small, elegant garden. "This is not in exchange for anything, it is simply for you to accept or decline."

"I, uh—oh?"

"I'd like to buy the house where you live. I realize," he added quickly, as Philion cleared his throat to tell him something he already knew, "that you do not own it. I have already spoken with the man who does—as you may know, he has been looking to sell—and the price he wants for it is within my means to pay." Only just, but he didn't say that.

Philion's eyes went very wide.

Varazda smiled. "He could probably get more for it, but don't tell him that."

"Ha ha, yes—er, no. Of course. Would you—if you—"

"I would need a superintendant to see to the upkeep of the building, since I live in Boukos. I thought of offering you the job and letting you and your wife live rent-free."

"Why?" asked Philion after a moment, sounding more puzzled than suspicious. "Why would you do that?"

"Because you're Damiskos's parents. Don't misunderstand. If I thought he wanted to consign you to the hounds of the Dark Valley, I would push you over the precipice myself and whistle for them—but he doesn't. He's not the kind of man who could ever turn his back on his family, and I love that about him. So if I can't eliminate you from our life, the next best thing, as I see it, is to keep tabs on you. I think if I became your landlord and employer, I'd be able to do that."

Philion cleared his throat several times. "That's—er. That's … "

"Probably a better deal than you would have got out of the Karganian fertilizer business, honestly," said Varazda. "Certainly less risky."

"Gods, yes. Real estate is the way to go. I've always said it. A wise decision. And very er—very generous of you."

"Mm," said Varazda. "Yes. We'll see."

Varazda and Damiskos's father returned to the dining room just as Niko was announcing the arrival of two new guests. No, three new guests. And "guests" was a stretch.

"What are you doing here?" Ino demanded of her mother and father.

"Coming to fetch you, of course," said Korinna. "We are staying with Agron Ephorbos and his family. Obviously we can't remain under Philion and Myrto's roof."

Philion glanced sidelong at Varazda, his allegiance shifting to the person who had offered him the easiest money.

"Obviously!" he agreed heartily. "For one thing, there aren't any beds for you to sleep in, haha! And you, Olympios? I didn't think I was going to see you again any time soon. Didn't want to, either. Suited me well enough. What are you doing here?"

"Olympios has been advising us," Korinna said before the advocate could speak. "We intend to sue your son for breach of promise to our daughter."

"You can't!" Ino cried, starting up from her couch. "He didn't!"

"Ah, but there you are mistaken, my dear," said Olympios, getting a word in past Korinna. "As your mother has confirmed, Damiskos Temnon did propose marriage to you, fifteen years ago, *and never made good his proposal.* Since you are now a widow—"

"What?" Chariton burst out, through a bark of laughter. "Fifteen years ago and she's a widow? Meaning she married someone else in the interim? But that's preposterous! He didn't breach his promise—she broke the engagement! She *married someone else.*" He was laughing too hard to continue.

"She is now free, and he should honour his promise," said Olympios with what dignity he could scrounge up. "We intend to make the case that—"

"No, see, I think what he was saying," said Lysandros,

thumping Chariton on the back because he seemed in danger of choking with laughter, "is that marrying someone else is sort of the definition of breaking an engagement?"

"Actually," said Dami, "her parents broke the engagement before she married the other fellow."

"Don't tell him that," said Lysandros, thumping Chariton again. "You'll kill him."

"What?" said Olympios, turning to Korinna and Simonides with a look of horror. "You—you didn't tell me that!"

Chariton had regained his composure enough to say, "Were you the same person who advised them that they could withhold their daughter's inheritance? Because they can't do that, either."

"What?" Olympios looked like a man beginning to hope he was having a bad dream. "No! That wasn't me. Did you honestly think you could *sue* him if *you* broke the engagement? Do you realize what a fool you've made me look?"

"Well, that doesn't take much work," Myrto remarked.

"What do you mean, we can't withhold her inheritance?" Korinna was doing her goose impression again, ignoring Olympios.

"Again, it hinges on her marriage." Chariton managed to confine himself to giggling. "Since she—excuse me. Since she was married, her father no longer controls her ability to inherit—since she is widowed—sorry—her late husband no longer controls it either, so that, absent any instructions left by her late husband, of which I gather there were none—excuse me. Er, yes. Absent any such instructions, no one controls her ability to inherit but herself. Legally, the thing—what is it again? Oh, the f—the f—" He became incapacitated with laughter again. "It's—hers. The thing—it's hers."

"The shit business," Aradne supplied, with relish.

"Vulgar," Simonides muttered.

"Niko!" Aradne called. "I think you should show these

people out. Ino, are you going to go with them? You're welcome to stay."

Ino sat back down on her couch, and there was a serenity about her expression as though she had made an important decision. It struck Varazda that she was speaking of more than Aradne's invitation when she said, composedly, "Yes. I will."

There was one more visitor that day, later in the afternoon. He declined to come in any further than the atrium, but he asked to speak to Damiskos. It was Helenos's father.

"I have come to express my thanks in person," he said, "for bringing my son's murderer to justice. Your friend will not need to testify at the trial. Phaia took her own life last night."

"I see," said Damiskos. So that was it. It was over. "I never had the chance to tell you, sir, that I am sorry for your loss."

Kontios Diophoros looked embarrassed. "Under the circumstances … "

"I know, but I was a credible suspect. If I had been in your position, I would have prosecuted me too."

Kontios smiled wryly. "It won't do my reputation any good, having wrongly prosecuted a hero of the Second Koryphos, but I doubt the episode will harm you, socially—which is some comfort. You came out of it rather well." After a moment he added, "I wish you and my son could have been friends. I never thought much of the friends he did have."

Damiskos and Varazda went for a walk around the neighbourhood in the evening, after most of the people had cleared out of Aradne's house. It was a substitute for their usual walk to and from their favourite bathhouse in Boukos. Damiskos lifted one of Varazda's hands as they walked, and turned it to look at his palm. The henna had faded a little, but the pattern was still visible. They walked on, hands linked.

They were headed for the island, not to eat fish this time, but just to stand on the bridge on the far side, leaning on the rail, looking out toward the sunset over the harbour. In Pheme the sun rose out of the mountains and set into the sea. There was a famous line about it in a poem, that Damiskos wished he could remember to quote now.

"So," he said instead, "it's all over. No second trial." *We can go home.* Why was it so difficult to say that?

"I'm glad. Not—" Varazda frowned. "Not glad that she killed herself, but that may only be because I'm still Zashian enough to dislike suicide. Glad that this won't all be drawn out any longer."

"Let's see," said Damiskos, to change the subject. "Ino's free of her parents, that's good, and Timiskos is going to go into business for himself, doing whatever it is he wants to do—"

"He's going to do a good job of it. That work he did on your mother's atrium is really first-class."

"My parents, speaking of my parents, are going to be your tenants—I can't believe you actually did that, and they actually agreed."

"Oh, your mother loves the idea. It was only your father I was worried about convincing. And that wasn't hard."

"Timiskos's debts are paid, Gorgion Pandares is off his back, for the time being at least. And may think twice about coming after our family again, because I'm pretty sure it was him you threw in the river. My parents got some of their furniture back. Who else is accounted for?"

"Korinna and her goblin—I mean husband—have slunk off with their tails between their legs. Oh, and your family's advocate has been humiliated, which I must say I found satisfying."

"Profoundly."

"Eurydemos ... well, it was a pleasure to see him sent packing by his boyfriend, but he's the type who never stays down for long—his inflated sense of his own self-worth buoys him up like a bladder."

Damiskos laughed. "Aradne and Nione, now—*that's* nice."

"Yes, they sorted themselves out beautifully, didn't they? I'm so proud of them. And it only took them about the same length of time that it took us."

"What? No, they've known each other since Aradne was a little girl."

"Oh, right. I knew that."

"No one comes close to beating our record for speed of falling in love."

Varazda snorted inelegantly. Damiskos lifted his hand to his lips and very lightly kissed his fingers.

"And us—are we ... all right?"

He didn't know how else to ask it. Part of him felt that he should ask forgiveness, for coming so close to giving up on their future together. But he also knew that Varazda had already forgiven him for that. What he wanted to know was just whether they could go back to Boukos now and carry on as before. Except—how had they been carrying on before? They'd been teetering on the edge of something, some permanence, and were they past that now, or not?

"I think so," said Varazda slowly, and it wasn't quite the resounding answer Damiskos found he had been hoping for. "There's something I've been wanting to say to you."

"Yes?"

He laughed, looking a little self-conscious. "I don't know how this is usually done, but I will do my best." He paused. "Damiskos Temnon, I want to ask for your hand in marriage."

Damiskos looked at him. He was perfectly serious. In one impossible sentence he had pushed past all the uncertainty and launched them onto uncharted water. It was absurd, and it was perfect. Damiskos gripped his hands.

"I accept."

Varazda's smile was like summer. "Really? Just like that? I expected you to say, 'What?' or 'How?' at the very least."

Damiskos laughed. "I guess 'how' is something we'll have to work out, but—to be married to you, Varazda, nothing in the world makes more sense to me than that."

"I know. That's what I want for you." He cupped Damiskos's face in his hands. "For both of us."

EPILOGUE

It was Turning Month, the first of the year, a propitious month for new beginnings, even though it was also cold and wet and celebrations had to be held indoors or under awnings. But the day was clear and crisp, and there had been no rain since last night. Clematis and almond trees were blooming in the quiet streets of Varazda's neighbourhood as he and Dami walked back from the Temple of Terza.

The words of the oath they had taken in the temple echoed in Varazda's mind. It was one that soldier couples often swore, promising lifelong fidelity in some very stern language. (There was rather a lot about blood.) When Dami had first told Varazda about it, he'd sounded hesitant, as if he was pretty sure Varazda wouldn't want to do it. "Well, there *is* this thing in my religion … " It had taken him weeks after their engagement to work himself up to mentioning it. It was very obvious that it was something he wanted to do.

There had been some preliminaries; Varazda had to sit through a couple of ceremonies and spend a night in the temple before he could participate in one of their rites, but that had honestly been quite interesting, like getting to know a particularly strange and serious branch of his lover's family.

Much less tiresome than dealing with Dami's actual family. And the other day, when Marzana's elder son had explained at great length why some theologians considered Terza to be an avatar of the Almighty, Varazda had actually been able to follow most of the argument.

Because of the military aspect of the whole thing, he was dressed for his wedding in a plain saffron-coloured tunic with his hair tied back and the smallest possible gold rings in his ears. He'd worn Dami's scarlet cloak on the way there in the chilly dawn, and now that the day had warmed slightly, he had thrown it back from his shoulders. He felt like a man, that morning, and he liked it.

They didn't talk, just walked arm-in-arm the way they liked to, and every so often they would glance at each other and smile.

There were tables set up in Saffron Alley, hung with garlands of all the greenery available at this time of year. Piled on dishes and in baskets was an absurd amount of food. Yazata had been cooking for days. Maia had popped in the door every so often to ask if they were having such-and-such, and say, "Oh, no, but you must!" if they said they weren't, and then go off to procure whatever it was.

But none of it was going to waste, Varazda realized, because the number of guests packed into the cul-de-sac when they arrived made them both stop and exchange startled glances.

"Did you ... did you want a big party like this?" Varazda asked, worried. He wasn't sure this was the sort of thing Dami enjoyed, but now that he thought about it he realized he had never asked.

"Yes," said Dami, hesitantly, as if it were an admission. "Did you?"

"I? Oh, of course! I love weddings."

"So do I."

"I just didn't think ... "

"That they were planning anything like this," Dami finished for him.

Varazda scanned the crowd. People from the embassy were there, and students and teachers from the dance studio, including a couple of Dami's new pupils, wearing their swords and looking very slick. Ino was there with a young man who must have been her stepson, and Timiskos sat next to them. Absolutely everyone from the neighbourhood was there, including a few who Varazda had always assumed disliked him; but perhaps they were there because they liked Dami better, or perhaps it was for the free food.

A knot of Ariston's friends lounged on the doorstep of the music shop. There was Maraz and a group of Yazata's friends, closer to the house. There was Marzana, hovering near the chair where Chereia was sitting—which he had probably fetched for her from the house and insisted she sit in, because she was expecting their third child.

There was Phormion, who owned the land at the end of the street where Xanthe was now stabled. Someone had hung a net bag of apples on the fence, so there was a distinct possibility that the horse herself was going to put in an appearance.

Yazata bustled out of the house wearing his new robe, bright red as befit a member of a Zashian bride's family, carrying a platter of fried sesame cakes. Kallisto pulled Ariston out of his way as he came down the steps. Behind him, Nione emerged from the house, serene and priestly in her Maiden's robes, followed by Aradne, with her gold butterflies in her hair. Remi popped out from under a table, chasing one of the other children, and Selene gave a loud honk—whether of outrage or joy, Varazda couldn't say.

He looked at Dami, intending to say something, but there were tears in Dami's eyes. So Varazda just slipped his arm around Dami's waist, and they stood there, waiting for their wedding guests to notice that they were home.

JOIN THE CLUB

Join my *Fragments Club* list to get exclusive short stories and snippets!

Sign up at **ajdemas.com**

LIST OF PLACES

Strong Wine is set in a fictional world loosely based on the cultures of the ancient Mediterranean. Here are some details about the places mentioned in the story.

Pseuchaia: A group of city-states, mostly on islands, with a common language and religion, usually in alliance with one another but not always.

Pheme: An island and a very large city on that island. Pheme is a republic and the most powerful city-state in the region. The city is located on the west coast of the island; the interior of the island is mountainous, and there are villages and seaside estates around the coast. The city of Pheme is built on seven hills: the Tetrina, Vallina, Goulina, Vernina, Portina, Rhina, and Skalina. The river Phira runs through the city.

Boukos: A city on an island of the same name, a short sea-voyage to the northwest of the island of Pheme. For the last eight years, Boukos has had a trade agreement with the kingdom of Zash. A permanent Zashian embassy was established seven years ago. None of the other Pseuchaian states has an official alliance with Zash. The governing body of Boukos is called the Basileon.

Zash/Sasia: A sprawling kingdom on the mainland to the east of the islands of Pseuchaia. Their language, religion, and culture are very different from those of Pseuchaia (and also diverse within the kingdom). Zash is what they call their land; Pseuchaians find this difficult to pronounce and so call it Sasia.

Suna: The main seat of the king of Zash.

Deshan Coast: A politically volatile region in the west of Zash. Damiskos served with the Phemian army in this region, and this is also where Varazda is from.

Gudul: An obscure provincial palace and city in Zash. This is where Varazda lived when he was enslaved.

Laothalia: Nione Kukara's villa on the north coast of the island of Pheme. This is where the events of *Sword Dance* took place.

ACKNOWLEDGMENTS

I started writing *Sword Dance* while I was pregnant with my daughter, who is now almost five years old. Over the time it has taken me to finish this series, I've had help from many wonderful people. I'm grateful, as always, to Alexandra Bolintineanu, for encouragement, practical plot help, and everything in between, and to my editor May Peterson for her excellent work getting this final book into shape. Vic Grey continues to blow me away with their amazing art that captures Dami and Varazda so well. And thanks again to Mary Beth Decker for her assistance, especially her excellent work on the cover copy. Finally, I'm grateful to my husband for his unwavering support and to my daughter for being a joy and an inspiration (literally, though happily she does not have a pet goose).

ALSO AVAILABLE

SOMETHING HUMAN

They met on a battlefield and saved each other's lives. It's not the way enemies-to-lovers usually works.

Adares comes from a civilization of democracy and indoor plumbing. Rus belongs to a tribe of tattooed, semi-nomadic horse-breeders. They meet in the aftermath of battle, when Rus saves Adares's life, and Adares returns the favour. As they shelter in an abandoned temple, a friendship neither of them could have imagined grows into a mutual attraction.

But Rus, whose people abhor love between men, is bound by an oath of celibacy, and Adares has a secret of his own that he cannot share. With their people poised for a long and bitter conflict, it seems too much to hope that these two men could turn their fleeting happiness into something lasting. Unless, of course, the relationship between them changes the course of their people's history altogether.

Something Human is a standalone m/m romance set in an imaginary ancient world, about two people bridging a cultural divide with the help of great sex, pedantic discussions about the gods, and bad jokes about standing stones.

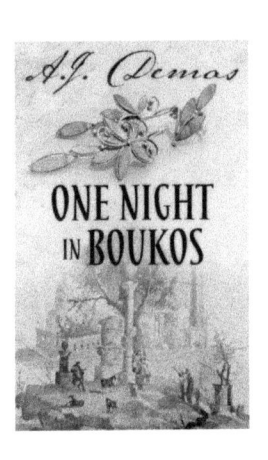

One Night in Boukos

On a night when the whole city is looking for love, two foreigners find it in the last place they expected.

The riotous Psobion festival is about to begin in the city of Boukos, and the ambassador from the straightlaced kingdom of Zash has gone missing. Ex-soldier Marzana, captain of the embassy guard, and the ambassador's secretary, the shrewd and urbane eunuch Bedar, are the only two who know.

Marzana still nurses the pain of an old heartbreak, and Bedar has too much on his plate to think of romance. Neither of them could imagine finding love in this strange, foreign city. But as they search desperately for their employer through the streets and taverns and brothels of Boukos, they find unexpected help from two of the locals: a beautiful widowed shopkeeper and a teenage prostitute.

Before the Zashians learn what became of their ambassador, they will have to deal with foreign bureaucracy, strange food, stranger local customs, and murderers. And they may lose their hearts in the process.

One Night in Boukos is a standalone romance featuring two couples, one m/f and one m/m.

ABOUT THE AUTHOR

A.J. Demas is an ex-academic who formerly studied and taught medieval literature, and now writes romance set in a fictional world based on an entirely different era. She lives in Ontario, Canada, with her husband and cute daughter.

Find out about upcoming books and more here:
www.ajdemas.com

A.J. also publishes fantasy and historical fiction with a metaphysical twist under a different name (her real one). You can find those here: www.alicedegan.com